THE
RIG

THE RI

by JOE DUCIE

HOUGHTON MIFFLIN HARCOURT
BOSTON   NEW YORK

www.hmhco.com

The text was set in Berling Lt Std.

Library of Congress Cataloging-in-Publication Data
Ducie, Joe.
The Rig / by Joe Ducie.
p. cm.
Summary: "Fifteen-year-old Will Drake has made a career
of breaking out from high-security prisons. His talents have
landed him at the Rig, a specialist juvenile holding facility
in the middle of the Arctic Ocean. No one can escape from
the Rig. No one except for Drake."—Provided by publisher
ISBN 978-0-544-50311-3
[1. Prisons—Fiction. 2. Escapes—Fiction.] I. Title.
PZ7.1.D83Ri 2015
[Fic]—dc23
2014029324

Manufactured in the United States of America
DOC 10 9 8 7 6 5 4 3 2 1
4500553939

For Sam,
who, a lot like Drake,
always comes out swinging.

1

HOME SWEET HOME

The Sikorsky SH-60 Seahawk flew low over the ocean, low enough that a cool mist splashed William Drake in the face through the open bay doors. He could taste salt on his lips and feel the roaring wind rush past his ears.

Handcuffed to a steel pivot loop attached to the floor of the chopper, Drake glared out at the miles of endless ocean. He had lost sight of the mainland nearly an hour ago, after takeoff from the holding center in St. John's harbor—the very edge of Newfoundland and Labrador on the North American continent. Nothing but dark, deep waters stretched over the horizon. The sky was bruised purple, heading toward nightfall.

It was cold aboard the chopper, but Drake refused to let his jailers see him shake. Also onboard were two armed guards, both wearing sealed gas masks and carrying sleek semiautomatic rifles. They sat, menacing and silent, by the cockpit doors, their eyes unseen behind tinted plastic. Drake was bound at the ankles and tied to a group of six other prisoners. Four girls and two boys, all about his age.

He had lost track of the days while on the run, but he knew that his fifteenth birthday had been in the last week or so. There was a good chance he was the youngest prisoner aboard, but that didn't make him the weakest.

Not by a long shot.

Strands of strawberry-blond hair hid one girl's face. She had started crying five minutes into the flight and hadn't stopped since. None of the others had tried to comfort her. A stocky boy on Drake's left, who had spiked purple hair—Drake tagged him as Mohawk—sneered at the girl. Drake knew little about where they were going, as the Rig was shrouded in secrecy, but he knew enough not to cry.

"Five miles out," a voice clouded in static transmitted into the cabin.

Drake turned his gaze back out to sea, scanning the horizon for their destination. He spotted it in the distance, rising out of the water like some dilapidated demon of steel and smoke.

The Rig.

An old oil platform that had been converted into the world's first floating rehabilitation center. The Rig was actually five platforms, one at each point of the compass, connected by networks of metal walkways and orange pipes, and a final platform in the middle of the structure. From the air, the Rig was shaped almost like a diamond.

Another cage, Drake thought bitterly.

He watched the Rig grow larger from his seat on the side of the chopper. In the vast and murky ocean, it was the only man-made structure. For all that it mattered this far out to sea, the Rig could have been the only dry land left in the world.

The chopper landed on the southern platform on a wide helipad marked with yellow paint. The shackles were unlocked from the chopper's floor, and Drake was offloaded along with his fellow prisoners. More faceless guardsmen met them here.

With a hard shove from a guard, Drake stumbled forward, shuffling in his ankle cuffs. The seven of them were lined up along the edge of the helipad. They stood shivering and alone as the Seahawk was quickly refueled by a ground crew and took off, on its way back to St. John's.

A large man dressed in a fine suit—too fine for this place, Drake thought—waddled up to them, his thumbs hooked into the loopholes of his pants and a smirk on his face. His tie was tucked into his belt, and his neck jiggled as he spoke.

"Good evening, ladies and gentlemen," he said, smiling at each of them in turn. "My name is Jonathan Rayland Storm. You may call me Warden Storm. Let me be the first to welcome you to the Rig." His gaze settled on Drake last of all, and he did not look away. The warden's smile turned into something nasty as they stared at each other.

"You must be my special case," he said, inclining an invisible hat. "Well, you ain't so special here, son. A few days of work in Tubes will see to that." He opened his arms and gestured to the group at large. "We live by rules here on my five platforms. As you can see, there is no escape. Nothing around you for a hundred miles but freezing water infested with some of the meanest sharks to ever grace God's green earth."

He dabbed at his brow with a cream-colored handkerchief.

"Only you won't find any of that earth around here, no matter how hard you look. So you will follow my rules. You

3

will call me Sir or Warden Storm," he said, repeating himself. "You will address all the guards as Officer.

"Alliance Systems, among other exciting ventures, provides the finest custodial services in the world, as some of you already know." The warden chortled. "Ten years ago, in 2015, after the eastern platform you see just over there was decommissioned, the Alliance built the rest of this place, and since then it has become the foremost center for violent offender rehabilitation on the planet. You are lucky to be here."

Drake tried hard to suppress a smirk at that and failed.

"If you've been sent to me, to my Rig, you are all criminals, no matter your age, and have been sentenced to no less than five years of rehabilitative incarceration by your respective national governments. This old girl is your home for the next half decade, if not more. You will hate it here. You will hate me. That's just fine. Keep your head down, do your work, and once your time is up, we will send you home as a productive member of society."

As the warden finished his introduction, Drake ran his eyes across the visible structure of the oil rig. He counted three guards behind Storm, plus the two from the helicopter. There was a shadowy figure stationed up in the command tower. Call that another prison officer.

That made at least six unique guards, all faceless and armed with automatic weapons and nasty-looking black batons. There'll be more, Drake thought, licking the salt from his lips.

Drake had known men like Warden Storm before. Men who sat in seats of power and absolute authority. Men who controlled everything about their private worlds. The faces of the men often changed, but in Drake's experience, they were always the same in one regard.

They were overconfident.

So Drake believed the warden when he spoke of shark-infested waters and the rules by which the prisoners were supposed to abide. He believed it as much as the man himself did. But his overconfidence, his arrogance made him overlook one key factor. One small yet important detail.

There is no escape, Warden Jonathan Rayland Storm had said, and it was there that he and Drake would have to disagree.

Because there wasn't a prison built—on God's green earth or otherwise—that could hold Will Drake.

2

PROCESSING

After the warden's speech, Drake and his chain gang were marched single file across the helipad and into the Rig, led down a gray corridor by four of the masked guards. Every two meters or so, a window looked out over the darkening ocean and the blinking orange lights along the perimeter of the other two visible platforms to the east and west. Mid-November and close to the Arctic Circle, the night would be cold.

The corridor took an abrupt turn to the right and opened into a larger room in the heart of the southern platform. Drake guessed that they were somewhere below the control tower he'd seen from the helipad. The floor was carpeted here, and a row of empty desks sat opposite a small kitchen. Along the far wall, five bunk beds were arranged in front of porthole windows. The last of the day's light shone across the room from the portholes, and the air smelled faintly of fried onions.

"Inside. Line up next to the central desk!" a guard barked.

Drake shuffled along at the back of the group. He thought it was just his imagination, but he was sure he could feel the floor moving beneath his feet, swaying with the ocean currents. At the front of the group, the girl who had been crying on the flight failed to stifle a particularly loud sob.

Mohawk pushed her hard in the back. "Shut up," he spat. She fell to her knees and wailed.

Drake stepped forward and smacked Mohawk upside his head with the edge of his steel cuffs. More surprised than hurt, Mohawk reeled back and raised his hands. He snarled and advanced on Drake with his fists clenched.

"Break it up!" A guard stepped between Drake and Mohawk. "Line up against the wall like good little daffodils now!"

Daffodils?

Drake did as he was told, ignoring the look of pure hatred from Mohawk.

The guard strapped his weapon to his chest armor and undid the clasp on his facemask. The molded plastic fell away to reveal a young man with a jovial smile. His brown hair was short at the sides and back, a military buzzcut, and his blue eyes seemed to sparkle almost sapphire in the half-light.

"There now," he said. "That's better." The three remaining guards kept their faces covered, weapons at the ready, and took up positions behind the smiling man. He began to pace back and forth in front of his captives. "There'll be no brawling here, my boys. Not while Marcus Brand is on watch!"

Brand . . . Drake filed the name away.

"Screw you, pig," Mohawk spat.

Without breaking pace, Brand slapped Mohawk hard enough to rattle the teeth in Drake's head. Mohawk snapped his head back with a cry, and droplets of blood sprayed from his mouth in a wicked arc.

7

"As I was saying," Brand continued. "Discipline, and a healthy respect for those in authority, will go a long way toward making your stay on the Rig that much more bearable. You will be here with us for some years. This is the entirety of your world from now on, and you can forget about luxuries such as trees or grass. Figure out early that it's best to do as you are told." He stopped pacing and crossed his hands behind his back.

"Tomorrow morning will be your induction meeting with Warden Storm. He will assign you a daily schedule, focused primarily on your platforms—boys on the western platform, girls on the northern—and a work program that you will adhere to at all times. Failure to do so will constitute a breach of the rules, and you will be punished accordingly. Am I clear?"

No one said a word. Strawberry Blonde whimpered while Mohawk licked the blood from his lips. The rest, except for Drake, simply nodded.

"Good," Brand said. "Now, you will be unlocked from your cuffs one at a time. When you are unlocked, you will step forward and Officer Hall will fit you with your very own Alliance tracker. A wristwatch, of a sort." He held up a thick black band that flashed the time, along with a stream of other data, in luminescent green numbers on a five-centimeter screen. "None of you will have any excuse for being late to work now, will you?"

Drake was unlocked first. He stepped forward and offered his left arm to the man behind the gas mask. Hall slapped it away and grabbed his right arm. The screen went over the back of his wrist, just above the steel handcuff, and snapped shut, uncomfortably tight.

Drake examined the watch while the other members of his group were each given one of their own. The heavy black metal band had sealed seamlessly around his wrist, and apart from the digital display and a single rectangular hole in the side, it was unremarkable.

The display flashed the time across the center of the screen, and a few numbers and symbols scrolled across the top-right-hand corner. Drake's read *$-182 AC.*

"Will someone please tell me what time it is?" Brand asked once every new inmate was wearing one of the bands.

No one spoke.

"Do not make me ask again, my little lawbreakers." He was still smiling, but it never touched his eyes. Something else smiled there, something not so kind. He rolled up the sleeves of his black sweater, below the armor, and crossed his arms over his chest. Drake thought he recognized the tattoo on Brand's left forearm—two swords crossed over a wreath and a silver crown, with the inscription "C-F '13" beneath the blades—but he didn't know from where.

He's dangerous, Drake thought. He enjoys his job.

"Half past eight," muttered the girl next to Drake.

"Thank you, my dear. Time for dinner before lights out at half nine. You'll sleep here in Processing tonight until you're assigned accommodations tomorrow. Oh, and just so you know, kids. You'll find it impossible to remove your trackers. There is good reason for this. They're also state-of-the-art Global Positioning Systems. They can track you to within a meter, no matter where you are in the world—and seeing as how your whole world for the next five years is the Rig, there won't be a moment Control can't find you." He grinned again, at Drake in particular. "Now, let's get you fed before naptime."

Still secured at the wrists, Drake and his six companions were herded over to the stainless-steel table next to the kitchen. The table was set with bowls of soup and hunks of bread. Plastic spoons had been provided for all. In the arm of each seat was a square device about the size of a smartphone. The device shone with a dull red light.

"Everyone sit," Brand said. "And wave your trackers over the scanners."

Drake waved his arm over the scanner embedded in the chair. It beeped as his tracker passed over it, and it turned a healthy shade of green. He also noticed that the display on his watch had changed. The counter on the screen now read **$-184 AC.**

"What does that mean?" he asked.

"I'm glad you asked, boy," Brand said. "Your tracker also keeps an account of how much it costs Alliance Systems to feed and house you during your stay." He chuckled. "This delicious meal before you costs two shiny Alliance credits. Your jumpsuits and flight to the Rig make up the remaining balance. A balance you owe the Alliance for your rehabilitation. Every meal you eat, every night you sleep must be paid for."

"And how do we pay?" asked an Asian boy opposite Drake. Black tribal tattoos crisscrossed his neck and up under his dark hairline. He had already finished half his bread and soup.

"You work, my boy." Brand clapped his hands together. "A day's work on the Rig will earn you, roughly, depending on the task, between fifteen and twenty-five credits. This will be used to provide your accommodation and food. Work hard, and you can spend the remainder on certain luxuries, such as candy or magazines. A fair system, yes?"

Drake grunted and ate his dinner. The soup was watery, and the meat could have been anything, but he was hungry.

Afterward, they were allowed five minutes each in a nearby washroom before being shown to one of the bunks. Brand undid Drake's cuff on his right wrist and attached it to a metal ring built into the wall. Tethered to the bunk, Drake had no choice but to lie down. The others were treated the same.

"One or more of us will be stationed nearby. Sleep well, kiddies," Brand said. "Lights out!"

Drake folded his pillow over and faced the wall. The only light was the faint glow of his tracker and the dull, blinking orange lights strung along the outside of the platform, shining in through the porthole. The only sound was the soft, muffled sobs from Strawberry Blonde in the bunk below.

He fell asleep at 2145 on the dot, according to his leash.

*　*　*

At 0217 Drake awoke with a cramp in his leg. He groaned and tried to shake it out. The other kids in the room were asleep, and someone—Mohawk, Drake guessed—was snoring. Drake rolled over as the pain in his leg eased, and he gazed out of his porthole at the continuous blinking lights along the outer shell of the Rig.

He saw a strange thing down below.

Hundreds—no, thousands—of tiny electric-blue lights danced back and forth just below the surface of the ocean, near the eastern platform. Like a swarm of fireflies, the lights darted to and fro in the water, casting the otherwise deep, dark sea in a soft, ethereal glow.

Drake watched, entranced, for close to an hour before—all at once—the lights vanished. It was some time before he drifted back to sleep.

STORM IN A TEACUP

The next morning, Drake had all but forgotten about the strange light show. He ate breakfast in silence around the steel table in Processing as one by one, Officer Brand delivered the prisoners to Warden Storm's office.

Mohawk went first, then Strawberry Blonde and all the others. Wherever they were going, they didn't come back the same way. Soon Drake sat alone at the table, with only one faceless guard and the dregs of his cereal for company. His tracker read *$-195 AC.*

For room and board, he thought grimly.

After about an hour, Brand returned for Drake. He was led up a narrow staircase in the heart of the control tower he'd seen from the helipad the night before. They walked past several doors that could be entered only with ID scanners and emerged in a room lined with computers and workstations and manned by more guards, and Drake made mental notes of all of it.

Brand, a hand on Drake's shoulder, led him across the floor

and up a single flight of stairs to a frosted-glass door. A plaque on the door read WARDEN STORM. Brand knocked once.

"Send him in."

Brand held the door for Drake and motioned him inside. He nodded at the warden and then stepped out.

"Good morning, Mr. Drake," Warden Storm said from behind a large, opulent desk. He was sipping tea from a fine china cup. "How was your first night on the Rig?"

Drake thought about the odd dancing lights and shrugged. "I suppose it was oil right."

Storm wore another immaculate suit over his bulky frame. "Ah, not only an escape artist, but a comedian. I have to say, I've been looking forward to your arrival for some days. Please, sit."

Drake sat and placed his cuffed hands in his lap. He glanced around the room—at the filing cabinets on the far wall underneath an open window overlooking the helipad far below, and at the ocean beyond that. The warden's office was decorated simply, with wood paneling and a skylight overhead. On the wall behind him was a collection of commendations and photographs from the United States Air Force. One picture showed Storm in the cockpit of a helicopter, flying through low, scrubby mountains.

"You like that one?" Storm asked. "My first tour, twenty years ago in Afghanistan. You weren't even born yet, son." He cleared his throat and turned to his computer. "Now, I am not foolish enough to assume that you will treat this facility any differently from your previous three incarcerations." Storm read from a display Drake couldn't see. "Trennimax, in France, well, that took no real brains, just courage. I must say, though, your escape from Cedarwood in the Alps was inspiring, crafting railway wheels in the metal shop and fitting them to a laundry cart. How did you know that the old track down the mountain was still operational?"

Drake shrugged. "I didn't."

"The devil's luck, hmm? Remarkable."

"Easy."

"Well, as it may." Storm turned from his screen and met Drake's eyes. "Are you a strong swimmer, Mr. Drake?"

"Used to churn through the water at East London Leisure when I was five. Don't imagine a hundred miles of ocean will be much more of a challenge."

Storm laughed. "If you wanted to try, son, I wouldn't stop you. There is no way down to the water from the Rig, just so you know. The jump alone—fifty meters—would kill you."

"I'll build a diving board."

"How did you escape from Harronway?"

"I walked out the front door."

"Come now. Warden Gomez was a friend of mine, before you embarrassed him and he had to be replaced. To this day, Alliance Systems hasn't been able to figure out how you did it. The morning of August thirty-first, you were simply gone."

Drake said nothing.

"Well, no matter. Your latest escape is why you've been sent here. Usually the punishment has to fit the crime—and the Rig takes only the worst of the worst. Murderers, violent offenders, and the like. You, as far as your record shows, are none of those things. Although you came close in Trafalgar Square, hmm? Which is why you may find your time here initially uncomfortable."

"That's fine, sir. I won't be staying long."

"I think it best we keep you busy." Storm tapped away on his computer again, and another square scanner flared to life in the arm of Drake's chair. "I think an intensive schedule will keep your mind off any foolish escape attempts. We wouldn't want you hurting yourself or others now, would we."

Drake kept quiet and let a long moment pass in silence.

The warden finally cleared his throat and gestured at the scanner.

"Swipe your tracker, Mr. Drake. The device will download your schedule for the next month. After that time, we will reassess how you're fitting in here, and modify your workload accordingly."

Drake swiped his wrist over the scanner, and his tracker beeped. A circular loading symbol covered the screen for a moment, and then the time returned, along with his debt. A new instruction ran along the bottom of the screen. It read:

Exercise: 0900–1000

The tracker made a harsh sound, and the screen flashed red.

Warning: You are outside the exercise area

"Ah, you'll be fined five credits for any breaches of your schedule, I'm afraid," Storm said. "And being here constitutes a breach. I'd hurry along, Mr. Drake. Officer Brand will show you onto the boys' platform."

4

ENEMIES

"You've got a job in Tubes, clearing pipes—that should keep you busy," Brand said as he unlocked Drake's wrist cuffs and led him down a corridor linking the southern platform to the central. The floor was made of reinforced clear plastic. Large silver-gray vents, hanging over the water, were fitted to the underside of the corridor. The ocean chopped and churned at least fifty meters below.

"Tubes?"

"You've been assigned a hefty workload. Tubes always needs hands clearing sand and grit. Good credits. You'll be one of the high earners, I'd wager." Brand snorted. "You'll have no other choice."

The Rig had not been used to drill into the ocean floor for more than ten years, yet the smell of grease and crude oil still clung to the structure. Drake imagined it was a smell he'd get used to, in time. Despite his bravado in Storm's office, he hadn't the first idea of how he was going to escape from this latest cage. But there would be a way. There always was.

From the central platform Brand led Drake west, into another corridor built out over the ocean. The western platform loomed before them, dark and dreary. They reached a set of barred steel doors at the end of the corridor, and Brand swiped his access card across the panel. The doors hissed open on slow hydraulic runners and revealed a whole new world.

For the first time, Drake got a look at the Rig's younger inhabitants. The male population, at least. He stood at the apex of a wide cellblock, at least sixty by sixty meters, looking down at several holding levels built into the walls of the structure, and into the heart of the western platform. Dozens of young men in green jumpsuits milled around an exercise yard ten levels below.

Drake was reminded of every prison movie he'd ever seen growing up, before his misdeeds had landed him in one.

A cadre of guards patrolled the levels above the exercise area. Drake counted seven—eight, including Brand, who led him down a series of interconnected walkways. They reached the guard level, just above the prisoners below, and Drake gazed over the railing.

Brand scanned the crowd and pointed at a small boy sitting on his own near a row of treadmills. "Tristan!"

The scrawny kid jumped and looked up, pushing his glasses up the bridge of his nose. "Sir?"

"This here's Drake. Fill him in on the details, would you?"

Brand stared at Drake and gestured at the final set of stairs down into the enclosed exercise area. "Well? I'm not going to hold your hand. Consider your induction over."

Drake headed down the stairway and met up with Tristan. Tristan's faded green uniform looked about two sizes too big, just like the wire-framed glasses on his face.

"I'm Michael," he said, and offered his hand tentatively, as if he were afraid that Drake might bite. "Michael Tristan."

"Will Drake." Drake shook his hand. The tracker on his wrist beeped and flashed green.

Entered exercise area

"So, you just get in last night? Already saw a few new faces this morning." Tristan shuffled nervously. "Where you from? You sound British."

"Yes. Last night. Yes. London." Drake shivered, and the hairs on the back of his neck stood up. He was being watched, and not just by the guards on the tier above.

"I'm from Perth, Western Australia. People from all over the world in here," Tristan said, but Drake ignored him.

He swept his gaze across the exercise area. Most of the boys were paying him no attention. A few sneered or stared at him blankly. He was trying to figure out the group dynamics, and who to watch out for. It had been the same in his other cages. There were always people to look out for—usually sooner rather than later.

Mohawk, the purple-haired kid from the chopper, was talking to a group of rough-looking boys near the weight wall and pointing at Drake.

"Who's the big fella the spiky-haired punk is talking to?"

Tristan followed his gaze and paled. That told Drake all he needed to know.

"Alan Grey," Tristan whispered. "He's—"

"Coming this way," Drake said. "I take it he's not the friendly type?"

Tristan was backing away as quickly as he could, no longer acknowledging Drake.

Standing his ground, Drake turned to the side as Grey approached, flanked by three large inmates on each side. Mohawk smirked at him from over Grey's shoulder.

"You're the tough guy, huh?" Grey said, crossing his arms over his chest. He had thick black hair and narrow, cruel eyes. His nose was flat, like a pig's, and rough stubble coated his cheeks. He was just less than six feet, and if Tristan's uniform had looked two sizes too big, Grey's looked far too small. His muscles bulged beneath the fabric. "Lot of tough guys here. What's your name?"

"Drake."

"Drake." Grey sneered. "Gaz says you disrespected him last night." He jerked his thumb at Mohawk. "Old mate of mine, is Gaz, from Trennimax. Thinks you owe him an apology, he does."

"I'm sorry," Drake said. "I'm sorry he's a scurrying little worm that beats on girls and goes crying behind the fanciest skirt in the yard when called on it."

Grey tried to grab his shoulder.

Drake slapped his hand away. A flash of anger crossed Grey's features and he lunged forward, faster than Drake thought he could move, and slammed his forehead into Drake's face.

Drake stumbled back, staggered by the blow and anticipating another. Blood spurted from his nose in a violent torrent. He ducked low and felt Grey's fist swing through the air above his head. No stranger to brawls, Drake launched a crippling kick into Grey's shin. If he didn't end it now, he'd find himself with worse odds later.

Grey groaned and fell to one knee. Drake spun on his haunches, swiped the bully's other leg out from under him, and slammed his fist into Grey's mouth. Grey hit the spongy floor of the exercise area hard and cursed.

Where are the guards? Drake wondered. He glanced up and saw Brand making his way slowly down the stairs. He had a smile on his face and seemed to be taking his time. The other officers watched from above, pointing and jeering.

One of Grey's friends came in from behind and wrapped his arms around Drake's chest, squeezing him tight as Grey got back to his feet.

"Hold him. I'm gonna break his damn jaw!"

Drake hauled his legs up into the air as Grey lunged at him. He timed it right, and his feet connected with Grey's chest. Drake thrust his weight back, using Grey's momentum against him, and the bully went down a second time, gasping for air.

The boy holding Drake was thrown back too, striking his head against one of the metal support pillars. Drake broke free.

With a roar, Grey rose again, glaring at Drake. For a moment Drake thought he saw an actual flash of furious red in Grey's eyes, but then Brand stepped between them and blew a shrill whistle.

"Enough!" He glanced over his shoulder. "You need to calm down, Mr. Grey. And Mr. Drake, fighting is prohibited. You'll both be fined fifty credits. Now walk away. All of you." Brand wasn't carrying his gun, but he held a long baton that hummed softly.

Electrified, Drake thought, wiping his bloody nose with his sleeve.

"This isn't over," Grey growled. He walked away, the rest of his gang following in his wake. Mohawk offered Drake a sly grin and flipped him off.

His tracker beeped.

Lessons: 1015–1215

"What does that mean?" Drake asked Michael Tristan.

"It means we've got lessons until lunch," Tristan said. He was looking at Drake in amazement. "Then work and dinner, followed by two hours' free time in the common area. Standard day in paradise. Do you know where you're working?"

"Tubes, apparently."

"Wow. You've been here five minutes and already made the worst possible enemy and been assigned the worst job on the Rig." Tristan chuckled. "Need to keep your head down, Drake."

5

LESSONS LEARNED

Heading up through the platform, Drake stemmed the blood from his busted nose with his sleeve. The bleeding stopped, thankfully, and his nose didn't feel broken. He was more concerned about a gash between the knuckles of his right hand, where he'd hit Grey in the face. He hadn't felt it at the time, but he must have struck one of the bully's teeth. Drake held his hand up, and a steady trickle of blood from the gash pooled along the edge of the tracker.

"Any bathrooms nearby, Tristan?"

Tristan nodded. "Next level up. This way. We've only got five minutes to get to the classrooms up top or we'll be fined, though." He held up his tracker, and Drake saw that he was actually in positive credits. His screen read *$134 AC*.

Drake checked his own. With the five credits lost in Warden Storm's office and the fine imposed by Brand, his screen now read *$-250 AC*. "How long have you been here, then?" he asked.

"A year and three months," Tristan said with a grim smile. "Only three and a half years to go—almost there. Heh."

"Yeah, me too." Drake was given a wide berth by the string of other inmates making their way up through the platform to wherever lessons were held. A steady clang of soft heels on steel rang up and down the large, nearly hollow structure. "So what are you in for?"

Tristan shrugged and muttered something below hearing. "Here's the bathroom. Two minutes, and then I'm going without you."

Drake let himself into the washroom using his good hand and was actually impressed with what he found. The floor was made of a white, rubbery material, and a line of urinals and cubicles followed the wall to a shower block. He headed over to a row of sinks below a long mirror that was locked behind a sheet of reinforced Perspex so it couldn't be smashed. Everything was spotless, which was what so impressed him—he'd seen some truly awful prison washrooms. The warden ran a tight ship, it seemed.

Running his bleeding hand under the cold faucet, he grabbed a handful of paper towels from the dispenser and cleaned himself up. The clear water ran crimson down the sink, and the gash in the back of his hand looked as if it needed stitching. He cursed and grabbed a few more paper towels to try to stem the bleeding.

"Is there a nurse or something?" he asked Tristan as he emerged from the washroom.

"There's the infirmary. Let's get up to class and show one of the guards there."

Drake let Tristan lead the way. They were at the back of the pack now, a few levels below the other inmates. The metal walkways ran parallel to the rows of what Drake assumed were the accommodations he was paying eleven credits a night for. As Tristan led him up another few levels, he lost sight of the cells, and the platform opened up onto another of those reinforced plastic walkways built over the water. Drake followed Tristan down the walkway and along the outer rim of the western platform.

The corridor led outside into a bright but chilly day. The cloudless blue sky bled into the darker blue of the ocean on the horizon, and the familiar taste of salt clung to the air. The top of the western platform had been cleared of drilling equipment a long time ago, but Drake could see the marks in the concrete where it had stood. A few dead insects—bees—littered the indentations in the concrete. Drake followed a line of yellow paint toward a wide, two-story complex that stretched the length of the platform. A few guards were stationed near the fenced-off edge of the platform, overlooking the water. They watched the crowd of boys move into the complex and held their weapons toward the floor.

Unsure if he'd seen these guards before, Drake added them to the growing count in his head. Unfortunately, he was beginning to see that the Rig was quite well staffed.

The two-story building atop the platform was modern, compared with the rest of the outer shell of the Rig. All the boys were filing into a room on the first floor. Still at the back of the group, Drake's and Tristan's trackers beeped last as they crossed the threshold of the wide-open space.

Entered western classroom

The room was larger than the classrooms Drake recalled from primary school and from the one year he'd attended high school before being sent into the system for his crimes.

Ten rows of white desks were bolted to the floor, each with a drawer and a chair. Red scanners for the trackers were built into the desks. Drake followed Tristan toward the front of the room, where a group of guards stood without masks—still armed. The three men and two women chatted among themselves, ignoring the prisoners. Drake thought about showing them his wounded hand, but they didn't look too friendly.

The rows of desks went across for ten seats as well, making a hundred desks in total. Drake saw that there was a computer embedded in the plastic surface of the desk, a touchscreen interface. He sat down next to Tristan at the end of the second row and, following suit, swiped his tracker over the sensor in the chair's arm. It beeped and turned green.

The screen flashed to life and presented Drake with three options in large blue squares: "English—Math—Science."

Drake pressed *Math*, and a screen of lessons popped up, numbered one through two hundred. Every lesson save the first was grayed out, so with no better place to start, he selected the first option. Half a dozen problems appeared on the screen. The first read

Q: 6 x 2
A: a) 10; b) 11; c) 12; d) 13

Multiplication problems—and ridiculously easy ones at that. Drake selected the right answers and flew through the first page. A fresh set of simple problems appeared on the screen.

He looked to Tristan, but the bespectacled boy had already started his lessons. He had removed a pad of paper and a pencil from the drawer in the side of the desk and was writing his answers down instead of using the touchscreen.

Tristan looked bored, and a quick glance at his screen showed similar, mundane problems. Drake glanced around the room. Of the hundred available desks, he estimated that about ninety were in use. Most of the inmates sat lazily in their chairs, idly pressing the screens and chatting to the people around them. A few made eye contact and sneered. Mohawk sat by himself across the room, apparently having been abandoned by his old mate Alan Grey.

Drake's gaze swept the room, but Grey and his gang of cronies were nowhere to be seen.

"Grey and his thugs aren't here?" he said to Tristan, making it a question.

Tristan shrugged. "Advanced lessons."

"Those morons? They can't have three brain cells between them."

Tristan shook his head and solved the next problem with ease and a sigh. Again, he wrote his answers down on paper instead of using the screen. Drake was going to ask him about the paper when someone tapped him on the shoulder.

He looked up. It was Officer Brand.

"With me, Balboa." He laughed. "The doctor will see you now."

Drake stood up. "Doctor?" He glanced at Tristan, who was doing his best to feign no interest.

"Just come on. Doc Lambros's office is upstairs. I don't want you bleeding all over my nice clean floors."

The blood from his split knuckle had slowed but not

stopped. Crimson drops seeped through the wad of paper towels covering the mess. Drake nodded and followed Brand out into the hall.

"Hold up your tracker. There's a good boy." From a collection of colored tags around his neck Brand swiped a green pass about the size of a credit card over the tracker. "Save you any more fines, huh? You're racking those up quite spectacularly already. Follow me."

Free movement, the screen read. Drake wondered what the blue, red, and yellow tags might do, and how he could acquire a set of his own.

Brand took off down the corridor, farther into the complex, at a steady clip. A spiral staircase at the end of the corridor led up to the second floor. As they climbed, Brand asked, "Found a way to escape yet?"

"Not yet," Drake said, gazing out the window at the distant horizon. No ships, no land, no nothing. "How long have you been here?"

"This shift block? Three weeks. On the Rig itself, five years." Brand grasped Drake's shoulder and pulled him to a stop outside a frosted-glass door. "I cycle off back to the mainland every eight weeks for a few weeks. We use the chopper—and only the chopper—so don't think you're getting off that way. Ha." He rapped on the door.

"Please come on in," a female voice chimed from inside the office.

"In you go—and behave yourself. I'll be just outside and will quite happily give you a wallop to match that nose if you cause any trouble."

28

"Right." Drake let himself in and shut the door in Brand's face.

"Hello, there," said a woman seated behind a large mahogany desk that was cluttered with files and paperwork. She stood and walked around the desk into the heart of the room. "I'm Dr. Acacia Lambros. You must be William."

Dr. Lambros was a short woman—just five feet and change. At a shave under six feet, Drake towered over her. She had pale skin and dark hair cut pixie-style, and she looked to be around thirty. A smattering of freckles covered her face, and she wore a professional business suit. The room itself, her office, was rather fancy. Aside from the desk, which held a state-of-the-art desktop computer, a row of bookcases lining the far wall were stuffed to bursting with leather-bound tomes. Twin windows overlooked the southern platform of the Rig and the ocean beyond. A high-backed leather chair rested at an angle in front of the desk. The carpet was soft underfoot, and a leather sofa sat behind a glass coffee table. Magazines were scattered over the table. Drake recognized one—*Peacekeeper*, an Alliance-issued magazine detailing the good work its private military arm, Crystal Force, was doing alongside the United Nations in hot spots around the globe.

Drake's mind flashed back to the night before and the tattoo he'd seen on Brand's arm. Twin swords crossed over a wreath under a silver crown. It was the same crest on the cover of *Peacekeeper* magazine. "C-F '13," the inscription under Brand's tattoo, stood for Crystal Force, and most likely the year he joined.

Damn, he could probably kill me just by blinking . . . Drake filed that troubling revelation away and concentrated on the present. Dr. Lambros was staring at him, letting him take in the new surroundings.

All in all, Drake had been expecting something a lot more . . . clinical, for a doctor's office.

"You're not a 'doctor' doctor, are you, Doctor?"

She smiled. It was friendly enough, and revealed shining white teeth. "I'm a practicing psychologist, Mr. Drake. The Rig's counselor for all the inmates here. We weren't supposed to meet until later in the week, after you'd had a chance to settle in, but fate had other plans, it seems." She gestured at his bloody hand. "And although I'm not part of the Rig's medical team, I have had quite enough training to take care of that little cut. Please, come and sit down."

Drake sat in the comfortable leather chair and rested his hand on the edge of the desk. Dr. Lambros fetched a large first-aid kit from atop the cabinets lining the right side of the room. The cabinets were labeled alphabetically: A–L, M–R, S–Z. Patient files. Drake wondered if he had one yet, perhaps transferred from Harronway, or from Cedarwood before that, and he concluded that he probably did.

"Now then," Dr. Lambros said. She pulled over a stool next to Drake, sat down, and put on a pair of surgical gloves from the first-aid kit. "Let's have a look at this hand."

The paper towels had done their best to stem the trickle of blood and had stuck to the gash. The cut stung as the doctor removed the wad of paper and revealed the wound.

"Yikes, that's a bit of a nasty one." She removed a spray canister of Betadine antiseptic from the kit and doused Drake's hand liberally with the brown, smelly liquid. "So tell me, William—or is it Will?"

He met her eyes and found them kind. "Will's fine."

"Will, then. How are you finding life on the Rig so far?"

Drake shrugged. "Same crap, different location. All these places are the same."

"Please don't curse in my office. And what do you mean by 'these places'?"

"Prisons."

"Best not to think of it as a prison, Will. You're in a rehabilitation facility—to get you back on the right track and back into society."

"By sticking me out in the middle of the Arctic Ocean hundreds of miles from society?" He snorted. "With a bunch of violent thugs, heavily armed guards, and God knows who else? Please."

Dr. Lambros chuckled as she threaded a string of thin cotton through the eye of a small needle. "Well that's one way of looking at it, I suppose. However the rehabilitative programs here are world-class, at the very forefront of academic and practical application. If you give it a chance, the Rig can help you. Now hush a minute while I disinfect this needle and sew you shut. Should only need four or so stitches."

Drake looked away as the needle pierced his skin. It was uncomfortable but didn't really hurt. A few minutes, and the doctor was done. She washed his hand and stuck a butterfly bandage over the stitches. All the medical waste went into a sealed bag and into the bin.

"Good as new, Will."

Drake flexed his hand and felt a gentle pull at the neat row of little stitches beneath the small bandage. He'd have to be careful with it for a day or two to avoid popping a stitch. "Thank you, Dr. Lambros."

"You're welcome." She cleaned up the rest of the mess and returned the first-aid kit to its proper place before sitting in her chair on the other side of the desk. "Now, since we have a few minutes, let's have a chat, shall we?"

"Sure."

"Officer Brand tells me you hurt your hand in an altercation in the exercise area this morning. What caused the fight, Will?"

Drake sat up a little straighter in the chair. "Oh, you know, an overabundance of world-class rehabilitation."

Dr. Lambros laughed. "We'll work on that attitude in the weeks to come. Do you know I can make recommendations to the Alliance about sentence reduction if you show signs of improvement?"

"I didn't know that, but I don't think the Alliance likes me that much."

"Fighting, however, is not a sign of improvement."

Drake frowned. "I didn't start the fight. One of the idiots I flew in with wanted a little payback, is all."

"Payback for what?"

"I . . . smacked him last night."

Dr. Lambros sighed. "I see."

Drake rubbed the back of his hand and felt that he had disappointed the woman across the desk. He had known her for only a quarter of an hour, but he liked her and so said nothing to fill the silence.

The doctor tapped a manila folder resting on her desk next to the computer. "I read your file—"

"I thought as much."

"—and there are several notes in there about other altercations. A particularly disturbing note about an incident in Cedarwood in which one of the boys lost his life."

A memory of a cold morning in the facility high up in the Alps flashed through his mind. He saw the smoke and the flames and heard the screams. One of many flawed escape attempts. He pushed those thoughts away. "Am I supposed to just let them hit me, then?"

Dr. Lambros raised her palms toward the ceiling. "No, but a little forethought could avoid such incidents altogether. I know you're a smart boy, Will, and yet you find yourself here—looking at five years before you'll even see land again."

Drake scowled. "I won't be here that long."

"Ah, yes. Your tendency toward escape, but I'm afraid there is no way off the Rig." She tapped a fountain pen against the edge of her desk. "How did you escape Harronway, incidentally?"

"I walked out the front door."

"No, you didn't. You couldn't have. Tell me, do you think you deserve to be here?"

"No."

"Really?" Dr. Lambros smiled again. Drake wasn't so sure he liked her anymore. "You were sentenced eighteen months ago in London for aggravated assault and a string of other offenses. Theft and arson, to name just two. Those aren't light offenses, Will, no matter your age."

"If I hadn't done what I did then, my mum would've died."

Drake thought back to that day in London — his sentencing. His mother had been too sick to attend. The judge had barely looked at him before sending him to juvenile detention for two years. From there he had disappeared into the Alliance Systems network, pulled from his hometown, his school and friends, and sent to Trennimax in France, then Cedarwood in the Alps, and then Harronway in Ireland after that. A busy year, all things said and done.

Drake ran a hand over his head. He'd always kept his dark hair short, but on the run in Ireland two weeks earlier he'd shaved it clean off to mask his appearance. I'll need to be cleverer next time, he thought. Because time is running out.

Dr. Lambros tapped her pen against her knee. "Yes, you lived with your mother in London, correct? It says here your parents are separated. Not a lot of info on your family life. Father is African American, mother originally from Poland. No siblings."

"And I haven't seen much of dear old dad in a decade," Drake muttered.

"You didn't see another choice, did you? When you committed your crimes. But what you did hurt a lot of people and caused a lot of damage. You need help, Will, and we can provide that here. Put you to work, offer counseling, and keep you busy. You'll know a trade by the time you leave us."

Drake said nothing and let out a long, slow breath.

"Well, it has been nice meeting you, at any rate." Dr. Lambros stood. "I don't want to have to repair you again, you hear? We'll speak again next week, once you're more settled — and once you've seen that there really is no way off the Rig. Try to put all thoughts of escape out of your mind, okay? Promise me now?"

"I promise," Drake lied.

She walked him to the door and opened it.

Brand leaned casually against the wall of the corridor. "He any trouble, Doc?"

"Not one bit," she said.

For the first time since meeting her, Drake saw Dr. Lambros lose her smile. She crossed her arms under her breasts and stared at Brand with an expression that, while not hostile, was not friendly. Drake suspected the good doctor did not care for Officer Marcus Brand.

"Good at escaping, this one," Brand said. Drake thought he was enjoying the doctor's discomfort. He slapped Drake on the shoulder and pulled him out into the hallway. "Not so good at running."

"Take care, Will. I will see you soon."

The doctor disappeared back into her office and Brand shoved Drake forward a step. "Come on, boy. Back to school."

6

TUBES

Drake spent the next hour or so tapping away at the touch-screen computer in the classroom. He couldn't move on to the next lesson without completing the first, but they didn't seem to get progressively harder. He wondered if the majority of the other inmates actually found the lessons challenging. Tristan certainly didn't, as he scribbled his answers on lined paper. All in all, Drake found it a monumental waste of time—but what else, at this point, did he have but time to waste?

At 1215, according to his tracker, the device beeped and displayed a new message:

Lunch: 1230–1330

Drake's stomach grumbled at the thought of food. Soggy cereal had been all he'd eaten, and after the poor night's sleep and the fight in the exercise area, he was running on fumes and heading toward empty. After less than twenty-four hours on the Rig, he could see that keeping his strength up would be vital for survival and, once he knew how, escape.

Sticking with Tristan, as the scrawny kid was proving useful in finding his way around and filling in the gaps in his knowledge, he followed the other inmates back down into the western platform. From there it was a jaunt across to a series of walkways stretching around the outer rim of the platform. Drake hadn't been this way before, but once they were out over the ocean again, he realized that they were heading for the center platform.

"Lunch is served in the core, huh?"

Tristan nodded. "Yeah. There's a large cafeteria, split right down the middle with the girls from the northern platform."

"We eat with the girls?" Drake raised an eyebrow. "That doesn't seem too clever, given some of the blokes in here."

"Well, not *with* them, technically. There's a fence keeping us separate, but you could talk to them, I suppose."

"I take it you never have."

Tristan ran a hand through his hair and shrugged. "What have I got to say?" he muttered.

The cafeteria was another of those large open spaces in the center of its platform, much like the exercise area. Drake could smell frying food before he saw the place. Two guards manned the entrance, and Drake tried to work out whether he'd seen them before or if they were new. Unfortunately, the uniforms were all uniform, and the facemasks made it impossible to tell them apart. He tentatively put his guard count at fifteen, probably more.

Are they all ex-members of Crystal Force? he wondered. Like Brand?

Stepping into the cafeteria, Drake found it to be much like Tristan's description. Rows of tables were bolted to the floor, and the space—like the washroom—was very clean. Beneath the scents of lunch was the tang of chemical cleaner. The kitchen was away to the left of the entrance, built along the entire far wall and through into the other half of the cafeteria, where the girls were separated from the boys by a chain-link fence.

Drake's tracker beeped as he crossed the precipice, and the credit count changed again. *$-254 AC.*

"Four bucks for lunch, then."

"As soon as you walk in, yeah. Holidays are coming up soon," Tristan said with an honest grin. "The price doubles, but we get proper pudding and roast potatoes."

All the inmates were lining up, a sea of green against the silver countertops holding stacks of lunch fare waiting to be served. The staff behind the counter were inmates themselves, being monitored by two guards at either end of the line.

Drake and Tristan fell into line and grabbed trays that held plates and cutlery made of some thick plastic that would be next to impossible to snap. As they shuffled forward in the line, Drake got to see what was on offer. The fried food he had smelled was french fries, with a fair helping of ketchup. The kitchen workers spooned a dollop of mixed vegetables, mashed together, and what looked like lentil soup in a plastic bowl onto their plates. The last worker in line placed a banana and an apple on the side of the tray.

As they reached the far end of the counter, plates full, Drake had his first glimpse of the female population of the Rig. They were lining up much like the boys, dressed in red jumpsuits instead of green. The barrier separating the two halves of the cafeteria kept them physically apart, but groups of boys and girls were chatting quite happily at the tables on either side of the barrier, as if it didn't exist.

"Can we just sit anywhere?" Drake asked.

"Best avoid some of the tables near the back by the fence. Grey and his gang usually hang around there. I sit on my own, mostly, in the middle over here."

Tristan moved away as if he didn't care whether Drake followed or not. Most likely he didn't.

"Hey, Drake, right? Drake?" Drake looked over his shoulder and saw Strawberry Blonde sitting just on the other side of the divide. She offered him a nervous smile. "Thanks for what you did last night. Smacking that guy. He was a jerk."

Her eyes were still puffy, but she was sitting at a table with three other girls. One of them, her red hair pulled back in a tight ponytail above sharp green eyes, gave him a wink.

"Don't worry about it," Drake said.

"Oh, okay. What happened to your nose?"

"Ran into a wall."

The other girls giggled, but the one with the red—or more like auburn—hair gave him a knowing smile and returned to her lunch.

Not knowing anyone else—anyone friendly or at least indifferent—Drake sat with Tristan in the middle of the cafeteria, and they ate their lunch in silence. He kept his head down and his eyes alert for any sign of Grey, but the pack leader was nowhere to be seen. Still, Drake didn't let himself relax. There would be a reckoning for what had happened that morning. Dr. Lambros may have been a qualified psychologist, but Drake thought that expecting the inmates not to fight was like jumping into the ocean and expecting not to get wet. More than a touch naive. He and Grey, and that punk Mohawk, were not done with one another yet.

"This isn't half bad, actually," Drake said, scraping the last of his lentil soup from the bottom of the bowl.

"Pretty bland, don't you think?"

"Maybe, but you're probably just used to all this fine cuisine. I was eating scraps while on the run. What's dinner like?"

"Much the same—more vegetables, and every other night is beef or chicken, with fish in between." Tristan waved his tracker through the air. "Costs five credits."

Drake nodded. In the heart of the center platform there were no windows overlooking the ocean, but he imagined that there were plenty of fish around nevertheless.

"So work after lunch, you said?"

Tristan took a bite of his apple. "That's right. Sucks you're in Tubes."

"How bad could it be?"

Tristan made a face, as if the apple were rotten. "Crawling around in the dark through the muck the Rig sucks up, clearing out pipes and vents? It's usually a punishment detail. Did you insult Warden Storm or something?"

"I told him I wouldn't be staying here long. Gonna swim back to Newfoundland."

Tristan laughed. "Going to escape, then?"

"Thinking about it, yeah."

"Aren't we all. You do know we're in the middle of the ocean, right? The temperature of the water alone would probably kill you, never mind the swim."

Drake shoved his tray aside. He had devoured everything, even the core of the apple. "Well, it's a work in progress."

"Best of luck to you then, Drake." Tristan snorted. "You're going to need it."

"So what's your job, then?"

"Ah, I'm on a pretty good thing there. I do the laundry. Bottom of this platform, just below the staff quarters." He showed Drake his hands. The skin around his fingernails was dry and flaky. "Although the detergent does mess with my skin."

"Sounds better than Tubes . . ." Drake muttered.

At 1330 his tracker beeped yet again and the message on the five-centimeter screen changed.

Work: 1400–1800

Assignment: Tubes, Eastern Platform

"Eastern platform," Drake said. "How do I get there?"

Tristan groaned. "Oh, man, they must really hate you."

"What? Why?"

"I've never done it myself, but I've heard a few stories from the others . . . Eastern Tubes is not only the sea pipes, the old crude pipes, but the Rig's . . . sewage."

Drake looked down at his tracker and back up at Tristan. "How lovely."

Tristan pointed to a group of inmates heading out of the lunch hall. "That lot are working Tubes. See their slumped shoulders, the constant scowl? Follow them, and you'll find your way."

"Right."

Resigning himself to the task ahead, Drake took off after the boys Tristan had pointed out. He fell in with the back of the group, moving through another of those clear plastic corridors built over the water. This one connected the center platform to the eastern. A slight breeze knocked the corridor, making it sway a little. Drake, at first alarmed, relaxed when the movement didn't seem to bother anyone else.

One of the older boys, his face covered in a scraggly beard, eyed Drake up and down. "You workin' Tubes or what?" he asked. His accent was a thick drawl, hard to place, and his dark skin put him from perhaps somewhere in the Middle East.

"Yeah," Drake replied.

Beard's eyes lit up. "Oh look out, boys, we got a fresher. Looks like you're not cleaning crap pipes today, Mario."

A tiny olive-skinned boy at the heart of the pack glanced at Drake and punched the air. "Ha! Thanks, Tommy."

"What are you talking about?" Drake asked.

The guy with the beard, Tommy, pressed his fingers into Drake's chest. "Freshers start at the bottom in Tubes." He gave a great, bellowing guffaw. "And when I say bottom, I mean bottom!"

The other five boys, and Mario, laughed. Drake recognized Tommy as the leader of this little cadre. "If it's all the same to you, mate—"

"It is all the same to me, mate, so you can bugger off if you think it's going to be any other way."

"I—"

"Unless the next words out of your bleedin' mouth are 'Thank you, Tommy,' we'll beat seven shades of snot out of you once we're inside. Guards don't come down the back of Tubes. Offends their sensibilities, it does."

Drake gritted his teeth and clenched his fists. He said nothing as they stepped onto the eastern platform through a set of guarded steel doors. Tommy took his silence for agreement and proceeded to put little Mario in a headlock and rub his hair with his fist.

"Ger'off, Tom!" Mario cried as the rest of the crew egged him on.

"Knock it off!" a guard barked.

Drake followed the Tubes crew down through the eastern platform. The first thing he noticed about this side of the Rig was that the upper levels were all open and exposed. The metal walkways and machinery that must have been used when the Rig was drilling for oil were all still in place. The eastern platform had not been converted into prisoner housing or offices or eating areas. It was as-built, as much as Drake could tell. He was no expert on oil rigs, but this—and not what he'd seen so far—was how he expected them to look.

The wind was chilly, and as the crew moved down the platform toward the water, the ocean spray stung Drake's face. They headed deeper into the platform, away from the edge and the spray and the network of old drill equipment and machinery, some of which hummed softly or rattled noisily on old motors. Drake pondered a set of old, rusted steel doors—locked with a shiny new chain—before they descended into the eastern platform's interior. The crew entered a building that thrummed and groaned with great gusts of air and the sound of water churning through a complex network, and Drake got his first look at the ducts and tubes that gave Tubes its name.

Yellow, blue, orange, and red pipes all converged in the center of a large room, about thirty meters across. The pipes shot up through the eastern platform, converging and diverging so many times that Drake found it hard to follow any particular one for too long.

"Right," Tommy said. "Jim, Argyle, and Wu, with me through levels eight to twelve. Mario, Greg, Neil, and the fresher, one to seven. Grab your hoses, boys."

Large spools of thick hose about the width of Drake's arm were resting on the floor near the doorway. They were long and heavy, not connected to any water source, and it took two of the crew to lift them. Drake shared the hose with Mario as they descended a level below the main junction to a set of older-looking rust-coated pipes.

"Plug the hose in here," Mario said, staring at Drake to make sure he was paying attention. He stood in front of a large panel of levers, switches, and needle gauges. "Prime the line here, so it's ready to spray, and set the pressure on the dial here. Higher the dial, higher the pressure. Got it?"

"Got it," Drake said.

The other two boys on Drake's crew — Greg and Neil — were using a large wrench to remove the cover of the nearest pipe. The release was well oiled, despite the general spottiness on the pipe, and gave way easily.

"Here's your gear," Mario said, and threw Drake a pair of thick leather gloves, worn and frayed, a heavy-duty plastic breathing mask, and a pair of swimming goggles. "Trust me, suit up. You'll be glad you did."

Drake put it on, and Mario shoved the hose into his hands. A small flashlight had been mounted just above the nozzle.

"Right, then, in you go."

"What? That's all the training?"

Mario gave him a thumbs-up. "In the tube, head left, there'll be a blockage about fifteen meters in, when the pipe widens. Always is on this one. You'll see it."

Drake wandered over to the uncovered pipe and stared inside. The channel was narrow and slick with some unspeakable grime. At best, he'd have to crawl on his hands and knees. "And if I refuse?"

Greg and Neil—Drake didn't know which was which—smirked and crossed their arms. Mario sighed. "Tommy wouldn't like that, buddy. No, sir, not one bit. He once forced me down this very pipe and locked me in the dark for an hour because I refused."

Outnumbered and alone, Drake sighed and stepped into the pipe. He dragged the hose in behind him and, after seeing no other way, got down on his hands and knees and headed left down the narrow tunnel into darkness and filth. He flicked on the light on his hose to guide the way.

Crawling through the pipe, he slipped and slid on what could have been grease and a decade of dirt, but he smelled the real mess before he saw it. An unholy stink of rotten fish, of refuse, and worse. Drake gagged into his collar. The stench forced tears from his eyes. He heard laughter from the crew behind him and kept crawling forward with the pressure hose nestled under his arm.

The space narrowed, and Drake, never claustrophobic in his life, felt the weight of a thousand tons of steel pressing down on him. He took a moment to reflect on just what his life had become, crawling through the bowels of a floating prison hundreds of miles from civilization and home. I'll escape from here. Whatever it takes, I'll escape.

The light at the end of the hose showed the pipe curving down and to the right just ahead, but the space also widened to twice its current size. Drake pressed on and managed to crawl up and onto his knees, keeping his head low. At the bottom of the pipe was the blockage—a mess of brown sludge congealed against a rusted grate that led God knows where.

"Nice . . ." Even through the mask, he could taste nothing but foul air. The larger pipe extended on past the grate and down to the left. A small circle of light could be seen in the distance. Curious, Drake started toward the light, but a voice from behind made him pause.

"Yeah, that's the block," Mario said, his voice muffled by his mask. Sludge and grime clung to his hair and clothes. Drake supposed he looked the same himself. "So what's taking so long? Fire the hose and let's get out of this muck."

"What's down that way?" Drake asked. He pointed the hose at the blockage and flipped the lever on the nozzle. A rumble of bubbling water caused the hose to whip like a snake in his hands, but he held strong.

"Overflow," Mario said. "Only if it's really bad do we end up down there, like after a storm or something."

Water burst from the hose in a high-pressure stream that blasted away the blockage. Mario helped guide the hose up and down in a wide, sweeping motion, forcing the congealed muck through the grate. In no time at all, the way was clear.

"Good enough job," Mario said, and slapped Drake on the shoulder. "Come on—we got about ten more pipes to go down here. Then the seawater pipes two floors up need scrubbing and greasing."

Great, Drake thought. His gaze lingered for a moment on that circle of light down the overflow pipe; then he turned and followed Mario back the way they had come.

The next four hours dragged by in a haze of crawling, gagging, and hosing. Mario stayed with Drake for the next few pipes, just to make sure he understood how to spray water at a blockage; then he disappeared to go to the "cleaner" pipes with the rest of the crew. Despite his best efforts, Drake was covered from head to toe in some of the worst grime the Rig had to offer. He was thankful for the gloves, the goggles, and the mask, if nothing else.

At 1745, according to Drake's tracker, Tommy ordered the hoses shut down and spooled away. He was spotless after the day's work, and the grin he gave Drake as he pulled himself out of the last pipe made Drake want to punch his teeth in. But he was too tired, too dirty, and too rundown for that.

After the climb back up the eastern platform, Drake followed the crew to a table near the corridor that led to the center platform. Sets of clean green jumpsuits, socks, shoes, and towels were stacked on the table. Drake collected a set and spent the twenty minutes before dinner blasting himself under the hot water in a washroom identical to the one he'd used that morning. He emerged with the smell and taste of Tubes still clinging to the back of his throat, but he felt better.

Sore, but better.

Beep!

Dinner: 1830–1930

* * *

Drake said little to Tristan at dinner that night, sitting at the same table as they had at lunch, mechanically shoveling food into his mouth one bite at a time. Tristan gave him a sympathetic look and concentrated on his own meal. Close to seven thirty, the dozens of trackers across the cafeteria beeped as one, updating the inmates yet again. Drake glanced at the screen. He was fast learning to hate the high-tech shackle.

Free time: 1930–2130

"So what do we do with our free time, Tristan?"

"I usually just read in my room, but there is a common area on the far side of our platform. Some TV, board games, table soccer, and snooker. A small library with a collection of old rigball games." He tapped his tracker. "Vending machines, too. You can swipe your credits for candy or juice. Or delicious Alliance-brand potato chips."

"I don't think I'm good for credits." After a day on the Rig, Drake owed the Alliance *$-259.* "Any fizzy drinks in those vending machines?"

Tristan shook his head. "The Alliance doesn't manufacture soda, so we don't get it."

Drake pushed his tray away and leaned back. Out of the corner of his eye he saw two guards, a man and a woman, without facemasks, walking down between the tables toward him.

"You're Drake, right?" the woman said. She held a black tablet computer about the size of a passport. The Alliance Systems silver crown was emblazoned on the back. Drake could see that beneath her armor her body was thick with cords of muscle. Below her blond hairline she had lines across her forehead that gave her a permanent scowl. "Need to sort you a bunk in one of the cells. Let's have a look at what's free. Anywhere in particular you want him, Hall?"

Officer Hall, who had slapped Drake's tracker on him the night before, shrugged. "Bit of a troublemaker, this one, but he's going nowhere unless he cuts his hand off." Hall snorted.

"I've got a spare bunk in thirty-six C, Officer Hall," Tristan said. "Ever since Anderson got sick and was sent back to the mainland."

Hall smiled grimly. "Sure. Why not? Let's put the two special cases together, Stein."

He took the tablet from Stein, pressed the screen a few times, and reached for the blue card among the colored set on the chain around his neck. Drake raised his tracker. The device made that familiar beep as the card was swiped across the display.

"All sorted. Thirty-six C, Drake. You'll find a towel, toothbrush, and other toiletries under the sink. Lights out is nine thirty on the dot. Your new penthouse suite will automatically lock at that time. Be in bed by then, or I will personally stick my foot up your ass and fine you fifty credits. Clear?"

"Crystal."

Hall gave him a funny look, as if he'd made a joke, and shook his head, muttering to himself as he moved away with Stein.

"Why'd he call you a special case?" Drake asked once they were gone.

"Don't worry about it." Tristan waved the question away. "I heard all about you at work today, though. You're kind of famous around here. Made the news and everything during your last escape. Did you really use a laundry cart at Cedarwood?"

"No, no. I lassoed some reindeer and flew a magic sleigh to freedom."

"How'd you get out of Harronway?"

"Front door was unlocked."

"No, really?"

Drake tilted his head and offered Tristan a sly grin. "Don't worry about it."

"I guess that's fair. So, want to go to the common room, then? Have a look around?"

Drake thought about it. He needed to know as much as he could about the Rig, all its many ins and outs, if he was going to have any hope of escape. But he was knackered. The day had been long, and the next day would be just the same.

He shook his head. "No. If it's all the same to you, can you show me where to find my bed?"

Tristan grinned. "Sure thing, roomie."

"Don't call me that."

Drake led the way to the western platform, confident in at least that much after his first day on the Rig. Back in the multitiered cellblock, overlooking the exercise area, Tristan took the lead down to the third floor and across the right side of even-numbered cells. A few other boys were about—Mario gave Drake a smirk and a high-five on his way past—but the cellblock was mostly empty.

"Your home away from home," Tristan said. A plaque on the white plaster wall read 36C. "I've been using the bottom bunk. My last cellmate, Carl Anderson, had the top, but he got sick and was sent back to civilization."

"Sick?"

Tristan tapped his forehead. "In here. Started waking up in the middle of the night, screaming about monsters." He grimaced. "It . . . wasn't pleasant."

Drake stepped into his cell. He'd caught a quick glimpse of one of the cells earlier in the day, before lessons. The Rig's accommodations were small but clean. Better than some, Drake thought. The cells were narrow, painted white. Bunk beds were bolted to the left wall, and a toilet-sink combination to the right. The door made up most of the third wall, and the fourth was a barred window of thick glass, overlooking the turbulent sea.

"Do you think the air up on the top bunk drove him mad?" he asked.

Tristan shrugged. "As you can see, it's not much. Lovely views of endless ocean while you take care of business, though. There's a curtain for privacy, and some drawers under the sink there, if you buy a book or something with your credits."

With the grand tour over, Tristan left him to it, slipping into his bunk and picking up a magazine that lay on his pillow. Drake's body ached from the day's work, so much so that he could barely face the climb up the short ladder to his bunk. Just get it over with, he thought.

He washed his face under the cool water from the sink and noticed a bunch of dead bees against the bottom of the window. What were bees doing all the way out here?

Too tired to give it much thought, Drake kicked off his shoes and climbed up into bed. With not so much as a good-night to the boy in the bunk below, Drake was asleep almost as soon as his head hit the pillow.

7

THE *TITAN*

The next day followed much the same pattern as the first, as did the day after that and the week that followed.

Drake learned within a week that life on the Rig was bound solely and always to the rigid device strapped to his wrist. He couldn't step more than half a meter outside of a designated area, at any time of the day, without the tracker buzzing and flashing red, imposing a five-credit fine for every offense.

"You going for the record or something?" Tristan asked one night, catching a glimpse of the display as he brushed his teeth before bed. As Drake clocked his first week on the Rig, his credits stood at *$-437.* That included the hundred or so he'd actually earned working in Tubes.

Still, Drake continued to push his limit, looking for blind spots or holes in the security net. In his not unimpressive experience, any prison was like a block of Swiss cheese—it stank and was full of holes. Ten days into his five-year sentence, it grated on him that he had yet to find even one flaw in Warden Storm's design. Although it took only a distance of half a meter outside the designated area on the center platform to set the tracker off, that could be pushed to three meters on the eastern platform during his work in Tubes. He guessed it was because the work area was quite large—it had to be, some of the pipes were pretty long—and the GPS net was a shade more lenient.

He had realized on his fourth night that he could, technically, be locked out of his cell at night, but only at a distance of half a meter from the door to 36C. Any farther would set the alarm buzzing.

Whether a blessing or not, Drake did not have another encounter with Alan Grey and his gang of meatheads following the fight on day one. He saw the thugs briefly from across the cafeteria on Sunday night at dinner—roast beef, a rare treat. The rest of the time found Grey and his followers conspicuously absent, at least to Drake.

"Advanced lessons," Tristan said when asked where they'd gone. "I don't know much about it. They were picked by Warden Storm."

Drake's small, bespectacled cellmate had fast become one of his main sources of information concerning the workings of the Rig and its people.

He met with Dr. Lambros eleven days after arriving on the Rig, the first time he had seen her since she stitched his hand. Drake had picked those stitches out on his eighth night, the wound all but healed. He thanked her again, and she offered him some gummi sweets, which he accepted with a grin.

"I see you've managed to avoid hitting anyone." She beamed. "This is good, Will. I'm glad you seem to be fitting in here." She glanced at a report on her desk. "Although you seem to be testing the boundaries of your tracker quite often. Sinking into quite a bit of debt, aren't you?"

"Alliance credits just aren't worth that much to me," he admitted. Although he knew better, Drake found himself liking this small woman more and more.

"You do know you need a positive balance of at least two hundred credits at the end of your time here before you'll be released, right?"

Drake frowned. "No, I didn't know that."

"The Rig isn't like those old, rundown government or state facilities, Will. The Alliance, rightfully, expects you to work, to build your character and gain responsibility, and, once your time is up, to pay your way back to St. John's."

Drake's liking for the good doctor varied, depending on his mood.

*   *   *

Of Warden Storm, Drake saw nothing. The man, as far as he could tell, did not deign to lower himself into the cellblock or the center platform at mealtimes. When Drake thought of him, he imagined the warden growing fat at the heart of the control tower, watching the cameras and laughing at Drake's growing frustration with the tracker.

Although he had to admit, if he'd been leashed like this at Harronway—maybe even Trennimax—escape would have been damn near impossible. The tracker would not have made much difference at Cedarwood, as his escape there had been at breakneck speed down Kleine Scheidegg to Grindelwald.

Drake still had nightmares about that rickety laundry cart swerving at sixty miles an hour down the snow-covered tracks.

The devil's own luck, he thought.

His count of the guards had settled at between twenty-five and thirty active officers on the Rig at any one time. The facemasks still made it impossible to be certain, so Drake had taken to watching how the guards held their weapons, how they walked, whether the stunning baton was hung from their left or right hand. The fact that they all carried semiautomatic rifles all the time still made him nervous. He'd never known prison guards stationed among the general population of inmates to be so heavily armed. They reminded him more of soldiers than of guards.

Well, Brand is a soldier.

All it would take was one inmate, or a group working together, to tackle a guard and swipe his weapon. Then what? Drake didn't want to think about it, but given his current situation, he found it hard to think of much else whenever he saw a guard.

On his twelfth day on the Rig, he learned of something that sent the escape gears spinning in his head. The helicopter wasn't the only transport that came to the Rig. After lunch that day, the Tubes crew were granted a small reprieve from their mucky work—for ninety minutes during the four-hour work period, at least. The hose refueling the Seahawk had ruptured on the helipad, and the crew was sent in to mop up the spill.

"Well, what's all this, then?" Drake asked Mario as they stepped out of Processing, in the shadow of the control tower, on the southern platform.

"All what?" Mario, while not overly friendly when Tommy was around, still spared Drake a bit of hassle.

"That ship."

"Eh?"

"That massive bloody ship over there!"

Drake pointed to what was perhaps the largest vessel he had ever seen up close. A cargo ship about the length of a football field, burnt orange under the sun, bearing the silver-crowned crest of Alliance Systems along its hull. Large white letters below the crest identified the ship as the *TITAN*.

"Oh yeah, that shows up every two weeks or so. Drops off food and supplies, I guess." Mario rubbed the back of his neck, blinking in the sun. He was more at home in a dark, dank pipe than in the world above. "What, you think we just throw a line off the Rig's edge and catch dinner every night? For a smart guy, Drake, you're not that smart."

"Keep it up and I'll lock you in the crap pipe, Mario."

Mario snorted and flipped Drake off.

Dozens of workers swarmed across the *Titan*'s deck, removing straps from piles of crates and containers stacked ten meters high. A large yellow crane built into the stern of the ship descended to collect the cargo and swing it up and around onto the Rig, where Warden Storm, Officer Brand, and a group of twelve guards accepted the delivery. The crane also collected a bunch of small shipping containers that rested on sleek hydraulic forklifts on the Rig and loaded them aboard the ship. Brand made sure that each container was firmly attached before the crane took it away.

Working under the sun was invigorating for a change, especially out in the open air, even if the weather was chilly.

Storm clouds threatened the horizon, but Drake rolled up his sleeves and got to work with the rest of the crew cleaning up the fuel spill.

Officers Hall and Stein monitored the crew and directed the cleanup. Drake threw sawdust on the helipad while Mario and Greg scrubbed with heavy wire-bristled brushes. Tommy and his boys scooped up the gooey, fuel-soaked dust into waiting barrels as the large crane on the ship offloaded more Alliance-stamped crates.

Drake kept an eye on the *Titan* as much as he could without arousing suspicion. He watched the ship for close to an hour. Near the end of the cleanup, large panels swung open at sea level in the ship's hull and a fleet of three matte-black speedboats emerged from within the behemoth.

Each small boat was manned by a crew of men who drove in circles around the mighty ship, churning up the dark water. Inspecting for damage? Drake wondered. The boats then vanished under the Rig, but Drake could hear the motors whirring below.

Soon the unexpected break from Tubes was over, and with two hours left of the workday, Drake found himself knee-deep in muck on the eastern platform. At least Mario had some good news at the end of the shift. Tubes crews operated on each platform, with the eastern being the worst, and rotated every two weeks. Tommy's crew switched to the western platform the next day, the boys' platform, below the exercise area. The female inmates took care of the northern and center, while the southern point of the diamond apparently didn't need workers.

Restless and unable to sleep in his bunk that night, Drake

heard the crane on the *Titan* swinging all through the night. When dawn broke, he watched the mighty ship sail away, her cargo hold stuffed with whatever Storm and Brand had loaded onboard.

Drake watched until the ship became a small dot on the broad horizon.

As the patterns of daily life took on a routine, Drake allowed himself to loosen up. He began to think that the fight with Grey had been forgotten; that the guards, while certainly armed, were more like the soft touches in his other prisons; and that the Rig was somehow familiar. But two and a half weeks to the day since he arrived on the diamond-shaped platform, he was reminded of just how far from normal things were.

"I mean you don't care, do you?" Tristan asked, standing next to Drake on one of the treadmills in the exercise area. Tristan walked at a steady pace. Drake was running his eighth mile, burning through pent-up energy and daydreaming about Flanders Road football fields back home.

"Not really, no." He had been on the Rig for eighteen days and had made little to no progress on his escape. Noting guard counts, shift patterns, supply runs, and the Rig's layout was all good and well, but he felt like a hamster on an exercise wheel—running nowhere fast.

"You're negative nearly six hundred credits now."

"What are they gonna do?" Drake asked between deep breaths. "Send me to jail?"

"You need credits to get off, you know, at the end of the five years."

Drake snorted. He liked Tristan, but the kid could be grating sometimes. Drake thought of himself, at fifteen, as older and wiser than his cellmate, but he had learned the other night that Tristan was nearly seventeen. His size and demeanor made him seem a lot younger. "When I go, it won't be on their terms, mate."

"Oh yeah, the escape. How's that working out for ya?"

"Swam halfway to the mainland last night before a cramp forced me to turn back."

"So that wasn't you snoring above me at two in the morning, then?"

Breathing hard, Drake slammed his fist on the treadmill's cool-down mode and began a slow jog. "A clever decoy made of papier-mâché and toothpaste."

"Genius. How'd they ever catch you after your last escapes?"

Drake sighed. "They knew which way I'd run . . ."

"Oh no. Look who's back." Tristan nodded toward the stairs behind Drake.

Drake stopped the treadmill and wiped the sweat from his face with a hand towel. He glanced over and cursed. Alan Grey, Mohawk, and his gang of toughs were descending into the exercise area. Officer Brand walked behind them and leaned casually against the handrail at the bottom of the stairs.

"Advanced lessons, wasn't it?" Drake said. His breathing was returning to normal after the run. "Gone for two weeks. Doesn't that seem odd to you?"

Tristan shrugged. "I try to stay off their radar. You should, too, given what happened last time."

Drake thought about wandering over and asking Grey just

where he'd been, but Tristan was right. He'd likely get his head caved in. Last time, he'd caught Grey and his gang unawares—they'd underestimated him—this time they'd swarm him and tear him apart. That's what Drake would've done if their roles were reversed.

"Right."

Drake spent the next quarter-hour doing a few sets of curls with the free weights. He could feel Grey's eyes on him from time to time. At 1000 his tracker beeped and advised of lessons for the next two hours. Drake was up to lesson fifty in the math department and had found that the problems failed to get any harder. He spent most of the time in class organizing in his head what he knew of the Rig.

"Come on, then," Tristan said.

Drake threw his towel over his shoulder and, feeling good after the workout, followed Tristan over to the stairs that led out of the area. Brand still leaned against the railing, facing away from them and chatting into his radio.

Drake felt the hairs on the back of his neck stand up, an innate sense of danger, and turned just as Grey moved in on him. The large, pig-faced bully held a long, sharp knife in his fist. The knife shone a bright white, as if it were ablaze. What? Drake's mind registered the strange weapon just after his instincts kicked in.

Grey struck at him with the glowing knife in a vicious lunge. Drake swung his left arm up to deflect the strike. The knife caught on his sleeve and cut through his skin as if it were tissue paper.

"Ah!"

Sizzling pain burned down his arm, and a spray of blood spattered the rubber matting of the exercise area. Grey snarled and advanced on him.

"Should've just taken your beating," he spat.

Drake pushed back on Grey's shoulders, and the knife swung between them, cutting his green jumpsuit open across his stomach and missing his flesh by the width of a playing card.

Grey swatted him away, and Drake stumbled back. Only a handful of seconds had passed since the attack began. Drake saw Tristan out of the corner of his eye. His cellmate reached over and swiped the baton hanging loose in its holster around Brand's waist. The guard spun with a cry and reached for Tristan, but the kid was too quick.

With a grunt, Tristan swung the baton and pressed the bright red button on the side, sending a humming charge through the business end. He struck Grey under his extended knife arm, and blue sparks flew.

Grey made a startled cry, something between a whimper and a scream. He fell to the mat, twitching and shaking. Drake lost sight of his strange knife.

Tristan stood, his arm still extended, looking stunned at what he'd just done—and pale.

"Put that down," Marcus Brand said, strolling onto the scene. Then, as if discussing the matter over drinks, he casually raised his sleek black rifle and fired.

A whip-crack sound exploded out of the barrel a split second before the bullet smacked into Tristan's chest.

Brand had shot him.

Drake's eyes bulged, and he felt as if the whole world had been drowned in thick, treacly crude oil. He felt his legs moving, but slowly, dredging through the oil. Tristan's arms flew back in slow motion. The electrified baton fell from his hand in a slow, lazy arc, and Drake watched his eyelids flutter closed.

Time sped up again, and Tristan hit the rubber floor with a dull thud.

"You bastard!" Drake roared. He balled his fists and advanced on Brand.

Brand swung his rifle around and pointed the barrel directly between Drake's eyes. A river of ice melted down his back as Brand pressed the hot barrel against his forehead and smirked.

"What was that, Mr. Drake?" Brand asked. "What did you call me?"

Quite a crowd had gathered in the half-minute since the fight began. Guards on the tiers above, inmates around the enclosed exercise area. Grey's gang hung back, forming a half circle around their fallen leader. The air trembled with tension but was quiet enough that Drake heard his heart pounding in his ears as drops of blood from his arm splashed against the floor.

"You . . . you shot him."

Brand laughed. "I certainly did. Look closer, Drake, you moron."

Glaring down the length of the rifle, Drake took a slow step back and looked at Tristan, expecting a bloody mess. The scrawny boy's glasses had fallen from his face, but there was no blood—no gunshot wound. A dart, about the size of Drake's thumb, stuck through his green jumpsuit in the nook below his left shoulder.

"Stunning rounds—nonlethal," Brand said, and spat on the mat next to Tristan. "More's the pity, huh? He'll have one helluva bruise and a headache when he wakes up, though."

Drake shook as he turned back to Brand.

"What's the matter, boy? Scared?"

The guards on the walkway above jeered and laughed. Four of them had descended to stand on the stairs behind Brand, weapons at the ready. The inmates looked on, some frightened, most solemn.

"No," Drake said carefully. "No, I'm not scared."

Brand scoffed and, after a long moment, lowered his rifle. "Why's your arm bleeding?"

Drake gestured over his shoulder. "Grey had a knife. Tristan must've seen him go for me. That's why he grabbed your baton."

"A knife? That looks more like a burn."

Drake actually took a moment to look at his arm. A long, jagged cut stretched from the crook of his elbow down his left forearm. But the wound looked . . . scorched. Cauterized, he thought. Half the cut was blackened and burned. It was still bleeding, but only a trickle compared with what it should have been.

"I saw the knife," Drake said. "It was shiny—no, bright. Glowing."

Brand's smile faded, and he glared over Drake's shoulder at the unconscious Grey and his gang. "Pick him up and get him

64

into his bunk," he snarled. The gang and Mohawk shuffled their feet. "Now!" Brand snapped.

"Warden'll want to know about this, Marcus," Officer Hall said, on the stairs behind Brand.

Brand nodded. "You," he said, pointing at Drake. "With me to the infirmary."

"What about the knife?" Drake asked.

"There was no knife, Mr. Drake."

"One of his gang must've taken—"

Brand grabbed him by the collar and pushed their faces together. "I swear, Drake, in front of God and all these witnesses, that if you don't follow me to the infirmary right now, I will snap your bleeding neck!"

Hot spittle sprayed Drake in the face. Worse, he believed every word the mad guard had spat.

The stairs cleared behind Brand as he turned on his heel and stomped away, expecting Drake to follow. Taking a tight rein on his anger lest he find himself on the receiving end of one of the trigger-happy guards, or worse, Drake knelt next to Tristan and scooped the small boy up into his arms.

Expecting a strain, Drake almost dropped him in surprise. Tristan weighed next to nothing. He was skin and bones beneath his jumpsuit. He mumbled incoherently below his breath as Drake carried him up the stairs, unconscious but alive, watched by at least six dozen pairs of quiet eyes.

The climb up the cellblock was slow and the stairs narrow, but Drake didn't let his burden fall, nor did he stop for rest. He was certain that Michael Tristan, the Rig's most unassuming and unintimidating resident, had just saved his life.

8

NURSE IRENE

The infirmary, Drake learned that morning, was on the roof of the center platform. A two-story building, similar to the classroom on top of the boys' platform, was built next to what looked like an open space that was surrounded by tiered seating. If he were anywhere else in the world, Drake would have thought he was looking at a small concrete sports field.

The reception desk inside the infirmary was unattended.

"Sit and wait," Brand ordered, and cast a sneer at Tristan in Drake's arms.

Brand stepped through a set of white double doors and left Drake in a waiting room that was similar to doctors' offices the world over. A row of neat cushioned chairs lined the wall next to a small table holding old magazines. Large indoor plants sat in the corners, and a wall of posters recommended flu shots, regular exercise, and a healthy diet.

Drake's arm stung. He stood there, tempted to follow Brand. Tristan may have been too small for even the featherweight division, but carrying him up ten flights and across platforms had created a knot of tension between Drake's shoulders. He wanted to put the boy down, but was left waiting alone for two minutes before Brand swung back through the doors and gestured him through.

The room beyond the waiting area looked far more like an infirmary. Rows of hospital beds lined the far wall, next to windows that let in a flood of sunlight. Medicine cabinets hung from the walls, and trolleys of bandages, medical equipment, and computers stood at the ready.

A tall, dark-skinned man with a pepper-white beard, dressed in a lab coat and glasses, smiled at Drake.

"Hello, young man. I'm Dr. Elias. Why don't you put him down on the bed over here. Gently now."

Drake grunted with relief and sat on the next bed once Tristan was set down. He rolled his shoulders to work out the knot and watched Dr. Elias lift Tristan's eyelids and shine a penlight into his eyes. "Hmm . . . did you have to shoot him, Brand?"

"Kid had a weapon and was using it, Doc," Brand said.

Dr. Elias carefully removed the dart in Tristan's shoulder and popped it in a silver pan. "He'll be out for a good hour or more, I expect. But he's breathing normally. We'll keep him overnight tonight and make sure he doesn't have a reaction to the dart."

"Whatever," Brand said. He reached for the set of colored cards around his neck and swiped one over Tristan's tracker. The red out-of-bounds warning screen faded to blue. "You, too, I guess."

Drake presented his arm and was granted free movement.

"Now let's have a look at that scratch," the doctor said. He was a large man, with broad shoulders and arms the width of tree trunks. Drake felt tiny, as Tristan must have felt around almost everyone, as the doctor took hold of his arm in his massive hands. "Hmm. Nasty."

Drake thought the doctor almost sounded pleased with his latest wound.

"An excellent opportunity for some of the apprentices to learn, don't you think, Nurse Rose?" Dr. Elias said.

Drake looked over his shoulder and saw a tall, thin woman wearing purple hospital scrubs. She must have been about a hundred years old. Her gray hair framed a wrinkled face composed of tiny, narrow eyes, a hooked nose, and pursed lips. The sour-faced woman nodded. "What d'you say, Brand? Pull a few of my girls out of lessons?" She had the voice of a lifelong smoker thrown in a blender.

Brand rolled his eyes and walked away, reaching for his radio.

"Does it hurt, young man?" Nurse Rose asked.

"No, it tickles."

"Well, let's get some antiseptic on it," Dr. Elias said. "The apprentices shouldn't be too long, and we'll have it cleaned up."

Drake thought of Grey's strange glowing knife. He looked over at Brand, talking into his receiver. *There was no knife, Mr. Drake.* What had the officer said to Dr. Elias before he and Tristan were allowed into the infirmary? Drake wondered. Why hadn't the doctor asked how the cut had happened?

As Dr. Elias dabbed the wound with cotton soaked in antiseptic, he mumbled to himself. "Oh yes, quite nasty."

He chuckled. "Impressively nasty."

Drake held his arm as steady as he could and said nothing.

"Excellent." Dr. Elias stood once he was finished with the antiseptic. "If you'll excuse me, I've some work to attend to."

Ten minutes later a guard Drake had never seen before—an older man with a skinhead and freckles—escorted a group of three young girls into the infirmary. A blonde, a brunette, and a redhead. Drake almost smiled. They were young, no more than eighteen, if that, and dressed in the red jumpsuits of the female inmate population.

"Right, girls," Nurse Rose said, hands on her hips. "Come and have a look at this and tell me what you'd do with it."

The girls gathered around Drake's bed and looked him up and down. Feeling as if he'd been put in a display case, he ran a hand back through his short, fuzzy hair. Nearly three weeks on the Rig had forced his shaved head to sprout dark brown.

"Well?" Nurse Rose said. "You've been listening and learning about this for the past three months. What would you do with him?"

One of the girls, the petite redhead whose hair was actually closer to auburn in the light, smirked. "Not much. I don't think he'd be able to handle it."

Drake laughed and was thankful that his dark skin helped hide the blood rising in his cheeks. He remembered seeing this girl before, on his first night, sitting with Strawberry Blonde in the cafeteria.

"Irene, behave yourself!" the nurse snapped. "Susan? Gemma?"

"Dab it with antiseptic?" Gemma said, unsure.

"Right, that's been done. What next?"

"Um . . . does it need stitching?" she asked.

"Good. That slice toward his elbow is still bleeding. The rest of the wound was cauterized during the accident—"

"Wasn't a bloody accident . . ." Drake muttered.

"—but he'll need stitches on that section. A nice row of fifteen, most likely. Any of you willing to learn?" Gemma and Susan sniffed and stepped back, looking at Drake's wound with disgust. "What about you, girlie?"

"You better not squeal or cry, kid," Irene said.

"Drake. My name is Will Drake."

Irene tilted her head, and her green eyes widened. "Harry Houdini himself? We'd heard on north that they'd moved you here."

"Enough chitchat," Nurse Rose said. She had Drake place his arm on an armrest as she swiveled around his bed on a stool, a set of sewing needles, thread, and bandages resting in a dish on her lap. "I'll get you started, Irene—pop these gloves on, dear—and then we'll have you prod him once or twice. Pull over that stool and watch closely. You two"—she pointed at Gemma and Susan—"entertain yourselves. I don't know why I bother with you girls sometimes . . ."

All in all, it took the nurse—and the apprentice, Irene—fifteen minutes to stitch and treat Drake's arm. He sat back and left them to it, thankful for the soothing burn cream they applied once the stitches were in. Every few minutes he'd look up and catch Irene staring at him. She held his eyes for an awkward amount of time, as if weighing and assessing him. Drake didn't quite know what to make of it.

"Now, Irene, wrap the wound in this gauze bandage. You'll have to come back every day for the next week or so, young man, to have the bandage changed," Nurse Rose said. "We'll give you two pills for the pain, which should help you sleep tonight. I'll go see to that." She wheeled away on her stool, leaving Drake alone with Irene. Gemma and Susan were busy chatting and leaning against the window.

"So what happened, then?" Irene asked. She brushed a loose strand of her hair away from her light green eyes.

"Knife."

Irene raised an eyebrow. "Was it on fire?"

Drake snorted. "It was, actually, yeah."

"Well, stranger things have happened around this place . . ."

That piqued Drake's interest. "Such as?"

Irene stared at him again, biting her lip. She took a deep breath and seemed to come to a decision. "Are you a good guy, Drake? Have you . . . been in the elevator on the eastern platform?" Her voice was lower than a whisper.

"I . . . no, I haven't."

With a dismissive sigh, she stood and turned to leave. Drake reached out and gently grasped her arm, just above her tracker. Her pale skin was soft and dashed with freckles. "Where's the elevator go? I work Tubes on that platform and haven't—"

Irene's arm spun in his grip, and she grasped his wrist hard, casting a quick look across the room at Nurse Rose pottering around the medicine cabinets. "Tubes? Listen to me carefully. There's a door near the base of the platform. A rusted old door that leads down a corridor full of old drilling equipment. Have you seen it?"

Drake knew what she was talking about. "Old rusted door, but locked with a new silver chain?"

Irene's eyes blazed. "Yes! Can you get through it?"

71

"A lot of the pipes we clean go under and over it. Never been that far through, though. Most of the blocks—"

"But you could, if you wanted?"

Drake shrugged. "What's so important?"

Irene dug her fingernails into his wrist. "I'll be waiting. On every fifth day at midnight. The fifth, the tenth, the fifteenth, and so on, you understand?" Drake could only nod. "If you can get there, and get me through that door, I'll show you something incredible."

"I—" Drake began.

"I'm trusting you, Will Drake," she whispered. "Don't breathe a word of this to anyone. Please just—"

"Two pills," Nurse Rose said, swiveling back around on her stool. She held one of those passport-size computer tablets in one hand and a tiny plastic cup with the pills in the other. "A little stronger than your average painkillers, but then that burn will start to sting, young man."

Irene let his wrist go and stepped away.

"How's it feel now?" Nurse Rose asked.

"Better, I guess. Thank you."

"Don't thank me yet. This little accident of yours will be costly." The nurse made a few swipes on the tablet. Drake's tracker beeped. He was now negative nearly seven hundred and fifty credits. As he knew all too well, health care wasn't cheap, especially where the Alliance was concerned.

The skinhead guard, who had been sitting and chatting with Brand at the reception desk, called over, "Are we done here, Rose? Can I take this lot back to class?"

"All done, Harry. Irene, make sure you scrub your hands thoroughly in the sink over there before you leave."

"Yes, Nurse Rose," Irene said, and cast Drake a quick, desperate look over her shoulder as she moved away.

Drake watched her go as the old nurse cleaned up the mess and disposed of the medical waste. Irene washed her hands, as instructed, and left with the other two girls. She did not look back again.

What was that all about? Drake wondered. Something incredible? He couldn't even begin to fathom just how he was supposed to reach the eastern platform at midnight, let alone without the tracker monitoring his every move. Did Irene know how to remove them? His mind spun with new possibilities, and he glared at the device strapped to his wrist with renewed purpose. You're coming off, he thought.

Tristan sat up with a cry, startling Drake out of his thoughts, and fell back with a whimper. He pressed a hand against his forehead and moaned. "Bloody hell, what happened? Drake?"

"Hey, buddy."

"I . . . Oh, God, I shocked him, didn't I?"

Drake snorted. "You shocked all of us, I reckon. Particularly Brand. He shot you with a stunning dart."

Tristan tried to sit up again and failed. "I feel terrible . . ."

"Not as bad as you're gonna feel when I've had a word, boy," Officer Brand said, storming over from reception. He slowly drew his baton and held the red trigger. Electricity thrummed through the weapon. "Now, let's have a review of the rules, shall we?"

For the next ten minutes Brand proceeded to shout and curse at Tristan until he was red in the face and almost bouncing on the spot. Tristan, his head already killing him, sank farther and farther back into the bed, as if the mattress could swallow him whole. What little color was left in his face drained away, leaving him on the verge of tears.

"This has gone to the warden, you understand?" Brand said, calming down and pausing for breath. "There'll be a review, boy. Personally, I'll be pushing for a reevaluation of your sentence. What you did was utterly unacceptable, and you're just lucky no one was killed!"

"And that's why," Drake said, wagging his finger, "you don't mess with another man's baton."

Brand turned his gaze on him and whispered, "One more word, Drake. Please, just say one more word."

Drake gave Brand a smile full of nothing but contempt. "Daffodils," he said.

9

HAPPY NEW YEAR

As Drake's first few weeks on the Rig bled into his first month, the morning of December 15 dawned with thick black storm clouds rolling in over the horizon. Despite his stolen whispers with Irene in the infirmary, he had made no progress with a plan to escape, let alone get his tracker off. He woke every morning to a sense of defeat and frustration that had to be pushed aside if he were to have any hope of making it off the Rig before he turned twenty.

By midmorning, the skies over the Rig were dark and impenetrable. Thunder rumbled, and flashes of electric-blue light danced among the clouds, accompanied by a biting wind that lashed the skin and rocked the Rig. Waves three meters high—and getting higher—slammed against the tiny collection of platforms standing alone in the middle of the Arctic Ocean.

This time Drake knew it wasn't his imagination. The floor beneath his feet was swaying. If he stared across at another platform at a fixed point, he could see the movement of the entire structure.

"This normal?" he asked Tristan as they left the classroom atop the boys' platform, heading for lunch. The first drops of rain splattered against the concrete—a drizzle that preceded a downpour.

Tristan nodded. "It's happened before. One day the wind was so bad, half the blokes got seasick." He stretched the word out until it became something horrible, a groan of the long-suffering. "Cellblock stank for days after that."

"Looking a bit flushed, Drake!" Mario said, chewing on a toothpick. "Tubes will be a mess tomorrow, *mi amigo*!" He threw his arm around Tristan's shoulders and grabbed his neck. "What about you, four eyes? We could use a runt like you in the small pipes!"

Tristan struggled unsuccessfully against Mario's grip. The rain was falling harder now, cold drops the size of silver dollars splashing Drake's arms.

"Let him go," Drake said, and pointed to the edge of the platform just three meters away. A fence at shoulder height was the only protection—except for the guards stationed along the perimeter—between the inmates and a swift fall into the sea far below. "Or we'll be seeing just how well you can swim."

Mario's smile faded a bit. He let Tristan go. "All right, just joking with the gringo, Drake. You know me. Everyone messes with little Mikey here, don't they, Mike?"

Tristan hunched his shoulders and pushed his glasses straight on his face.

"Not anymore," Drake said. He sighed inwardly—it was trouble like this that had gotten his friend Aaron killed at

Cedarwood. Drake hadn't made much in the way of friends since then. "Or they're messing with me, too. Got it?"

Mario tried for a smile, "Yeah, Drake. Sure I got it. Only playing, anyway." He darted away, keeping Drake between himself and the edge of the platform.

"You didn't have to do that," Tristan said quietly as they resumed the walk to lunch.

"What happens if the Rig has to be evacuated?" Drake asked as a particularly violent gust of wind made the platform moan.

"There are evacuation crafts below some of the platforms. At least that's what I was told . . . I've never actually seen them."

"There'd have to be something, wouldn't there? I mean we're on a goddamn oil rig in the middle of nowhere."

Tristan made a face, masking a brief worry. "Yeah, there's the lifeboats, that's what I heard."

Later that night, after lights out, the storm broke in earnest against the Rig. Confined to their cell, Drake and Tristan rode out the worst of it as best they could. The entire platform was shaking as waves of tremendous power and height crashed against the pillars that kept the Rig afloat. The rain fell so fast and thick outside their window that Drake couldn't even see the orange lights that lit up the Rig at night, alerting ships to its presence.

Tristan had been right about the seasickness. Drake's cell-mate was up and retching over the toilet every five minutes, holding his stomach and groaning. At this point he was just throwing up water and little else. Drake felt woozy as well, so he concentrated on the task at hand. He'd nicked a pen lid from the classroom that morning and was working the pointed end into the keyhole on his tracker.

After a month on the Rig, Drake had come to the realization that the tracker problem would have to be solved before he had any hope of escape. Or of meeting that Irene girl . . . The massive amounts of fines he had gained exploring the boundaries of the device had convinced him of that. So far he'd tried the lock against a paper clip found in the common room, a prong on the plastic sporks they used for meals, and now the ballpoint pen lid.

Nada.

Drake was no expert on lock picking—in fact, he had no idea what he was doing. But it was better than nothing, and it made him feel that some progress was being made. He was confident that if he could get the device off, a plan of escape would present itself. The tracker had been activated even before it was snapped around his wrist in Processing a month earlier, which led him to the shaky conclusion that, perhaps, he could remove it without setting off any alarms. It couldn't sense whether or not it was attached to his wrist. If he could get the device off, he could move unimpeded—even make it seem to whoever was monitoring the devices that he was somewhere else entirely. In the month he'd been here, that seemed like the greatest flaw in the Rig's security. The cruel and heavy-handed staff relied too much on the leashes strapped to the inmates. Drake had never once seen a guard actually poke his head into the cell at night.

Drake worked the pen lid back and forth in the narrow

rectangular lock, listening closely for clicks and feeling for resistance. The point of the lid was about three centimeters long, and it slipped into the hole all the way to the cap. The more Drake fiddled with it, the more warped and stretched the plastic lid became. After half an hour of fruitless trying, Drake tossed the lid aside, afraid of breaking the point off in the tracker and ruining any future attempts.

He rolled over to face the wall and tried to sleep—but sleep was long in coming. Images of the Rig's delicate spine snapping and plunging into the freezing water plagued him until a gray and lifeless dawn broke through the rain.

* * *

The weather cleared up after the storm into a brisk but sunny week.

As Mario had promised, Tubes was a nightmare after the storm. The Rig had soaked up—God knows how—mounds of seaweed and sand. The working day was extended for the crews through free time and beyond lights out to get the pipes cleared and keep the mighty prison running. For the first time since he arrived, Drake saw the technicians from the control tower out and about, making repairs and checking the dials and readouts on dozens of machines. He stumbled into his cell around midnight, escorted by a guard, for three nights in a row.

On the fourth day after the storm, he was afforded a brief reprieve from the work, as his latest session with Dr. Lambros had rolled around. Drake had been looking forward to a change of pace, and she provided just that. At the very least, it was an opportunity to stop looking over his shoulder for Alan Grey or worrying about all the guards with rifles and batons.

"Good afternoon, Will," the psychologist said. She removed her wire-frame glasses and smiled. "How are you this week? Bit of a scare with that storm, wasn't it?"

"Yeah. I only just managed to keep my dinner down. Is the Rig supposed to sway like that?"

Dr. Lambros nodded. "Oh yes. I've been here nearly eighteen months, and we've had a few wild nights, I can tell you."

"What happens if we have to evacuate?" Tristan hadn't been so sure, and Drake was honestly curious. If he could force an evacuation somehow . . . Easier to escape when he wasn't a hundred or more miles out at sea.

"There are lifeboats under this and the northern platform. In that very unlikely event, you'd proceed through the outer shell, and one of the winches would lower you down—along with ten or so others—into one of the rafts. You weren't told all this when you arrived?"

"No."

"Oh, well, now you know. I'm sure someone just overlooked that in your induction."

Drake weighed the idea, then nodded slowly. His induction had been a bowl of cold soup and five minutes of butting heads with Warden Storm. He was certain something more was going on at the Rig. Something secret. He thought of Irene, the urgency in her eyes, and of Grey's "advanced lessons."

"So what should we talk about today?" Dr. Lambros asked.

"You've been here nearly five weeks now. One month down!" She made that sound almost like a good thing.

"Only fifty-nine to go . . ." Drake muttered, and made a little puffing sound between his pursed lips. During lunch, Brand had delivered the news that his work schedule would continue—Tubes for another month, on Warden Storm's order. "You know, you may be the only friendly person in this place."

"Have you been making friends?" the doctor asked. She made a few quick notes on the pad before her. Her desk was always cluttered, but even more so today. Drake liked that. He liked her, now that he thought about it, and the wall of qualifications behind her desk.

"Friends . . ." Drake mused. "No, no friends."

"My report says you got into a bit of trouble a few weeks back—another fight with Alan Grey. What have I told you about fighting? Michael Tristan stole a guard's weapon in the assault. I hear rumors it was to protect you."

"I didn't ask him to watch my back. Little bastard took a beating for it, too. If Grey catches up with him . . ."

Dr. Lambros tsked. "Please don't curse in my office, Will. And what he did sounds like a friend to me, if you were being attacked. A touch brazen perhaps, but loyalty like that—in this place—can be dangerous, you know."

"I don't have any friends," Drake insisted, and thumped his fist against the arm of the leather chair. "Last friend I had . . ."

"Yes? Go on?" She smiled warmly.

"Last friend I had . . . I got him killed," Drake said flatly. He took a deep breath. May as well get it all out. "He was my cellmate at Cedarwood. His name was Aaron. You said something about it the first time we met, with the fire in the laundry."

"It's all in your file, yes. They also say you tried to pull him out, that it was an accident."

Drake shook his head. "Does it say the only reason he was there is because we were stealing tools to escape? I sent him. My fault."

"No, it doesn't say that. But the fire was caused by faulty wiring, yes?"

Drake nodded. "That's what they said."

"You can't blame yourself for wanting out of these places, Will," Dr. Lambros said, and put her pen down. "Get back to the real world—to video games, the Internet, sports, junk food, girls—but you do understand that your behavior isn't conducive to those things, to functioning within society. That's why you're here, because right now, here is the best place for you."

"You think I'm escaping for . . . for what? Cheeseburgers and Internet porn?" Drake gave her a wintry, humorless smile. "That's pathetic."

"Why do you want to escape?"

He waved the question away and rubbed at his eyes. To say he was tired was an understatement. "You've got your reports and your files—figure it out, Dr. Lambros."

* * *

Christmas Day came and went with very little fanfare on the Rig, despite the extra-special food Tristan had promised the night of Drake's arrival. Roasted potatoes and a sticky date pudding for lunch. A few of the boys, somehow, received care packages from their homes dotted about the globe. Outgoing mail was restricted on the Rig, an Alliance rule, but apparently exceptions could be made.

There was no work break, either. Drake's tracker beeped, as he'd known it would, for his shift on the Tubes crew. Tommy, Mario, and the boys had been back on the eastern platform for just under a week. Drake had long since tired of the drudgery, but having no say in the matter—and not wanting to make any more enemies than he already had—he kept doing the work.

A cold, near-freezing breeze whistled through the eastern platform that afternoon. Drake's hand nearly froze to the hose as he swept the tubes clean on the fifth level. Having been at it a month, he'd suggested to Tommy a week back that they request an extra hose and split the teams into three. Drake and Mario, Greg and Neil, and get the work done twice as fast. Tommy had told him to piss off, but the hose was there the next day. Greg and Neil hadn't been too pleased, as the amount of pipes Drake had to clean had been cut in half—work they now had to do, but as always, Mario seemed to enjoy it.

They were all done by five, and Drake emerged from his tube with his stomach grumbling. Thoughts of food on Christmas Day made him think of his mother and the feasts she used to spend days preparing in advance. He spent a few minutes wondering, among other things, whether she was enjoying Christmas dinner with Nanna Vera next door on Tilbury Road, back home in East London.

Stuffed turkey from Arnie's butchers down the road, and then blackberry pie and ice cream for dessert.

"Drake, with me," Tommy said, pulling him from what were fast becoming sad, hungry thoughts. "You got one last job for the day."

Drake followed Tommy down a level, along the exposed outer rim of the eastern platform, past the rusted door with the new chain that so intrigued apprentice nurse Irene, and back around to a massive collection of what looked like boilers and tanks, all connected via a network of vents and small gas pipes.

"What's this, then?" Drake asked. The slick grime from the day's work was drying in his short hair. Seeing as how he had no means of shaving his head, he wanted to wash the muck out before it became permanent.

"Rig's heating system," Tommy said. "Hot water, air conditioning, water treatment, and de-sal." He pointed to the boilers and tanks, all of them rumbling and tumbling. Subtle vibrations echoed through the steel walkway. "We need to clean the filters in the heating duct there."

"We?"

"You, Drake." Tommy pointed to a ladder alongside one of the wide silver vents. "Up you go, remove that panel there, hop inside, and replace the dirty filter with this clean one." The Tubes crew leader reached into a cardboard box at the base of the ladder and removed a rectangular piece of plastic, crisscrossed with metal mesh.

"The heating on? I don't want to get fried."

Tommy slapped his forehead. "What was I thinking? Damn, son, you'd think it was my first day on the job." He stepped over to a panel of dials, levers, and buttons, made a few adjustments to the dials, and the sound of air rushing through the vents overhead became a low hum. "Two and a half years I've been doing this, Drake. Now get up there. You've got five minutes before the heating automatically cycles back up. Warden don't like to be cold."

Drake tucked the new filter under his arm and began to climb the ladder. The vent was only about three meters above his head, but carrying the filter made the climb difficult.

"So the eastern platform heats the whole Rig, huh?" he asked Tommy as he fiddled with the sliding panel on the vent.

"That's right. If we don't keep this running, we'll freeze in January, when the cold really sets in."

The whole Rig . . . Drake thought as he slid the panel loose and crawled up into the vent. A burst of balmy air hit him in the face and warmed him through. That means it's all connected. Those silver vents running under the clear corridors between platforms . . . they're air ducts, all leading back to the eastern platform. Learn something new every day.

With all the muck and grime still clinging to him from the pipe work, changing the filter proved to be a lesson in patience. The vent was caked in dust and fluff, but he managed to swap the old filter for the new. Drake cursed as unlatching the screen caused a plume of dust to explode into his face. The dust stuck to him as if he'd been tarred and feathered.

Tommy smirked as he came down the ladder. "Merry Christmas."

Drake tossed the old filter at his head.

* * *

New Year's passed with as much fanfare as Christmas, and Drake was awake to see it as his tracker crossed over from 2359 to 0000 on December 31.

"Happy New Year," Tristan muttered in the darkness from his bottom bunk. "Two thousand twenty-six. I think I'll go traveling. Take a gap year away from this place. Yup, sounds good."

The first few weeks of January were bitter cold. Arctic winds covered the pipes and outer layers of the Rig in frost. Tubes became an almost full-time job, and two extra crews were assembled from the inmates to deice and thaw the critical systems. Once again, the trained engineers and technicians journeyed down from the warmth of the control tower to supervise.

During free time on January 15, Drake sat idle in one of the chairs in the common room, overlooking, as all the outer rooms did, the vast, empty ocean. Today was his two-month anniversary. He had spent exactly eight weeks on the Rig and had come no closer to figuring out how not to spend the next two hundred and fifty-two weeks here. He had long since given up on trying to pick the lock on his tracker. However the device was held together, it wasn't with a tumbler or any normal lock. Perhaps if I break my thumb, I could slip it off . . . he thought. No, I'd never get it over the wrist.

Overhead, the flat-screen TVs drilled into the walls churned through Alliance-approved programming. "Join Crystal Force—Enhance, Explore, Excel—and make a difference today!" Or the always popular "Alliance Systems—safeguarding the future of corrections across the world. Providing humane rehabilitative facilities, the Alliance is committed to global safety."

"Drake, fancy a game of pool?" Mario asked.

Drake gave him a brief grin. "Think I'm off to bed, actually, mate. Storm's rolling in—Tubes'll be a mess by tomorrow."

"Suit yourself. Want me to come read you a bedtime story?"

Drake considered, then shook his head. "Screw you and your story."

Mario flipped him off and darted away. "Greg! Game of pool?"

The walk down four tiers from the common room was as dull as ever. The scent of the Rig, old crude oil and salt, could never be completely masked by the air-conditioning system or the cleaning crews. No, that was a smell that had seeped into the Rig's bones, as surely as weary resignation was seeping into Drake's. If he didn't get off this platform soon, he was sure he'd go mad. As mad as Tristan's last cellmate. Drake hadn't seen Tristan since breakfast. He'd been called away by Hall to the control tower—Warden Storm wanted to see him. Nothing good could come of that, Drake had thought at the time.

Five years is too long . . .

Drake entered 36C and washed his face in the sink. Places like this, in Drake's experience, hurt the people they claimed to help. They did more harm than good. Kids who made mistakes, who were forced into crime by trial or circumstance, were served justice from the courts, sentenced away, and all but forgotten. The Rig, and places like it, screwed people up. Sure, the violent and disturbed people needed help, to be restrained from harming themselves and others, but at what point did justice become vengeance? As far as Drake was concerned, the Alliance—and the governments across the world that supported the Alliance—had long since crossed that line.

Lost in his thoughts, he didn't hear Tristan shuffle into their cell until the kid sank down on his bed and muttered, "Another year."

Drake spat out a mouthful of toothpaste. "Eh?"

"They put another year on my sentence for swiping Brand's baton." He heaved a massive sigh and whispered, "I'm back at the start . . ."

Drake finished brushing his teeth in silence, not quite knowing what to say. Tristan had only done what he'd done to protect Drake—to save his life. Grey would've stuck him for sure with his strange glowing knife if Tristan hadn't acted. What had Brand said? *There was no knife, Mr. Drake.*

He felt guilty for what had happened to Tristan, but it wasn't his problem, and what could he do about it, in the end? Take him with you when you escape, whispered a small voice in the back of his mind. Drake shook his head. He didn't have an escape plan, not even the fuzzy outline of one, and he'd learned well at Cedarwood not to make friends.

"Sorry," he said, climbing up onto the top bunk. "That's rough."

"'S not your fault," Tristan muttered, half his face squished into his pillow.

As Drake slipped into bed, he thought he'd never heard so much defeat in one voice. He bit his lip, lying in silence for a long moment, and then he sighed. "I never said thanks, did I? For what you did."

"I'd ask you to buy me a Twix or something from the vending machines, but . . . what's your score now?"

Drake glanced at his tracker. *$-995.* "Closing in on the full thousand. I'll have it by morning." He tapped the tracker against the wall. "You know, these things really are pretty damn secure."

"Not as secure as you think . . ." Tristan muttered.

"Say what?"

Tristan was quiet for a long moment, and then Drake heard him take a deep breath. "You asked what I did to get here? Why I'm a 'special case,' like you?"

Drake sat up. "Yes?"

"I . . . I did something, and a lot of people got hurt. Some died."

"What did you—"

"You've seen me in lessons, right? How I use the pen and paper and don't actually touch the computer."

"Yeah."

"That's because I'm not allowed to touch a computer again." Tristan sniffed. "Well, not for the next five years, according to the judge who threw me to the Alliance down in Perth. Don't think they care about the lessons anyway."

Drake agreed. He was sure there was more to the Rig than he and Tristan knew. He was certain that some of the inmates were in on the secret—Alan Grey and his gang—and he was certain that it was dangerous. Very dangerous. He thought of Irene. *I'll be waiting. On every fifth day at midnight.* "Something strange is going on in this place, mate."

"You only just getting that, huh?" Tristan laughed bitterly.

Their trackers beeped as one, marking half past nine and

lights out. The automatic steel cell door slid across, locking them in for another night. The overhead light flickered and died, leaving nothing but flashing lights along the outside of the platform, casting the dancing shadows along the cell wall blood-red.

"Why aren't you allowed to touch a computer?"

Tristan sighed. "Because last time I did, eight people died. God, eight people died." He moaned, and Drake heard him shuffling around. "It wasn't like I meant to do it, but it happened, and that's why I'm a special case, Drake. Most of the kids in here, they . . . they did mean to do what they did. To kill or . . . or worse, I guess. They knew what they were doing. Mine was an accident."

Drake said nothing. Tristan was working his way toward whatever he wanted to say, moving in slow circles around the truth.

"My dad's a software engineer. He's pretty good with computers, and I used to watch him all the time. He'd teach me things. By the time I was five, I knew three coding languages and was working on my fourth. My dad was good with them, but I was a natural. I could do anything online, anything. They used to call it hacking, once upon a time. Now it falls under the International Cyber Terrorism Act."

"Call what hacking?"

"I was one of the best by the time I was twelve. Diving in and out of networks—civilian, military, it didn't matter. I was . . . I've thought about it a lot since coming here. I was too clever. That's what happened. In the end, I was too clever, and I didn't see all the people I was affecting. All I saw was the display, you know. Lines of code, numbers on a screen, moving information back and forth like it was a game."

Drake kept silent, which Tristan took as an invitation to continue.

"By the time I was thirteen, I'd figured out that people were willing to pay for access to the networks, or to have those networks destroyed, modified, unlocked, and dispersed . . . Everything is connected these days, Will. I mean everything. I could hack into NATO using one of the consoles behind the counter at Burger King."

"Really?"

Tristan chuckled grimly. "No, not really, but you get the idea. I was good."

"So what happened?"

"Like I said, I didn't see the people, you know. Just the screen. I . . . I shut down the power grid for all of Perth one night. A million people in the dark. Sounded cool, you know, and I wanted to see if I could do it. They still use the old Cerco systems down there . . ."

Drake didn't know what that was, but from the tone of Tristan's voice he imagined it was something outdated. "So you switched off the lights?"

"All of Perth, in the dark, in the middle of summer, where the heat often forces power cuts anyway. The generator at Princess Margaret Hospital couldn't handle it, and blew. Eight patients there died, and a whole load more got a lot worse."

Drake could almost feel the wave of despair from the bunk below.

"One of the patients was only nine years old . . ."

"Damn, mate," Drake said. "I . . . I don't know what to say. So they caught you and threw you in here?"

"They didn't catch me. Like I said, I was good. One of the best for my age, even. No way they could have found me." There was pride in Tristan's voice, but also regret. "I turned myself in."

Silence reigned in the small cell for a few minutes. "I don't want to talk about it anymore, Will." Tristan sighed, and Drake was thankful for the dark, because he thought he heard tears in that sigh. Last thing he needed was the awkwardness that would follow seeing Tristan cry. "Let's just say I deserve to be here and leave it at that."

Thinking of how isolated the Rig was from the real world, of Tubes and the heavy-handed tactics of the guards, particularly Brand, and of that line between justice and vengeance, Drake said, "I don't think anyone deserves to be here, mate."

"Yeah," Tristan said. "Maybe not."

Something Tristan had said clicked over in Drake's mind. *Not as secure as you think . . .*

"Tristan, do you know how to get the trackers off?"

Nothing but silence from the bottom bunk. After a minute, Drake turned to face the wall, thinking that Tristan was done talking for the night. Then, a moment later, a tiny, almost inaudible word floated up from below.

"Yes . . ."

10

RIGBALL

Drake tried, in the weeks following Tristan's revelation, to en-
list his help in removing the tracker, but his cellmate wouldn't
budge. His reluctance irked Drake, who didn't like to rely on
anyone for anything, but despite his best efforts, he had failed
to come up with a way of removing it himself, short of cutting
off his hand. Despite his frustration, Drake needed Tristan.
But Tristan seemed resigned to a fate that saw them both
spending the next five years on the Rig.

In the first week of February, Tommy cornered Drake after
work in Tubes and handed him an old, faded jumpsuit.

Drake held the suit up and raised an eyebrow. The number
10 was scrawled crudely on the back in black spray paint.
Ruby-red stains also dotted the collar, the sleeves, and—well,
most of the suit. Drake didn't like to think what those stains
might be.

"What's all this, then, Tommy?"

Tommy stroked his beard and grinned. As of two nights
earlier, he was officially eighteen and one of the Rig's adult

inmates. Drake almost envied the two years he had left on his sentence. "You ever heard of rigball, William?"

"Don't call me that, and no, no I haven't."

"Well, you're our crew's new rigball wingman. Congratulations."

Mario punched the air and applauded. Greg and Neil, as always, glared and smirked.

"No, thanks," Drake said, and tossed the suit back at Tommy.

Tommy's smile faded. "We need a sixth since Anderson was sent home, and you're it, Drake. We all saw you fight your first day here. You can look after yourself, which is what rigball is all—"

"*No* means no, mate." Drake ran a hand back through his hair. He could do that now—his fuzzy dark brown hair was fast becoming a mop. Last time he'd had hair this long was years ago.

"Did we mention," Mario said casually, "that we're one of only two teams in the league? And the other is captained by none other than Alan Grey, your best mate?"

Drake considered, then nodded. "Is that so?"

Tommy pushed the jumpsuit jersey into Drake's chest. "You play, or you're on crap tubes until you do."

"The winter league starts up in a couple of weeks," Greg growled, stroking the scraggly mess on his chin that he thought passed for a beard. "We get to practice Wednesdays and Fridays during free time, on the field up on top of the center platform."

Drake recalled seeing the "field" during his excursion to the infirmary. He had seen tiered seating surrounding a concrete slab, with two worn nets at either end. Hard to call something

94

so devoid of plant life a field, but then they all were on an oil rig being called a prison.

"What are the rules?" Drake asked, turning the jumpsuit over in his hands.

"You ever played lacrosse?" Mario asked.

"Years ago, during PE at school. The one with the sticks and the ball?"

"That's the one. Well, rigball is just like lacrosse, only more . . . electrifying." Mario snorted, and Tommy slapped him upside his head.

"The rackets are magnetized; so is the ball. When we're in control, going to score, we have to pass the ball between three of our rackets before a goal can be made. The other side can intercept, steal possession." Tommy waved his hand back and forth and chuckled. "Body checking is not only allowed, but encouraged. That's where you come in, Drake. None of these pansies would dare touch Grey out on the field, but we figure you've got nothing to lose."

Drake actually laughed. "He's going to kill me anyway, huh? Might as well make myself useful before then."

Tommy grinned and clapped him on the shoulder. "Now you're being a team player."

Drake glanced at the wicked scar tissue that stretched in a thin line across his arm from Grey's knife attack. A little payback was more than deserved, and if he could do it without any headaches from the guards . . .

He slung the jersey over his shoulder. "Practice tomorrow night, then?"

The next night, a cool snap to the air, wind that had picked up a chill from shelves of ice breaking free to the north, had

Drake shivering in his jumpsuit, bouncing on his toes as Tommy and the boys handed out battered bicycle helmets from a large wooden trunk, along with shin and elbow pads and thin chestplates. Drake and Mario had just hauled the trunk up five tiers of cells and across platforms with the help of a large boy Drake had never met before named Emir. The team's goalkeeper, he was from Turkey and spoke no English.

The sweat running down Drake's back threatened to freeze as he watched his breath mist in the air under a cloudless sky scattered with roughly ten billion stars.

The field atop the center platform had been fitted with a few more features since Drake had last seen it. The infirmary building was all quiet, save for a few lights shining between the blinds. He wondered if Irene was in there, and he thought it more likely that she was in whatever passed for the girls' common room on the northern platform. Fresh white paint marked the borders of the field—a football pitch made of stone—and at either end stood a goal about the size of an ice-hockey net. Strung above each hockey net was a board of circular lights, three in a row, that looked as if it had been stolen from a traffic intersection. A separate raised box of seats, with a shaded tin roof, stood behind the far net. A simple scoreboard hung from the roof of the box seating.

"What are the lights above the nets for?" Drake asked.

"That's so we can see how many passes we've made. Remember, three before we can score, and it resets if we lose possession," Mario said. He hefted a long, thin racket from the trunk and tossed it to Drake.

Drake caught it, and his eyes widened at the weight. The handle was wooden, reinforced with strips of thin steel and wrapped with what looked like gauze bandages. There was a small button embedded in the handle about halfway along its length. At the top, an oval-shaped plate was ringed with an array of small metal lumps, interconnected by wires that ran into the handle and backed against a net of hard, stretched leather.

"Switch it on like this." Mario flicked a switch at the base of the racket, and a tiny blue light lit up the plate.

"Wait—" Tommy cried.

Half a dozen rackets were thrown from the trunk as something exploded from within it and flew through the air. Drake only had time to gasp before a heavy metal sphere, about the size of a tennis ball, smashed into his racket and tore it from his arm. The racket landed with a dull clunk, its handle sticking straight up and humming softly.

Emir, the large Turkish goalkeeper, grunted harsh laughter.

"Blimey," Drake said as Tommy gave Mario yet another slap. He hefted his racket back up, with the ball in the net. It was heavy but manageable if he was expecting the ball. He gave the racket a practice toss, but the ball was well and truly stuck to its magnetized net.

As the other boys picked up their rackets from the mess Mario had caused, Tommy explained a few more of the rules. "If you've got possession, as you do now, then you've got to pass within three seconds or we'll be penalized. Understood? Better to lose possession than hold it too long, because that gives the other team time to organize their field."

"How do I"—Drake lifted the racket over his shoulder and swung with all his might, but the ball remained stuck to the net—"toss it?"

Mario snorted. "Thought a guy your age would've figured that out by now."

Greg and Neil laughed as Tommy pointed to the small black button on the handle of the racket. "Swing just like you did then, and hit that button when you've got the aim right. Let's do a practice one."

Tommy jogged across the hard concrete field, stopping about a dozen meters away. He switched his racket on and, under starlight and the pale, poor lights blinking along the top of the platform, gestured at Drake.

With a shrug, Drake lunged forward and hurled the rigball as hard as he could. The racket swung over his head, and at the top of the arc—when he got the aim right—he pressed the button in the handle.

The ball flew from his net, straight for Tommy, and snapped back as if on a tight elastic band. For the second time, the force of the impact pulled the racket from Drake's hands.

"You're supposed to keep the net demagnetized until the ball's properly away," Mario said, tutting and shaking his head. "Keep the button pressed a good second or two after you've hurled it."

"Right." Of course. Drake lined up another shot, and this time the ball flew true, if a little wide, as Tommy had to take a staggering step to the side, into Tommy's racket, striking the net with a loud chime.

"If the scoreboard was switched on, you'd see a light in one of those traffic lights," Neil said, pointing to the goals at either end of the field.

"Yeah, I get it." Drake flexed his arm. He'd need a bit more practice if he didn't want to wrench his shoulder from its socket.

Neil scoffed. "Sure, you get it. Let's see how well you do when Grey's thugs are throwing that thing at your head and smashing you into the ground."

Drake exhaled a cloud of misty, warm air into the cold air and picked up his helmet. "I'll be right, mate. I've got a bicycle hat."

Later that night, just before lights out, Drake stumbled into 36C covered in welts and bruises, cursing the sport of rigball. He hadn't stayed cold for long up on the center platform. No, no. Tommy had seen to that. After an hour and a half of running drills and tossing a heavy metal ball at one another as hard and fast as they could, Drake had been ready to strip down to his boxer shorts. All the rules of rigball, possibly the most dangerous sport he had ever played, fumbled around in his head. Three passes to a goal . . . The keeper doesn't get a racket, just catcher's mitts . . . No, checking above the shoulder is a foul . . .

Tristan, lying on his bunk and reading his tech magazines purchased from the vending machines in the common room, chuckled when he saw him. Drake was sure that Tristan was the only one on the Rig who bothered with those magazines. *I guess if he can't touch a computer, he can at least read about them,* he thought.

"I can't believe you signed up for rigball," Tristan said. "I've been here for two seasons of it, and do you know how many bones have been broken?"

"No . . ."

"I don't think the infirmary does either. There's a reason they built the field next to the doctor's office, you know."

Drake chuckled and went over to the sink. He found it a touch too painful and didn't bother to wash. The climb up the ladder into his bunk was the Rig's worst torture yet, but he sighed with relief once he was up on his paper-thin mattress and cardboard pillow. The trackers beeped over 2130 a moment later, and the solid steel cell door slid closed, sealing them in yet another night.

"If I die in my sleep," Drake groaned, watching the orange lights from outside play along the wall, "bury me at sea, would you?"

"Sure thing."

Staring at his tracker as the minutes ticked by toward ten o'clock, Drake cursed the device and tried, once again, to pull it from his wrist. He attempted to weasel his fingers under the edge, between his skin and the hard shell, but it was clamped on too tight. He smacked it hard against the bed frame, but that barely scratched the finish of the device.

"These things," he muttered, "are really well made. What say you get this thing off me now, Tristan?"

"You know I can't touch them, Will," Tristan said, a note of honest regret in his voice. "Besides, what if I do get it off? What's your next move? The guards are all over this place, half the doors between platforms are sealed and need swipe cards, and let's mention the security cameras, shall we?"

"We shall not."

"I just don't see it, you know." Tristan paused. "I mean, say you get through all that—and you won't—what next? There's a hundred miles of ocean, at least, between the Rig and the mainland."

Drake thought of Tubes, of the vast array of vents and wide conduits that interconnected the diamond-shaped platforms of the Rig. "I've been secretly whittling a canoe out of soap, elbow grease, unicorn tears, and a teaspoon of shenanigans. Almost ready to set sail, if only I could get this damn tracker off."

"Can I see the canoe?"

"You can, yes, if you use your imagination."

Tristan chuckled and then fell silent.

Drake held his breath. He could almost hear Tristan's mind working, weighing up whether or not to help him.

"I . . . I could do it," he said finally. "But what if you got hurt?" The last was barely a whisper, and Drake knew that Tristan was thinking of the people he had hurt the last time he'd messed with computers.

"I'm already getting hurt, mate, and . . ." He paused, wondering just what to say. Drake needed to escape—for reasons more important to him than anything in his life. "Look, you'll just have to trust me, but if you don't help me, if I can't escape . . . then someone is going to get hurt. Maybe . . . maybe even die."

Tristan sighed. He was quiet again for a few minutes, shuffling around in his bunk. Drake heard him sit up as the orange lights danced on the walls, playing with the shadows like the tide washing in and out.

"I'll try," he said. "I'll give it a shot, I guess. But you have to understand that it may not work, okay?"

Drake swallowed hard and felt a flutter of excitement rise

up from his stomach and into his throat. He shivered as goose bumps rippled up and down his arms. "Thanks."

"Give me a week or so. I'll need to gather a few things, then explain to you how hard this is going to be."

"How you gonna do it?"

"You can't just hit it with a hammer, okay? Although I'm sure you've considered it. Best that'll do is shatter your wrist. I'm going to have to think about it and . . . Look, just leave it for now, Will. I said I'll do it, I just need time."

Time was the one thing Drake had in buckets, and the one thing of which he was running short. But he kept his peace for now, thanked Tristan again, and rolled over in his bunk.

As always, sleep was a long time in coming.

* * *

That Saturday was the first rigball game of the winter season. Drake's welts and bruises had barely had time to purple from the training session the night before, but he was excited—and a touch nervous—to get out on the field and play the game properly against Grey and his thugs.

He'd felt the eyes of the entire cafeteria on him that morning at breakfast. Whispers and half-heard rumors suggested that there was quite a betting pool on the match, particularly on whether Grey would pummel Drake or vice versa.

"Yeah," Mario said as they warmed up on the side of the field just after lunch. Three hours were set aside for the game, a rare treat and break from work hours. "The odds on you aren't good, *mi amigo*. I got three Snickers bars that say Grey pounds you into the ground."

"You bet against me?"

Mario nodded and laughed. "I may have been caught with the murder weapon in my hand, but I'm not an idiot."

Grey and his team of five large boys were half the field away, getting ready up on the tiered seating. They were laughing and joking, pointing at Drake and his team. Drake thought, Christ, look at the size of him . . . Grey had torn the sleeves from a black jumpsuit, and his thick arms bulged with muscle. It had been two weeks since Drake had seen him, and he'd doubled in size. That's impossible. More and more, Drake wondered just what was involved in advanced lessons.

The inmates from both platforms were allowed to attend the games, and Drake noticed with mild curiosity that on the other side of the field, a team of girls was slipping into safety gear and picking up rackets. With each game running an hour, according to Tommy, the girls played first. They had a much more civilized match, as Captain Tommy put it, with four teams instead of just two, which actually lent a better structure for a season of games.

The boys, on the other hand, could only ever field two teams—no one else wanted to go up against Grey, let alone actually beat the bully. Where the girls had a proper league, the boys' matches came down to who could hit the hardest and best out of the seven-game season.

Drake donned his helmet, leaving it unbuckled temporarily, and sat on the first row of seating next to Mario and the boys. He was more anxious than excited as the guards shepherded the rest of the inmate population up from their respective platforms and they began to fill the seats.

There was a fair turnout on both sides of the field. Drake

estimated that most of the Rig's inhabitants had come up for the game. The boxed seating behind the far goal at the north end of the field held a slew of guards and some of the prison's staff. Warden Storm sat laughing with Dr. Elias and Brand in the center of the box. Other guards positioned themselves on duty around the edge of the playing field. Drake scanned the box for Dr. Lambros but didn't see the tiny woman.

He also spent a few minutes scanning the girls' seating, looking for the blaze of auburn hair that belonged to Irene. She wasn't there, as far as he could tell. Perhaps she was playing. Last in a long line of inmates, Michael Tristan wandered up, shoulders slumped and hands stuffed in his pockets. He gave Drake half a smile through pursed lips and chuckled.

"Good luck, Will," he said, and climbed up a row to sit behind Tommy's team. "I've only been to one of these games, but I do remember that Grey liked to go for the knees."

Mario winced and rubbed at his own knee, glancing over his shoulder at Tristan. "Ain't that the truth . . ."

"Thanks for coming out," Drake said. The butterflies in his stomach felt as if they'd been doused in petrol and set alight. He fidgeted in his seat, more than eager just to get playing.

But the girls played first, and when their match started, Drake got a good look at just how hard and brutal the sport of rigball could be. He didn't know or recognize any of the girls as they arrayed themselves across the field, one team wearing red, the other green. The core of the team aligned on the center circle, waiting for the guard who was refereeing the match to drop the magnetized ball.

The game began with the blowing of a loud air horn.

The Reds threw themselves into the Greens with such force that it was clear from the start which was the superior team. Drake watched the mess unfold as the Reds swiped and swapped the ball with the ease of long practice. By halftime they were six goals to nothing and had bloodied the Greens quite harshly. It took a lot for a foul to be called in rigball, and by game's end the Reds had pulled away twelve to three.

It was all over at the sound of the air horn. The Greens limped from the field utterly defeated, bleeding, and, in one case, cradling a broken wrist.

The other two teams in the girls' league played next, and this game was much more evenly matched. The contact and body checking were faster and harder, and spots of bright red blood lay cooling on the concrete field before too long. Dressed in red and green jumpsuits again, the game ended in a two–two tie. Both teams stumbled from the field to steady applause from the staff box and the inmates in the stands.

"God, I'd let her hit me with a racket all day long," Mario said, nudging Drake in the ribs and pointing to one of the Reds. Drake was a little surprised to see that it was the girl from his flight in, Strawberry Blonde, who had cried the whole way and most of the first night. Life on the Rig had toughened her up, it seemed.

A ten-minute break allowed Tommy's team to check their gear and slip into their pads. Drake wasn't sure, but he could sense that the first two games had only been a warm-up for the crowd. The real game, his game, was about to begin — and the sharks in the stands could smell blood.

Moving in somewhat of a nervous daze, he followed the

rest of his team out onto the field and took up his position on the wing, just as he had in practice. Grey's team lined up against them and looked intimidating in their dyed black jumpsuits. Drake was breathing hard and remembered only at the last minute before the ball was dropped to turn his racket on.

The horn blew.

The game began.

Drake, new to the game and barely familiar with the rules, clung to his wing. He took large sidesteps down the field, keeping his racket at the ready as possession moved one way or the other. The rigball sang as it zoomed across the field, clanging from racket to racket. Grey's team was brutal.

For their part, Tommy and the boys gave as good as they got, in most cases. None of them got closer to Grey himself than half a meter—and none of them dared make contact. The large, pig-faced bully wore a smirk during the entire first half, tossing the rigball with casual ease halfway down the field with each throw. He made it look effortless. Drake was sweating, and his arm was stinging just from the half dozen throws he'd had. A near miss with the opposing wingman almost gave Mario a black eye. He hit the ground hard and came up laughing.

"Drake!" Tommy cried, and tossed the rigball down the wing.

Drake's racket thrummed as the ball slammed into his net. He turned and ran—heading for goal with three of Grey's black-suited thugs on his tail. Mario darted ahead of him, gesturing with his racket.

"Pass it, Will!"

The referee, running along as well, blew a shrill whistle and awarded a foul to Grey's team.

Drake came to a stop, confused.

"You have to pass," Mario said, shaking Drake's helmet. "Three seconds, or you foul. You have to pass!"

Damn. Drake had forgotten one of the simpler rules. He shook his head, ignored the jeers from the crowd, and ran back up the wing as Grey's team took possession.

From there, the game descended into a grudge match, with all but Grey open for full contact. The referee blew more fouls in the next ten minutes than in the entirety of the girls' games, and they had been cruel enough.

Despite the beating Drake's team took in the first half, the score was tied at nil–all when the guard blew the air horn, signaling halftime. Tommy limped off the field with a goofy smile on his face. Mario's teeth were bloody from a split lip. Greg and Neil had matching black eyes. Emir was uninjured, as was Drake, but that had been more from luck than anything else. None of the team had given Drake much in the way of possession after that first error.

"Why the hell are you still smiling?" Drake asked Mario as the Spanish boy swashed water around his mouth and spat it out on the ground.

Mario beamed. "We're still tied. If we can keep this up, it'll be the first time Grey hasn't won. A tie's better than losing, yeah?"

Drake leaned against his racket and shrugged. Grey was whispering furiously to his team in a tight-knit circle, still on the field. He sensed Drake's gaze and gave him a glare that should have sent the Rig frozen into the sea. "I guess, but what'll he do if we actually win?"

Mario seemed to consider this for the first time. He blinked and shook his head. "He'll take it out on you, *mi amigo*."

The air horn blew again five minutes later, and the teams took to the field, switching goals and, for Drake, wings. He clenched the racket hard, intending to make this half count. He wanted to beat Grey, for no other reason than to take away the bully's perfect record. Never mind the knife attack, this was about something more important—showing the musclebound goon that he didn't scare everyone on the Rig.

Whatever Grey fed his team during halftime, they had absorbed, and they now vented against Tommy's team with an all-out assault. Drake was fairly safe, stuck on the wing, as most of the action in a game of rigball centered around the three key players in midfield—the offense.

Still, he was thrown to the ground more than once. He grazed his knuckles on the elbow pads of the opposing wingman and took a racket to the cheek, splitting the skin below his eye. Mario was pummeled into the ground, laughing every time and somehow managing to claw back to his feet after every knock.

Drake intercepted a toss from Grey in the last two minutes of the game. The scores were still tied, and the air blowing in off the Arctic Ocean felt hot with tension. Drake tossed the ball across the field to Greg, and the first light above their goal lit up.

"To me!" Tommy roared, farther downfield.

Two lights.

Mario, as fast as lightning, darted under Grey's large arm, narrowly missing the blunt end of Grey's racket, and ran across the concrete surface. "I'm open!"

Tommy hurled the ball, his aim perfect, and it sailed into Mario's racket.

Three lights.

Mario spun on his heel and pelted down the field, covering the last five meters before the goal. Drake had fallen back after his pass, guarding his wing and blocking one of Grey's players from joining the attack that was about to go down in the goal square.

The crowd whooped and cheered as Mario raised his racket. All that stood between him and the goal was the keeper. He threw the rigball with an almighty cry, and it sailed toward the net.

Somehow, Grey was there. The ball flew into his racket, and the lights above the goal reset. A murmur of disappointment shuddered through the crowd.

Grey set off down the field, running hard. He passed the ball right on the cusp of three seconds to the wingman opposite Drake. Neil grappled with him and took an elbow to the face for his trouble. His nose gushed blood, but the referee called no foul.

Drake took lunging steps up the field, light on his toes, keeping parallel with the wingman. Grey had come up the middle, as the wingman with possession hurled the ball over Grey's head to the man Drake was marking. He caught it solidly, edging Drake's racket out with a swift elbow to the ribs.

"Back to me!" Grey roared, his voice a dull bellow that echoed across the field and the stands. For all his muscle, he could really move.

The ball sailed into his racket, making three passes. Grey's team had the chance to score, with seconds left on the clock.

Drake felt a surge of anger and bared his teeth in a snarl. He swept the legs out from under the wingman who had just thrown to Grey, leaped over him as he fell, and darted after the large bully. Grey was fast—but Drake, at least fifty kilos lighter, was faster.

He got out in front of Grey as Grey made for the goal. Emir stood at the ready, knees bent and eyes focused, but Drake stepped between them, racket raised.

For the smallest fraction of time, the space between heartbeats, Drake and Grey locked eyes. The game was about to go either way. In that split second, Drake saw twin points of actual fire flare in Grey's eyes. Pinpoints of shining crimson swam across his pupils.

Then they connected.

Grey tackled Drake with the force of a freight train hitting a soup can. Drake was literally thrown up and off his feet. His legs flailed uselessly, scrambling for purchase, as the air was forced from his lungs in a violent gust. He flipped head over heels, saw the ground and the stands of gaping inmates before gravity decided to switch back on and he hit the concrete hard, landing on his head. He heard a loud crack and thought for a moment it was his neck, but then his helmet fell away, split cleanly down the middle.

His eyes . . . Drake thought, gasping for air. What the hell?

Grey slammed the rigball into the goal a second before

the air horn announced game's end, and the crowd exploded. Half the boys in the stands were up stamping their feet and hollering. Drake heard one or two chants, drowned in curse words, directed his way. He laughed them off, chuckling as his abused lungs managed to suck in a mouthful or two of cool, salty air.

The game was over.

Tommy's team, and Drake, had lost.

11

MAGNETS

"Good afternoon, Will," Dr. Lambros said. Beams of bright sunlight shone through the blinds behind her desk, illuminating the room. "You're looking a little rough around the edges today. How'd you get that cut on your cheek?"

Drake took a seat in Lambros's office, inhaling the smell of her old books and polished mahogany desk. "Rigball," he said, and stroked the scab under his eye. Work in Tubes the last few days had been torture—he'd gotten a lot more bruises and scrapes during the game than he'd realized.

At least Tommy and the boys didn't blame him for failing to stop Grey during the dying seconds. None of them could say, as Drake flipped through the air and cracked his helmet in half, that he hadn't tried.

Dr. Lambros shook her head. "Such a violent sport. I've told the warden that it does no good, just gives you boys an excuse to batter each other, but he's of a mind that it's team building."

"I didn't see you at the game."

"Why would I want to see it?" She leaned forward in her chair and removed her glasses. "Really, Will, do I strike you as the type to enjoy blood sport?"

She surely did not. To Drake, she had become the only person on the Rig, save perhaps Tristan, that he thought he might trust. And he wasn't sure about Tristan—he was a nice enough person, but weak. He thought he belonged here, and that was something that would never sit right with Drake. No one belonged in this place, so far removed from the real world and . . . and from oversight. The Alliance could do whatever they wanted out here, away from prying eyes. The guards—Brand, at least—were former private military and had no trouble beating the inmates. If Drake thought he had to spend close to five more years here, he might just try the swim.

"What's on your mind this week, Will?" the doctor asked. "You're closing in on three months now. I'm pleased to see you've taken a lot of steps in the right direction. We can probably look at pushing our meetings back to once a month now."

Drake was surprised to find that he felt a sliver of disappointment. He quite liked these meetings, and not just because he got out of work for an hour or two. He had wondered—when not thinking of escape—what it was about the small psychologist that put him almost at ease. It had come to him the previous night, as he lay awake into the early hours of the morning. Dr. Acacia Lambros reminded him of his mother. The way she spoke, the way she smiled.

"If you think so," he said.

"I remember our first meeting. You were full of fire and anger about being sent here to the Rig. It's good to see you've settled into the routine somewhat. No more thoughts of a daring escape? You can't fly out of here, you know. And no more fighting?"

Drake looked down at his left arm, at the crooked pink scar tissue that contrasted glaringly against his dark skin. He'd yet to pay Grey back for that. "No, just rigball."

"Which amounts to the same thing, doesn't it?"

"I—" Drake considered, then nodded. "I'd say that's a pretty fair assessment, actually."

"He sees the light!" Dr. Lambros clapped. "Now, talk to me about what's on your mind."

"Alan Grey," he said, and was surprised he said anything at all. Apart from Tristan and a few of the Tubes crew, Drake hadn't voiced his concerns about Grey and his gang to anyone.

"You know I can't talk about any other inmates, Will," she said, but there was an edge to her voice.

Drake leaned back in his chair. He was willing to bet any hope of escape from the Rig that Alan Grey wasn't one of the good doctor's clients. In fact, he'd take that bet a step further and wager that none of Grey's gang attended these sessions. Which left him wondering . . .

"They don't come to see you, do they?" Drake asked. "Why not? Does Irene, from the girls' platform, come? She's a redhead."

"Irene Finlay? How did you meet her?"

Again, Drake could read the look on her face. No, Irene—Finlay—did not have scheduled meetings—and that bothered Dr. Lambros.

Drake licked his lips and decided to share a concern he'd

had since learning of Grey's "advanced lessons," or whatever he was doing.

"I think they're up to something. I think whatever they're up to is happening through a locked door on the eastern platform." Drake took a deep breath and thought of Irene. She had trusted him in the infirmary, when she probably shouldn't have. "I mean I don't see him for weeks at a time. Where is he?"

Dr. Lambros shrugged. "Perhaps I'll have a chat with the warden and see if I can't find out a little bit more about it. Honestly, though, Will, I think you're worrying over nothing."

Drake snorted. "He tried to kill me not so long ago. I'd rather know where the bastard is and what he's up to."

"Please don't curse in my office," Dr. Lambros chided, and offered him a brown paper bag. "Care for a strawberry bonbon, Will?"

* * *

The rest of February fell into much the same routine to which Drake had grown accustomed. Life on the Rig ticked idly by, governed for the inmates solely by the trackers. Having stopped pushing his luck with the boundaries so much, Drake had actually managed to bring his debt to the Alliance down somewhat. He sat at *$-1356*, which, although not on the runway and heading toward a gate, had come down a few hundred credits from the upper stratosphere. Tristan even took pity on him and bought him a candy bar from the common room one night.

"You won't clear that debt inside a year," he said, and threw Drake a Snickers as he lazed on his bunk during free time.

"So make this last." Tristan had been enjoying a few relatively uneventful months since he'd swiped Brand's baton and word had got around that Drake didn't like anyone messing with his roommate.

Drake stared at the chocolate for a moment, unsure just what to say. He mumbled thanks and returned to staring at the ceiling, a rather incomplete map of the Rig's vent system dancing through his head.

"When are you going to tell me about your plan to get this tracker off?" Drake asked a few minutes later, around a mouthful of peanuts and caramel.

Tristan chuckled. "Trust me, I'm working on it. My rough assessment of a week should've been closer to a month."

Two more Saturdays came and went, as did two more games of rigball. Tommy's team, having enjoyed a near tie on the first match, were trounced both times by Grey and his thugs. They did better the second game, as Grey was out sick and his team played a man down, but the sheer size and ferocity of the rest of the team, while not making up for a player of Grey's immense size, still afforded them victory.

Tommy was impressed with Drake's playing, however, and promoted him on the Tubes crew to, as he put it, "No more than three crap tubes a shift." A high honor, indeed.

Near the end of the month, the *Titan* returned to resupply the Rig. Drake watched the freight ship from his cell, still amazed at its length and wondering how something so heavy could stay afloat. Those tiny speedboats emerged from the hull, just as before, and inspected the ship and the pillars of the Rig's platforms for damage. He watched the crew offload on the southern platform, using the tall crane on the ship's stern. As before, a whole bunch of Alliance-stamped crates and small shipping containers were also loaded onto the *Titan*. Waste? Drake wondered. What else? Strange that both Warden Storm and Dr. Elias oversaw the loading as the sun set to the west and darkness cast a blanket of shadow over the Rig.

By the next morning, the *Titan* was gone, and February became March.

Down on the eastern platform clearing pipes, Drake thought the weather had a little less bite to it. The seasons were changing, the icy conditions becoming more favorable. He expected the Rig to be extremely cold year round, given its location in the middle of the bloody Arctic Ocean, but a few degrees warmer made all the difference to his frozen fingers and toes after he emerged sodden and stinking from a pipe.

Still, staring out at the ocean from his window in 36C that night, his forehead pressed against the tough Perspex, Drake couldn't help but find it harder than usual to temper his frustration. The Alliance had sent him to the Rig because the place had a perfect record—it was inescapable—and nothing he had done so far had gone any length toward tarnishing that record. Would he see his sixteenth birthday here? His seventeenth? Or, all said and done, his twentieth? He was nearly four months, a third of a year, on the Rig, and no closer to escape. With little else to do, he stood thinking these thoughts for close to an hour, until Tristan returned, trying hard to suppress a smile.

"I've got it," he said, keeping his voice an excited whisper. "What I was looking for."

Drake stepped away from the window. "What's that now?"

"Come sit over here and keep your voice down."

Curious, Drake did as instructed. He was lost for a moment; then his eyes widened. "You mean for getting this off?" He tapped his tracker. "Tristan, how?"

"You see that narrow hole on the side of the tracker? Like a keyhole without the curves? That's how we trip the system, even without the proper key."

Drake considered the keyhole and then nodded. "Okay . . . I tried working it with a pen lid, with no luck. So how does it work?"

"It's a hole for an electromagnetic key," Tristan said, speaking almost to himself. "I've seen them before. Knowing that tells me a lot about how the trackers work."

Drake stared into the hole. It didn't look like anything special to him. "And how do you know that?"

Tristan smiled a touch sadly. "From my past misdeeds. Sometimes, to break into a network, you actually have to be in the building. About two and a half years ago I was trying to get into an insurance company's files—all that personal data is worth a fortune online—but it was on a completely self-contained drive within the building. I had to break in and use a terminal on-site. Getting the security cameras to loop safe footage was easy, but the back door was sealed with an electromagnetic lock at night. Physical security, you know—ugh."

"Electromagnetic?"

"Yeah. Think of it kind of like a really strong clamp. It's not, but that'll do. They're impossible to force manually with anything less than a tank, or about fifteen hundred pounds of pressure."

"So how did you break it?"

Tristan shook his head. "That's just it—you can't break them." He dug around in his pocket and produced a handful of tiny magnets, some stuck together and others repelled. Half were circular, some were semicircles, a bunch of them were shiny and cube shaped. The rest were thin bars about the length of a fingernail. "But you can confuse them."

"Confuse them?"

Tristan dug around in his other pocket and produced another handful of small fridge magnets in the shape of bananas and strawberries, and two floppy pictures of St. John's—the nearest port to the Rig—that had magnetic backing. "It'll be trial and error, and we'll have to be careful, or we could blow the power of the entire tracker, which will bring the guards, but if I can confuse the magnets in the lock within your tracker . . . it may just pop open."

Drake felt a surge of excitement. "You actually know what you're talking about, don't you?"

Tristan sighed. "That's why I'm in prison."

"Okay, sorry. So tell me how it works—how all of this"—he gestured at the various magnets on the bed—"will do the trick."

"It may not," Tristan admitted. "But I'd be very surprised if it doesn't. As I said, the trick will be doing it carefully enough that we don't disrupt the power to the entire tracker. You'll disappear from the monitoring display up in Control if that happens, and then I imagine all manner of alarms will sound."

"Not conducive to sneaking about and escaping, is it?"

"No."

Tristan played with the magnets, sorting what repelled

from what didn't. He made two large piles and every so often slipped a bunch of different magnets into a third, smaller pile. The cube-shaped magnets dominated this pile.

Drake picked up one of the cubes. "What's so special about these?" he asked. The magnet was heavier than he thought it would be. He tossed it at the bed frame and it stuck fast, with a resounding chime.

"Nickel-plated neodymium," Tristan said, as if that explained everything. He finished sorting and looked up at Drake. "You know, the strongest type of permanent magnet they make? Head actuators on hard disks? Never mind. I pulled these out of the back of the lifter and compressor in the laundry tonight. Took me a week to loosen the panel without being spotted. These piles came from the common room. I swiped these thin ones from cabinet latches, and the half circles from the extractor fan above the toilet."

Drake looked up at the ceiling. "The extractor fan?"

"Yeah. Don't use the extractor fan."

Drake laughed. "You think they'll do the trick?"

"Properly aligned with the magnets in the tracker, that thing will fly off your arm." Tristan frowned and pushed his glasses back up the bridge of his nose. "But again, we're going for subtlety here."

The casual confidence in his voice was at odds with the quiet, shuffling boy Drake had met nearly four long months earlier. For the first time, he was seeing Michael Tristan in his element. The kid was smart—spooky smart—and he knew it.

"Okay, the magnets are a start," Tristan said. "But we'll be needing some other materials. A small power source, like a watch battery—it doesn't need to be strong—and some copper coil wire. With that, I can create a key, I suppose, that should unlock the tracker."

Drake didn't have any idea where he'd be able to swipe a power source—yet—but his mind flicked to the defunct machinery at the bottom of the eastern platform, in Tubes, through the worst of the muck. Or maybe one of the vending machines in the common room? No, they'd notice that. Who wore a watch? Dr. Lambros. He didn't want to steal from her. Probably the eastern platform, then. Loose wires and, possibly, more magnets abounded down there. He swallowed, thinking, Ugh . . . no one said this would be easy.

"I'm still not clear how it'll work."

Tristan nodded. "It is a bit complex to begin with. Took me three weeks to trip my first lock back in Perth." He turned his right forearm toward the ceiling, exposing the underside of his tracker, and ran his finger along the almost imperceptible seam that bound it to his wrist. "Imagine magnets of varying polarity, either north or south, all along the length of this thing. Our key will have to match that varying polarity exactly, you understand. North to north, south to south, and so on . . . or the armature plate, that fifteen-hundred-pound pressure thing, won't release. Sounds simple, right?"

Drake nodded slowly. "Yeah, but we can't see the polarity of the magnets in the tracker, or even how many there are."

"Good. You're beginning to see the problem and how much you'll owe me once this is done."

Drake thought more on what was fast becoming a headache. He was keeping up with what Tristan was saying, but only just. "Say there are five magnets in the tracker . . . that would mean, what, the key would have to be assembled a certain number of ways in order to find the right combination of magnets to unlock the tracker?"

Tristan pointed at him. "Now you're getting it. It's pretty simple to extrapolate the variables."

"What?"

"Count the possible combinations."

"Oh."

"Yeah, so each magnet along the length of the tracker is either north or south. Two variables to each magnet, right? If there are five, like in your example, then that's a possible thirty-two key combinations."

Drake perked up. "Not so many."

"That's if there are five. The number of combinations doubles for each additional magnet over your five. Six magnets, sixty-four possible combinations. Seven, then one hundred and twenty-eight. Ten magnets, God help us, is a thousand and twenty-four combinations."

"Okay." Drake tapped his tracker against the edge of the bed, producing a dull metal click, as if that would force the device to release and save them all the hassle. "Let's hope for less than ten, then."

"Twelve magnets would be a possible four thousand and ninety-six combinations."

"Bugger."

"Indeed."

Drake and Tristan sat in silence for a moment, contemplating the challenge ahead. "So we'll start at one magnet and work our way up, I guess," said Drake.

"Logical way to do it, yeah, but there'll definitely be more than one."

"How'd you know that?"

Tristan smiled grimly. "Because this won't work if there isn't."

"Ah. Do you think the magnets in my tracker are in the same order as yours?"

Tristan shrugged. "No idea. I've never seen the keys they use to take these things off. Could be each tracker comes with its own magnetic key, aligned with the magnets in that particular tracker."

Drake thought that sounded about right. Given what he understood of the electromagnetic locking process so far, a master key was probably the stuff of fairy tale. "These magnets don't fit the lock on the side of the tracker," he pointed out.

"No, they don't. Which is why I've got the neodymium magnets for a little extra kick. Only way this has any chance of working, actually. Our key will work by aligning with the magnets inside the tracker along the underside, or perhaps to either side of the underside. We'll see."

"How will it work? I'm not getting that."

Tristan removed his glasses and rubbed his eyes. He looked tired, but he answered the question. "The key we're creating works by using a pulsating magnetic field. It'll cause the magnets in the tracker to vibrate—perhaps violently, if we're not careful—at between thirty and fifty vibrations a second. The key, arranged in the right order of polarity, will cause the bolt to release."

"Hopefully without interrupting the power to the rest of the tracker."

"Right. Keep that in mind."

Drake took a deep breath and exhaled slowly. "This could take a while."

Tristan stood up and began transferring his piles of magnets to the drawers under the sink. "Well, I've got about five years. How about you?"

12

UNLEASHED

In the first week of March, Tommy's Tubes crew was reassigned to maintenance duty on the southern platform of the Rig. Drake didn't mind, as it meant less time crawling through grime-stricken pipes and dusty vents. He had an idea there'd be plenty of that coming his way once Tristan managed to build a key to unlock his tracker.

The final materials necessary to construct the key—a copper coil and power source—had, quite literally, been thrust into Drake's hands during rigball practice the night before.

The racket.

Powered by an internal source, magnetized, and, in essence, according to Tristan, almost what they were trying to build anyway—just on a much smaller and more refined, complex scale—the racket was perfect. After practice, Drake offered to clear away and store the equipment. The other boys shrugged and left him to it. In the short time before lights out, Drake had simply snapped one of the rackets and stolen its innards, a string of circular lithium watch batteries and a handful of wiring and magnets, stuffing the whole mess into his jumpsuit and heading back to 36C. He tossed the broken racket over the edge of the Rig and into the cold, dark waters of the Arctic.

Tristan had been impressed. The wire and the batteries were exactly what he needed. He said they could start working on the combination key as early as the next night.

Tonight, Drake thought, as Warden Storm waddled toward him and the Tubes crew, skirting around the Seahawk helicopter resting on the helipad. Now what could he want?

Apart from brief glimpses and at the rigball games, Drake had seen nothing of the Rig's warden since his induction meeting in the man's office. Brand accompanied the warden, one hand resting on his rifle, glaring at Tommy's crew as if they'd been caught trying to do something silly, like escape.

Storm wore another fine suit. The white jacket was pristine, and a wide-rimmed Stetson adorned his large head. His thumbs were tucked into his belt buckle. Tristan had told him that the warden sent a suit down to the laundry on the center platform once a day to be dry-cleaned and pressed. The man took care of his appearance, much in the way he took care of the Rig.

In the four months since Drake had been imprisoned there, he was still grudgingly impressed by how clean everything was. From the washrooms to the cafeteria, from the cells to the corridors. Half the inmates were on cleaning crews—not as dirty as Tubes—but cleaning crews nevertheless. They could never quite mask the taste of the sea, or the old scent of crude oil, under their chemical cleaners, but they gave a good job of it. Warden Storm seemed to care more for the Rig than for the inmates under his charge.

"Good afternoon, gentlemen," Storm said. "And what a glorious afternoon it is on my beautiful rig. Can you smell that marvelous sea air? Good to be out in the sun, eh, and away from those tubes?"

"Yes, sir," Tommy said. He was standing up straight and proper. The rest of the crew murmured similar sentiments. Drake kept his silence.

"That's a good boy," the warden said. "You've done a good job these last few years, Mr. Nasim, keeping this old girl's insides running smoothly."

Tommy beamed at the praise. "Thank you, sir."

"And you almost had Alan Grey's team in the game last Saturday, didn't you, boys?"

Mario was sporting two black eyes to match the split lip he'd earned during the first match, nearly four weeks earlier. He'd managed to keep splitting it, week after week. "We'll get them this Saturday, Warden. You watch."

Brand snorted.

"I'm sure you'll give it your best," Storm said seriously. He clearly didn't think they stood a chance.

With four games left of the season, Grey's team only had to win once more to secure victory for the winter league—but it wasn't about winning, never had been, and Drake suspected the warden knew that. No, the rigball games were about power—power and dominance. Grey had both, from his size and cruelty alone, but this way everyone on the Rig never forgot it. When they saw him pounding Tommy's team into the concrete, saw the blood spilled . . .

What Drake didn't know was why Grey was so special.

Why the warden, and Brand, and a handful of the other guards—Hall and Stein, to name just two—treated him not as another prisoner, but almost as if they were on even footing here. The more Drake thought about it, the less sense it made. He wondered if Dr. Lambros would be able to tell him anything more in their next meeting, two days away, on Friday. Drake had been looking forward to the meeting all week long. She was the only adult within a hundred miles who treated him with even an ounce of respect.

"Now, to business," Warden Storm said. "This Monday the Rig will be playing host to the executive board of the Alliance. I don't have to tell you all to be on your best behavior." The warden's gaze lingered on Drake for a long moment. "Lucien Whitmore himself will be here, boys. Yes, yes, the head honcho. He's coming to inspect how we do things here on the Rig, how smoothly this facility runs, and how well you're all doing under our supervision."

Whitmore . . . The man who controlled the Alliance. He was coming to the Rig. Drake knew little about the multi-billionaire beyond the clips he saw on TV of him at charity events, giving press conferences, or traveling to the hot spots around the world where Crystal Force, the private military arm of the Alliance, operated. He was a young man, for someone in his position, Drake had always thought. He recalled some story from a year or two earlier about how Whitmore had taken over Alliance Systems after his father had retired, or something.

"You are all, in your own unconventional way, employees of the Alliance," Warden Storm continued. "Lucien Whitmore is your boss, your employer, as much as he is mine. This is your workplace, and you want the Rig to make a good impression, yes?"

Tommy nodded enthusiastically. Drake had to relax his fists.

"Good boys." The warden tipped his hat back and gestured to one of the supply sheds connected to the Processing building, just across the platform. "In those sheds you'll find pavilion tents and trestle tables that need assembling. Over the next few days the Seahawk here will be busy ferrying caterers and Mr. Whitmore's personal security staff from the mainland to the Rig. Weather reports show clear skies all weekend, so Officer Brand and I have decided there's no time like the present to begin preparations. He'll be supervising you boys for the next few days."

Oh . . . great.

Almost anything beat Tubes, although after spending the best part of four months crawling around the insides of the eastern platform, Drake had grown somewhat used to the muck and the stench. However, an afternoon in the sun was a rare treat, even with Brand barking orders and snide comments. Drake had found that he liked working with his hands, keeping things running in Tubes and now constructing the tents and tables in the courtyard out in front of Processing.

If not for the fact that he was working for the Alliance, he could almost have enjoyed the job.

As evening fell the next night, Drake flipped through Tristan's tech magazines as Tristan assembled, disassembled, and reassembled the magnetic key, keeping his tracker arm flat on the bed so Tristan could run the combinations along the seam of the device. So far, they'd had no luck, although

Drake thought he felt something vibrating in the tracker at one point the night before.

They were already up to a seven-magnet key, which meant a possible hundred and twenty-eight combinations. Tristan muttered to himself as he worked, keeping track of the polarity of the magnets in his head, never skipping a combination or growing frustrated. Drake marveled, at first, at how Tristan could keep all those numbers swirling around in his mind, but he soon grew bored. He'd hoped, however unlikely it seemed, that his cellmate would crack the tracker on the first night.

The key worked on the ninety-seventh combination.

Drake was on the verge of falling asleep when he felt the tracker vibrating and the bolt release. The device fell away from his wrist, but given the months it had been strapped to him, he could feel it as if it were still attached.

At first neither he nor Tristan could process what had just happened. The tracker was life on the Rig—the small, five-centimeter display governed everything. Every hour of their schedule, twenty-four hours a day, seven days a week. Drake's tracker now lay face-down on Tristan's mattress, looking like nothing more than what it was. A tiny, not so powerful computer locked inside a plastic band.

Drake sucked in a harsh breath at the same moment as Tristan let out a long, slow sigh. "Is it . . ." Drake swallowed. "Is it still working?"

Tristan carefully picked up Drake's tracker and turned it over so they could see the display.

It was 2355, five minutes to midnight, and Drake owed the Alliance nearly thirteen hundred credits.

"Well," Tristan said, and chuckled. "That was easy."

"Yeah." Drake wasn't sure he trusted his voice just yet. He rubbed at his wrist where the tracker had sat. The skin was tender—and hairy. "Um, thanks."

"Told you it'd work." Tristan cast a quick glance at the cell door and the thin window, as if he expected Brand or Warden Storm to be glancing back at him. "Now what?" he said.

"Now we put it back on."

"What?"

It was Drake's turn to chuckle. "You think I'm escaping tonight? Blimey, mate, unless you can throw some magnets at that door and at every security camera between here and the chopper—which I can't fly, by the way—I'm not going anywhere."

Tristan blinked, then nodded. "Right. Of course."

Drake slipped the tracker back over his wrist and snapped the lock closed. He felt the bolt latch, and the device was as secure on his arm as it had ever been. "Let me see if I can work the key and get it off again."

Tristan handed him the row of seven magnets, about ten centimeters long and wrapped in copper wire coiled around the battery stolen from the rigball racket. Drake pressed it against the seam of his tracker.

Nothing happened. His heart leaped into his throat.

"Turn it around," Tristan said.

Drake did, and felt the magnets vibrate suddenly. The tracker snapped open again as the bolt released and fell from his wrist.

"This evens the playing field somewhat," he mused, and clapped Tristan on the shoulder.

The tracker went back on his wrist a third time, but it no longer felt like a leash. The device felt like an ally now, a way to turn the Rig's own system against itself. A fit of honest laughter burst from Drake, and Tristan caught it. They sat rocking back and forth on the bottom bunk, holding their sides and trying to stifle the gasps and cries. Tears ran down Drake's cheeks, and he thought he might die if he didn't stop to take a breath sometime soon.

Ten minutes later, still chuckling softly, Drake was up on his own bunk. Tristan's magnificent key was stuffed down the side of his bed in a hole he'd torn in the mattress. Thinking thoughts of escape, Drake folded his pillow in half and turned to face the wall. For the first time since he'd arrived on the Rig, sleep was swift and true.

* * *

The next day, as Drake strolled up to the top of the western platform for his meeting with Dr. Lambros, he did so with a smile on his face. All day long the tracker had felt like nothing more than a bracelet—an expensive, fancy bracelet to be sure—but one he could remove whenever he saw fit.

Entering the classroom complex after lunch, Drake headed along the white-walled corridor and up the spiral stairs to Dr. Lambros's office on the second floor. He knocked on the frosted glass.

"Enter," a deep male voice said from within.

Drake frowned and let himself in. The first thing he noticed were the sealed cardboard boxes sitting in front of the empty bookshelves. The leather sofa had been pushed back, and Dr. Lambros's pictures, her qualifications, were stacked haphazardly on one of the cushions.

A thin, pale man wearing a turtleneck sweater sat behind the fine desk, looking down his nose at Drake over a pair of half-moon spectacles. He put down a fancy fountain pen. "William Drake?"

"Yes," Drake said. He didn't step into the office. "Who are you?"

The man pointed at the seat in front of the desk. What had once been a comfortable, high-backed leather chair was now a plastic foldout. "Sit down, William. Let's get this over with."

Drake bristled. "Get what over with? Where's Dr. Lambros?"

"Dr. Acacia Lambros is no longer aboard this facility or employed by the Alliance," he said. "She left two days ago to pursue other opportunities. I'm her replacement. Dr. Farrington."

Drake glanced at the empty bookshelves and the stacks of photo frames on the sofa. The frame on top of the pile, Dr. Lambros's undergraduate degree, had a web of cracks running through the glass. "She just left?"

"Did I stutter? Take a seat, Mr. Drake."

"No, I don't think I will."

Farrington shrugged and returned to his paperwork. The sound of his fountain pen scratching across the page was like nails on a chalkboard. "Then get back to work—and close the door on your way out."

* * *

Later that day, at dinner, Drake sat in silence at his usual table with Tristan. Something felt very wrong about Dr. Lambros's abrupt departure. He kept playing over in his mind the brief two minutes he'd spent in her office. The glass in the cracked frame bothered him, as did the arrival of Dr. Farrington. Behind that desk, the man had looked like a skeleton wearing a thin skin suit.

She didn't just leave, did she? Maybe she *had* left, and Drake had misjudged her character. Perhaps he was just another file to her, another number in a long list of numbers—a kid who couldn't do anything right and had been sent to prison for his crimes.

Care for a strawberry bonbon, Will?

Drake slammed his fist into the table, startling Tristan, and took a deep breath.

He did not believe for a moment that she had gone to "pursue other opportunities," as Farrington had put it. Two days ago? Drake had seen the Seahawk flying in and out these last few days, busy with preparations for Lucien Whitmore's arrival, and he had not seen Dr. Lambros leave. She would've said goodbye!

Drake's worry for the doctor was matched only by worry for his own neck. If she had started asking questions based on Drake's suspicions about Grey and the locked doors on the eastern platform, had she confronted Brand and Storm? Had she mentioned his name? What if Irene's name had come up somehow?

Worst of all, had Drake's concerns gotten her hurt? Did Drake think the warden and his number one guard were capable of hurting one of their own? She never liked Brand, whispered a voice in his head. You saw that on your first day here. But why would she have to leave? To hide what was happening on the eastern platform? Drake swallowed. He had no proof of anything, but he believed he'd come to the right conclusion all the same.

"You okay, Will?" Tristan asked.

Drake shook his head.

The hairs on the back of his neck tingled and stood to attention—someone had just walked over his grave. Taking slow, measured spoonfuls of lentil soup, Drake looked over to the swinging cafeteria doors and saw Marcus Brand standing there, staring straight at him from across the hall.

Brand held his gaze, cocking his thumb and forefinger like a gun, and shot Drake another of his all-too-friendly grins.

13

BENEATH THE DEEP BLUE SEA

The southern platform was abuzz with activity the morning of Monday the tenth of March. Lucien Whitmore would be arriving at some point in the afternoon, and Drake knew that Warden Storm was keen to impress.

As such, inmates were told that under no circumstances were they to stray from their assigned duties that day. The guards issued strict and stringent warnings at breakfast that anyone caught doing something they weren't supposed to be doing would be dealt with severely.

"If any of you sneeze without asking permission first," Brand warned, standing at the head of the cafeteria flanked by four masked guards on either side, "by God, my little lawbreakers, there will be hell to pay."

Drake spooned his porridge into his mouth and ignored most of the bluster. He was more convinced than ever that something was amiss on the Rig. Dr. Lambros's abrupt departure—disappearance—had dissuaded him of any lingering doubts. He decided to sneak away before lights out that very night, leaving his tracker in 36C, and see what he could find. If he could make it as far as the eastern platform, perhaps Irene would be waiting.

I'll be waiting. On every fifth day at midnight. The fifth, the tenth, the fifteenth, and so on, you understand?

Irene Finlay, one of the inmates Dr. Lambros had not been permitted to see during her counseling sessions. Would she be there? What about her tracker? A flutter of unease and nervousness clawed at Drake's gut, but he forced another mouthful of thick porridge down his throat. He'd need his strength later on. It had been some months since he'd met Irene at the infirmary and seen the insistence in her eyes about getting behind those rusted and locked doors, but Drake wanted to know more. He'd use the heating ducts or the overflow in the lower levels of Tubes, if he had to, but he was going through those doors—whether or not Irene was waiting for him.

Drake finished his breakfast and checked the time on his tracker—which was now nothing more than a disguise. Coming up for 0900 and almost time to head for the exercise area. Then lessons, followed by lunch, then work in Tubes and dinner. The Rig ran like clockwork. Drake intended to use that system to his advantage, and no one—not Storm or Brand or even Lucien Whitmore himself—would stop him.

It was the longest day Drake had spent on the Rig so far. The minutes crawled toward dusk, and his time in Tubes had never gone so slowly. He tried to keep from staring at his tracker every two minutes, but he was anxious about the evening. So much could go wrong—but he had to know what was happening here.

He forced himself to eat the fish curry for dinner, if only to try to settle his nerves. After dinner, during the two hours of free time before lights out, he and Tristan headed back to their cell to prepare.

"Okay," Drake said, retrieving the magnetic key from within his mattress. "You sure you're okay with this?"

"For the last time, yes," Tristan said, exasperated. "If anyone notices, I'll just tell them I had no idea you weren't in your bunk."

"Good, I suppose." Drake collected a few other items from around the room. Specifically, a thin bar of steel with a narrow, flat head—a makeshift screwdriver without a handle that he'd nicked off one of the machines down in Tubes that afternoon—and a black felt-tip marker he'd borrowed from the art supplies in the common room. It was 2030. Only an hour before the cell doors would automatically lock for the night. Drake's plan called for him and Tristan to be in the bathroom on the ninth tier of the cellblock by no later than nine.

Fifteen minutes before the hour, Drake removed his tracker and stashed it under his pillow. He didn't know how closely the security cameras were monitored, given how effective the trackers were when they couldn't be removed, but this was, perhaps, the most risky part of the plan—moving up through the cellblock without his tracker. If anyone in Control was paying particularly close attention to the cameras that night, they'd see two William Drakes. One as a GPS dot in his cell and another moving about freely.

A risk he'd have to take.

"Ready?"

Tristan nodded, then shrugged.

"Let's go, then."

Feeling almost naked out on the tiers without his tracker, Drake hunched his shoulders and tried to act normal as he and Tristan ascended the platform toward the washroom on the ninth level. From there, Drake knew, the vents ran under the corridor to the center platform—he'd studied them enough over the last few months—and represented his best chance of reaching the eastern platform.

No one intercepted them; no alarm bells rang. Trying to suppress nervous grins, Drake and Tristan entered the washroom without being accosted.

"Made it—" Tristan began.

Drake cleared his throat and pointed across the washroom. One of the stalls was occupied.

Tristan nodded, and they made themselves busy, standing around the urinals until whoever was in the stall cleared out. Drake couldn't help but stare into the mirror, up at the metal vent in the ceiling positioned just over the row of sinks.

A flush of water came from the occupied stall, and Emir emerged. He grunted in Drake's direction, scrubbed his hands, and left.

"Right, then. You need to keep an eye out while I unscrew this thing."

Tristan stepped back outside the washroom, and Drake hauled himself up onto the sink underneath the vent. The sink wobbled but took his weight, though he had to bend his neck to avoid hitting his head on the ceiling. He retrieved the makeshift screwdriver from his pocket and began working on the screws that held the vent cover in place. Warm air blew into his face from the outlet, a good sign that the vent was connected to the heating system. The heat vents ran straight to the boiler tanks on the eastern platform, or as near as Drake could tell.

The cover was held in place with crosshead screws, and after some wiggling, he managed to loosen the first one—just as Tristan stepped back into the bathroom.

Drake leaped down from the sink and dashed into one of the stalls. He heard the door swing open, footsteps outside in the washroom, several pairs, and then the tinkle of urine against porcelain.

"All clear," Tristan said a minute later, and headed back outside on watch.

Drake hauled himself back up onto the sink and worked the screws loose one at a time, slipping them into his pocket. The vent was only about half a meter wide, and he knew this would be a tight fit if he could scramble up into it at all.

The vent outlet didn't fall away, which was exactly what Drake hoped would happen. The cover was wedged in tight, which meant that with some help from Tristan, they'd be able to replace the cover over the vent once he was inside, without replacing the screws. No one would notice some missing screws, but there would be questions if the entire cover were removed.

Drake slipped his hands between the vent slats and pulled gently. The cover fell away, showering him with specks of plaster and plumes of dust. Coughing but smiling, he pushed the cover back over the vent. It held steady.

He stepped down from the sink again and out of the washroom, four tiny screws jingling in his pocket. Tristan was leaning against the railing of the tier, looking down over the exercise area nine floors below.

"We're good," Drake said, casting a glance up and down their level. "Quickly now, while no one's coming."

Drake and Tristan stepped back into the bathroom and moved fast, having rehearsed this part of the plan several times in their cell the night before. Back up on the sink, Drake removed the vent cover and handed it down to Tristan. Then, wasting no time, he reached up into the vent and scrambled for purchase.

Drake had picked this vent, and not the ones on the levels above or below, for a particular reason. This one rose vertically into the ceiling for only about ten centimeters before it curved horizontally. Standing on his tiptoes on the edge of the wobbly sink, he could just reach the horizontal pathway with his hands. There was no way he could pull himself up, however, and that's where Tristan came in again.

Placing the vent cover on the floor, Tristan linked his hands under Drake's foot and heaved him up as high as he could. Standing at five feet and change, that wasn't very high, but it was enough for Drake to get his head and shoulders up into the vent. He sneezed as dust tickled his nose, but he managed to get his elbows over the curve and onto flat metal. From there, he wiggled his way into the tight vent and was surprised to find it widened by another fifteen centimeters or so once he was up and in. He couldn't turn around, not when the vent was this narrow, but he'd be able to crawl forward.

"It look okay?" Tristan called from below.

"Just get the cover back on and get out of here!" Drake replied, trying to keep his voice low.

"Right."

Drake heard scrambling from the washroom below as

Tristan pulled himself up onto the sink with the vent cover. A moment later, after some grumbling and squeaking, Tristan said, "It's on. Are you good?"

"I'm good. Just remember to be here in the morning."

"Got it. Be careful, Will."

Drake heard him step down from the sink, heard the washroom door open and close, and then he was alone in the ceiling.

Dim slivers of light from the washroom below lit up the vent for about three meters ahead. Beyond that, he could make out nothing. He had ten hours or so until the cell doors opened in the morning. In another fifteen minutes it would be lights out, and no turning back.

There's already no turning back, whispered the voice in his head. Come on, this is the exciting part!

Drake took a deep breath and let it out slowly. Then he began to crawl into the dark, making as little noise as possible. Tubes had more than prepared him for shuffling through narrow spaces. If anything, this vent was a treat, being devoid of muck and slime from the sea.

He rounded a curve in the vent, and the darkness began to recede. Up ahead he could see more outlet vents and mesh coverings, which allowed pale light to stream in and highlight the path. After another ten meters he came to his first crossroad. The vent veered away to the left, moving slightly down, or up and to the right.

After a moment's indecision, playing over the layout of the Rig in his mind, Drake thought that down and to the left might lead him to the transparent corridor that connected the western platform to the center. He reached into his pocket and pulled out the felt-tip pen. As he turned left, he drew an arrow on the roof of the vent just above his head, pointing back the way he had come. Underneath this arrow, he scrawled the number 1.

The vent widened again, so much so that Drake could turn around if he wanted, but only on his stomach. Moving past one of the overflow vents, he looked down and saw some of the inmates fooling around in the common room below in the last few minutes before lights out. He was less than three meters above their heads, but they had no idea he was there.

I'm on the right track, he thought.

Up ahead, the path once again split in two directions, and Drake took the right route this time, marking the vent over his head with another arrow leading back and the number 2. For the next half-hour Drake navigated the vents, trying to visualize the layout in his mind and head as far east as he could. At one point he was up and over the tiered cellblock, looking down at a drop of fifty meters to the exercise area far below. At the next point he'd somehow gotten turned around and found one of his arrows, number 7, leading back the way he'd come.

At times the vents grew warmer, but never uncomfortably so, and once, he had to spin onto his back and pull himself up through a Z-shaped bend. His jumpsuit was, at this point, covered in dust. Still, it beat the grime and worse from down in Tubes.

Eventually Drake got to where he wanted to be.

The vent narrowed again, and stretched out from head to toe, he had to pull his arms ahead of him and shuffle forward as best he could. A mesh panel on the side of the vent showed him the underside of the clear walkway between platforms, and if he pressed his face against it, he could see the cold ocean far below.

Elated, Drake crossed, unseen and undetected, from the western platform to the center—well and truly out of bounds.

In time, after navigating below a maze of familiar corridors overhead, he found himself over the cafeteria. The dining hall was quiet and the lights dim. Strange to see all these places empty, Drake thought. Strange to be off the Rig's stringent schedule at all. The path diverged just ahead, straight on or down toward the left and the heart of the center platform. In the rough blueprints he'd been keeping in his head, Drake guessed that the guards' quarters were down that way. Probably best avoided.

Sticking primarily to vents that moved ahead or seemed to hug the outer shell of the platform, Drake crawled onward into the night. He estimated that he'd been in the vents for just over an hour when he heard muffled voices from below. Drake took a slow, deep breath and held it in. A nearby outlet vent gave him a view of Hall and Stein, two of the Rig's most hated guards after Brand, marching along a corridor Drake wasn't sure he recognized.

"Yeah, they're going down tonight," Stein said. "Warden has them all eating prime ribs and caviar on the south platform now, but they're going tonight."

"Does Doc Elias know . . ." Hall trailed away, out of Drake's hearing range.

Giving it a few minutes before he moved again, Drake shuffled forward. The next vent led down and to the right.

He made his mark in black felt-tip and journeyed on. He felt a cool breeze blowing from this direction and thought it might be the corridor to the eastern platform, but unless his sense of direction had failed him completely, it was more likely the crossing from center to south.

Thinking on it for a moment, Drake convinced himself that yes, it was the wrong corridor, and he continued on past the turn. If I head straight as far as I can now, and then head left, he thought, that should put me in line with the eastern corridor.

Ten minutes later, the vents did just that, and Drake made the crossing from the center to the eastern platform. He suppressed gleeful chuckles as he moved silent and unseen through the night, more than fifty meters above the Arctic Ocean. No prison, he thought. No prison can hold me.

He crawled into the eastern platform, and it felt, in a way, like coming home. He was a few levels too high, but once he found his way down to the heart of the platform, he'd start to recognize certain walkways and pipes from Tubes. As he'd noted during his first visit here, most of the eastern platform was exposed to the outside elements, and the vents grew a lot colder as he descended toward the ocean.

I'm probably not in the heating vents after all, Drake thought. These vents are all too open for hot air to travel any real distance from the boilers. More likely these are for ventilation or something. The why of the vents didn't matter as much as the destination—and Drake had come farther tonight than he'd dared hope on his first expedition about the Rig without his tracker.

He discovered a few minutes later that the vents ran parallel with the upper levels of Tubes—the nicer pipes that Tommy's lot always got to clean—and knowing where he was, Drake began searching for a way out of the vent. Access panels were every six meters or so, he knew, the next few levels down, but the configuration of the vents was different here. He crawled over a drop of about six meters that certainly would've put him on the next level down, but he'd have no way back if the vent did something stupid, such as come to a dead end.

Eventually he came to a section of disused and old drilling equipment, visible through a mesh screen in the side of the vent. Listening carefully for a few minutes, he decided that he was alone, and he pressed his weight against the screen as hard as he could. The mesh warped outward, creating a thin gap of about ten centimeters.

"Come on . . ." he groaned, and put his shoulder into it. The screws gave way on the left side, and the screen, with surprisingly little noise, flew open. Drake almost tumbled from the vent, but caught himself with a gasp.

He lowered himself down, covered in dust, onto the midlevels of the eastern platform.

Wasting no time, he clung to the shadows as much as he could and made his way down through the cool night air toward the rusted doors with the shiny padlock. He encountered no one and nothing on his way, and he crouched down behind some pipes just opposite the door, about five meters away and out of sight in case any guards happened along.

He looked down at his tracker to check the time, but of

course it wasn't there. He chuckled softly to himself and continued to wait. He couldn't have been up in the vents more than two hours, which put the time somewhere close to eleven, if not just after. Too early for Irene, if she was coming.

He settled in for a bit of a wait, shoving his hands into his pockets to keep them warm against the biting wind rolling in off the ocean.

I'll give her ninety minutes. If she doesn't show by then, I'm having a look through that door by myself.

With nothing but time to kill, Drake began wondering why he was waiting for Irene at all. He didn't know for sure that she'd even come, and he certainly didn't need her—or anyone's—help when it came to escaping. Got that tracker off by yourself, did you? Drake shook his head and chalked it up to curiosity. Perhaps there was something she could do to help.

No more than an hour later Drake found himself almost dozing, shivering from the Arctic wind. He yawned—and the dark walkway away to his left, lit only by intermittent flashes from the orange beacons strung along the edge of the platform, yawned with him.

He strained his ears and listened. Had he heard anything at all? A guard?

A minute later, and he heard the creak again. This time he was sure of it.

Irene Finlay, sleeves rolled up on her red jumpsuit and her hair tied back in a ponytail, stepped into the circle of light from the bulb above the rusted doors. She jiggled the shiny padlock, perhaps hoping it was unlocked, and she cursed.

Casting a quick look at her surroundings, she dug a thin metal bar from within her jumpsuit and jammed it into the lock.

Drake watched her for a moment, wondering whether to give away his position. Is she alone? he wondered.

Deciding that she was, he stood up and cleared his throat. "Nice night for a stroll, don't you think?"

Irene jumped out of her skin and dropped her lockpick. "You're here," she said, her eyes wide and amazed. She ran over to him and seized his wrist. "You're actually here! How on earth—"

"How'd you get your tracker off?" Drake asked.

Irene was silent for a moment and let his wrist fall. "How'd you get yours off?"

"Magnets."

"Magnets? Really?"

"Yeah. Now tell me how you did it."

Irene considered, then shook her head. "Not magnets. I'll tell you later, once you get me through this door."

"Why should I?"

"Because you won't believe what's on the other side. Now come on, we've got to be quick—they come this way all the time at night."

Drake didn't have to be told who "they" were. From Irene's tone alone, he knew she meant the Rig's demented staff. Still, he took a moment longer to assess his current situation. Could he trust this girl he'd met only once before? Was it even about trust? No, not really, because more than anything right then, Drake wanted to know what was going on aboard the Rig.

"Okay," he said. "Follow me back this way. There's a tube

that leads to an overflow, a level above us, and I'm pretty sure it overflows through whatever is beyond this door."

"A tube?" Irene whispered, jogging in Drake's wake.

Drake chuckled. "Yeah—a little less cushy than the vent you just crawled out of. Hope you don't mind getting a bit dirty, Irene."

Drake led her through the familiar maze of gauge and dial-covered machinery and old drilling equipment. Back in Tubes, he was in his element, and he quickly grabbed the meter wrench the crew used to pry the thick pipes open and set to work.

"Help me, would you? This usually takes two."

Together they unscrewed the bolt securing the cap, and Drake heaved the iron lid away, revealing the dark insides of the mucky pipe. Irene gagged and covered her mouth.

"Oh that's foul . . ." she said. "You want me to go in there?"

"Hey, this is actually pretty clean. You're welcome, by the way."

"I think I might be sick."

Drake shrugged as he unclipped a flashlight from the nozzle on one of the furled hoses he'd packed away just over six hours ago. Funny to be here at night. "I do it ten times a day. Look, this was the first pipe I ever cleaned when I arrived here near on four months ago. We'll have to crawl for the first bit, but then it widens and you can crouch on your feet."

"But it stinks."

"That's life on the Rig, Miss Finlay."

Irene sighed. "Suppose you think that sounded clever. Well, you go first, but if this doesn't go where you say it does . . ."

Drake pictured the layout of the eastern platform, the levels and the pipes, and nodded to himself. If there was one thing he knew about this platform, it was the pipes. "I can't see it going anywhere else. We'll come out above whatever's beyond those rusty doors. Now follow me."

A few centimeters of cold, filthy water sat on the bottom of the pipe, and despite his words of a moment ago, Drake grimaced as he lowered himself into it. He shuffled forward, minding his head, and was pleased when he looked back and saw Irene lowering herself into the pipe.

She gasped. "Oh God, is this what I think it is?"

"Mostly," Drake said. "But also probably a lot worse. Come on, it gets better ahead."

He flicked on the light and began to crawl through the pipe. Irene followed and gagged in his wake.

The pipe somehow seemed more menacing at night, but as Drake had promised, the cylinder began to widen, and before long he was up on his feet, taking quick strides into the bottom of the channel as it curved down to the right. Near the blockage grates he waited for Irene to catch up and then pointed to the overflow chute Mario had shown him on his first day. The chute extended on and down to the left. A small circle of flashing orange light could be seen in the distance.

"I've never been down there," Drake admitted, and tapped his head. "But if my math is okay, we should be right on top of where you want to go."

Irene shoved him aside and took the lead. "Then try to keep up with me, Will Drake."

He grinned. "By all means."

The overflow pipe did just what it promised—overflowed,

right above the choppy, dark waters of the ocean below. Drake's math had been off, after all.

"Well, this is no good," Irene muttered.

The pipe was wide enough that they could squeeze together side by side, wet and covered in muck, and gaze up at the night sky. Spray from the ocean struck them in the face, cold and salty. Damn . . . but it has to be close, Drake thought.

"Follow me," he said. He reached up, clinging to the rim of the pipe overhead, pulled himself up and out—briefly over the ocean—and found what he was looking for. "Irene, we're here."

Atop the pipe, an opening in the twisted metal and endless network of walkways led back into the heart of the platform, and to a view of a familiar set of rusted doors—the reverse side of those doors.

Irene scrambled up behind Drake, and they entered what looked like a dilapidated junkyard.

Hunks of old machinery, broken down and scavenged for parts long ago, littered the space. A high ceiling split the levels of the platform, and Drake knew that if he could see through that ceiling, he'd glimpse the boiler tanks, the heating system, and, away to the left, the pipe he and Irene had uncapped.

"Bloody hell," Irene said. "You were actually right."

"No need to sound so surprised."

"Shut up and follow me, Will."

Drake sighed and did as he was told. He followed Irene through the piles of junk to a cleared corridor that led from the locked doors to what looked like . . .

"Is that the elevator you told me about?" Drake asked. "It's big."

"It sure is." Irene dashed across the junkyard and gazed up at the wide elevator car, at the system of pulleys and counterweights on top of it that were bolted to the ceiling. She pressed her thumb against the call button half a dozen times, bouncing on the spot in excitement.

The doors didn't open, and Drake saw why. "Look, there's a panel for an access card. It won't open without one."

"Damn it, you're right. I missed that . . ."

A thought occurred to Drake. "But we're in the lower Tubes—the next stop down is the ocean. So where's this elevator going anyway? It's wide, as well. Like for freight or something?"

Irene grinned. "Now you're beginning to see, right? We have to get in there, Will."

"How? I don't have an access card. Do you?"

"No, I don't."

Somewhat defeated, Drake and Irene stepped away from the elevator to the edge of the junk piles littering the lowest level of the platform. They stood, silent for a moment, and Drake could hear the swell of the ocean crashing against the pillars below. The warden had told him, on his first day, that there was no way down to the water.

What else has he lied about? Drake was beginning to think a whole lot.

"Can we climb up on top of it, do you think?" Irene asked. "Give me a boost."

"What for?"

"It's an elevator, right? That means there's a shaft. I'm going to check and see if there's a ladder."

With no better idea, Drake linked his fingers and put his

back against the elevator. Irene slipped her foot into his hands and steadied herself, holding on to his shoulders. "Ready?"

"Yep."

With a grunt, Drake heaved her up by her foot, and Irene pulled herself onto the roof of the elevator car.

Drake took a step back so he could see her standing amid the pulleys and weights. "See anything?"

"No, nothing. Wait! Yes, there's a gap between the car and the wall, and like concrete handholds built into it, leading down."

Drake didn't like the sound of that. "Give me a hand up."

Irene's beaming face appeared over the rim of the elevator, and she reached down to grasp his hand. "Ready?" she asked.

Drake lifted his foot against the car doors and, with Irene's help, scrambled up the side. The top of the car smelled of grease and machinery and wobbled slightly as he moved across it. Irene had been right about the handholds leading down the back of the shaft. A ladder built into the wall itself.

"I'm game if you are," she said, and nudged Drake in the ribs.

"Ladies first, then."

Irene rolled her eyes and stepped off the car, gripping the handholds and steadying herself before taking a step down. She disappeared out of sight, and Drake steeled himself, worried that he was going to hear her slip and then scream as she plummeted down the shaft to depths unknown.

Shaking his head, he stepped off the car and followed her down.

The shaft was dark, but not entirely. Light from the junkyard did reach into the depths, and Drake could make out the bottom of the shaft—a good fifty meters below. Blimey, he thought, it goes down under the ocean, as deep as the platform is tall.

"See, this is easy," Irene said just beneath him a few minutes later. "I can't believe—oh, oh damn."

"What is it?" Drake looked down and saw that she had stepped off the ladder onto a ledge about a meter below. He saw the problem immediately. "The ladder doesn't go all the way down."

He joined her on the tiny ledge, their backs pressed against the wall. The junction box for the elevator was locked to their right. One step forward would mean a swift and fatal drop of about a dozen meters to the bottom of the shaft.

"We need a rope or, or a . . ." Irene huffed.

"We have one," Drake said, staring straight ahead. It was hard to see through the dull gloom, but the elevator cable hung in the air just in front of their faces.

Irene was silent for a long moment. "You're not serious."

Drake stretched his arm out and touched the cable with his fingertips. It wasn't slick with grease or oil. Most likely it lifted one of the counterweights as the car rose and fell.

"I'm halfway down an elevator shaft built below the Arctic Ocean with a girl who won't stop smiling. Who's being serious anymore?"

"This is the best first date I've ever been on," Irene said. Drake raised an eyebrow, and Irene laughed. She swatted his arm. "Were you any good at rope climb back in England, Will?"

"Didn't have a rope to climb, where I went to school." He

took a deep breath. "It's only about ten meters, yeah? Take two minutes."

"I don't think I can do it," Irene admitted.

"How much do you weigh?"

"Oh, charming. You ask all the girls that?"

"Well then, you're not going to like my next question. Want to climb down on my back?"

Irene squeezed Drake's upper arm and frowned. "You're not overly bound with muscles, you know. Do you think you can hold us both?"

"Oi, I'll leave you here if you keep that up."

Irene chuckled and gazed down the shaft. She licked her lips and looked back at Drake. "My life in your hands, Will."

Taking a moment to build his nerve, Drake reached out and gripped the steel cable with both hands. He stood like that for a second, stretched over the shaft, then stepped out and locked his ankles around the cable. It was taut, but there was some give to the line, and he swung back and forth a few centimeters.

Irene waited for him to stop swaying before she reached out, placed her hands on his shoulders, and wrapped her whole body around his back. Her legs came up around his waist, feet wrapped around the cable, gripping Drake almost like a vise.

"Loosen up a bit, please," he whispered. Irene's weight wasn't too much for him to handle, but he began to feel the strain in his biceps almost straightaway. "Now, let's be quick about it."

Drake was anything but quick as he lowered himself and

Irene down the shaft. He had to let the cable go with one hand and reach down, gripping the cable tight again before lowering his other hand, half a meter at a time. His ankles remained locked tight around the cable—not that it would have done much good if his arms gave way.

He didn't want to think about how they were going to get back up.

Drake's hands were becoming a touch sweaty. He started wiping his palms on the knees of Irene's jumpsuit every time he lowered them down another half meter or so.

"How you doing?" she asked.

"Fine and dandy like—"

The cable vibrated in his hands, and the sound of whirring machinery filled the shaft. Drake's heart leaped into his throat, but he clung tight to the cable and, dreading what he was about to see, looked up.

The freight elevator was coming down the shaft and picking up speed.

Oh.

Crap.

"Damn it—hurry!" Irene whispered in his ear, her breath hot and panicked.

Drake began to move, taking larger sweeps of the cable between his hands. The descent jarred his arm with each sweep, threatening to tear his shoulders from their sockets. Irene's hands dug painfully into his neck, and her legs about his waist bit hard. The cable began to shake in his hands as the elevator approached—a descending behemoth threatening to knock them to their death.

"Ah . . ." Drake fought against the burning strain in his arms and shoulders. He looked up and saw the elevator closing in on them fast. He looked down and saw about five or six meters of open air to the bottom of the shaft.

"Faster!" Irene said.

Drake loosened his grip and slid down the cable. At first it was just uncomfortable, but the friction soon took over and set his palms on fire. He gritted his teeth and bit back a scream as the cable shredded his hands. A few meters above the bottom of the shaft, his flayed hands could no longer hold the steel rope.

Drake and Irene fell—quickly and suddenly. Too quickly. Too suddenly. They hit the ground hard, Irene on top of Drake. Air exploded from his lungs in a vicious torrent, forcing breathless gasps, but that was small pain compared with the fire eating his hands.

The elevator car drew closer, and through the pain Drake knew that they would never be able to get out of the shaft in time. He could see no vents, no tubes—nothing to slink through. Why would there be anything this far below the surface? If they had time, perhaps they could wedge the doors open—doors that led to whatever secrets were buried under the Rig.

But there was no time.

Hot tears stung Drake's cheeks from the pain in his hands. Irene rolled off him and onto the cool stone floor at his side, next to the vast array of pulleys and counterweights built into the shaft. Drake was dead, and he knew it. And he'd gotten her killed, too.

"Irene, I'm sorry—"

"Shut up!" she whispered.

"But—"

The car came down on top of them, and Irene slapped her hand across Drake's mouth. Shrieking brakes rang out and rattled Drake's brain. The car came to a screeching halt just half a meter above their heads, sealing them in darkness that was peppered with small circles of light coming through the porous floor of the freight elevator.

Muffled voices from inside—Drake thought one belonged to Warden Storm—and then footsteps, shoes and heels clicking against metal as the elevator doors pinged open and the occupants stepped out.

Drake and Irene lay next to each other in the dark for a long minute. The darkness, spoiled only by the dim light shining through from the car, did nothing to calm the nagging thought that they were at least fifty meters below sea level, trapped and alone.

Irene removed her hand from his mouth. "Okay, I think they're all gone," she whispered. "You okay?"

"My hands . . . they feel cold." Drake's voice was tight with pain. "No."

He was almost thankful for the half-light. He didn't want to see the extent of the damage the cable had done.

"Let me see," Irene said.

He felt her soft fingers slip down his arm, feeling her way in the dark. She touched his wrist and paused. Drake didn't feel her hand on his palms or fingers—they stung too fiercely—but from the way her arm tensed against his, he knew she must have found something bad.

"Oh," she said. "Oh, Christ."

"Yeah?"

"Yeah."

Drake could almost hear her biting her lip. "Let me try something . . ."

"What could you possibly—"

A flash of brilliant cerulean light lit up the shaft, and the fire in his right palm went out. Drake could feel his skin tingling across his fingers. He looked down and saw an amazing thing. The flesh on his hands was rippling, as if still water had been cast with a pebble, and knitting itself back together. It took only a moment before the mysterious warm light faded, but before it was done, his hands were whole and unscarred.

Irene gasped and stifled a whimper. She was panting hard, as if she'd run a mile. "Does that feel better?" she asked.

"Better . . . ?" Drake was gobsmacked. "What in the hell was that?"

"I think there's a panel in the floor of the elevator car. Here, look." Irene pointed to a latch just above Drake's head. "I can almost . . . can you reach it?"

Drake turned onto his side and used his miraculously healed hands to work the bolt from the lock. It came free with a few good tugs. "Help me push."

With Irene's help, Drake managed to lift and squirm up through the panel in the floor. The light in the car was better, burning from a halogen bulb bar. He examined his hands, amazed and . . . frightened.

"Are you going to help me up or what?" Irene asked. She had wedged herself between the counterweights and the floor panel. "Give me a hand."

"I had a scar," Drake said. "On the back of my hand from . . . from where I tried to . . . pull Aaron out of the blaze at Cedarwood. It's gone." He reached down and gave Irene his hand. With a bit of shifting, she managed to worm her way into the car.

Irene rolled her shoulders and stood up. She tilted her head, and her neck cracked. "Oh, that's better."

"That was like magic, what you did. You . . . you just healed my hands."

"I did, yeah."

Drake tried to clean the blood and grease from his hands on his jumpsuit. "What the hell are they teaching you in the infirmary?"

She laughed. "I didn't learn that in the infirmary." Her laughter faded, and the look on her face became pensive as she turned to face the elevator doors. "No, I learned that through these doors."

"What? So you've been down here before?"

"Oh yes, didn't I mention it? I've been trying to get back for six months."

Drake saw her eyeing the button panel and stepped between it and her. "What's down here, Irene?"

She offered him a dazzling smile. "Magic. It's hard to explain, but we've come this far, Will." She put a hand against the doors. Drake wondered if she were about to blast the metal off its hinges with a bolt of lightning, Jedi-style. "Come with me a little further and see what they're doing here."

Drake had suspected that the Rig was hiding its secrets. But nothing like this—never anything like this. He hesitated. The entrance to the freight elevator above was unguarded, he knew, and there was no slot for an access card inside the car. He could take the elevator back up and avoid whatever madness was waiting beyond these doors.

Drake entertained that idea for all of three seconds before stepping to the side and pressing his back against the wall. "Hide there, just out of sight, in case anyone's waiting outside."

Irene suppressed a smile and did as he said.

Drake's fingers hovered over the two outward-facing arrows on the button panel for a moment. He strained his ears, listening for any sound beyond the doors, and then pressed the button. The doors slid open, and Drake beheld something breathtaking.

A wide, arched walkway shot as straight as a bullet out from the elevator. An eerie blue light covered the walkway, and the curved walls were made of some kind of reinforced glass, at least ten centimeters thick. Drake gasped and stepped out into a cold, silent bubble below the surface of the ocean.

"Neat, huh?" Irene said.

"I'd say so . . . " Drake was reminded of the London Aquarium, of the conveyor belt that took you around and under the water, shielded from the sea creatures by this same sort of glass. Heavy, bright floodlights were attached to the outside of the bubble, illuminating the dark water in all directions.

"We better be quick. There's nowhere to hide along here."

Irene took Drake's hand and pulled him along. His neck turned every which way as he tried to take in the view from outside. As they ran, keeping their footfalls as quiet as possible, Drake saw a ridge of underwater rock stretching away to the left.

The rock was speckled with glowing electric-blue light. He thought back to his first night on the Rig, to the strange light show he'd seen outside the window in Processing. This was the same light, only locked in rock dozens of meters below the surface. A school of bioluminescent fish swam past the window, their eyes shining blue.

"Wait a minute . . ." Drake said, pulling Irene to a halt. He pressed his face against the glass, trying to see farther down. The rock descended into the inky depths below, studded with that locked-in light the whole way down. "What is it?"

"Magic," Irene said. "Now hurry. If someone comes back this way, we're dead."

The walkway ran for about thirty meters toward a portal of artificial light. A huge shadow extended in the water above the portal, on the outside of the glass, and it took Drake a moment to realize what he was seeing.

A massive underwater complex had been built beneath the Rig—connected to the prison by this bubbled path. He let out a breath he hadn't known he was holding, as they ducked through the portal of light and into the complex.

Drake and Irene entered a wide-open space that was crisscrossed with metal walkways leading up and down and all around. This felt like more familiar ground, like the Rig. Drake heard the faint sound of machinery and what he thought might have been a vast turbine somewhere above. The air was fresh, and as he swallowed, his ears popped. Wherever they were, the pressure was being regulated.

"Do you think there are cameras around? Like up on the Rig?" Drake asked.

Irene pulled him toward a set of metal stairs that led downward, deeper underwater, and deeper into the complex. "I doubt it," she said. "They wouldn't want anybody seeing what they're doing down here."

"Who's 'they'? The Alliance?"

Irene nodded.

"And how do you know what they're doing down here?"

"Like I said, I've been here before. This way."

The stairs descended into a narrow corridor built along the edge of the complex. As quiet as mice, Drake and Irene jogged down the corridor and lost sight of the network of steel walkways and the roar of distant machinery. Windows of reinforced glass, at least three meters high by the same across, ran along the length of the corridor. More of that glowing rock shone with neon light, casting the corridor in shades of ghostly blue.

Drake kept his eyes open and his ears strained for any sign of people, but all was quiet. The corridor branched off as they reached the edge of the complex. Another corridor led to the right, and what looked like a viewing platform made entirely of glass was to the left, dark and concealed save for the uncanny light from the rock outside. Irene led Drake this way, out of sight, and together they sat down against the wall, hidden from view if anyone happened to be using the corridor they'd traveled down.

"This is amazing," Drake said. He could look through the glass-bottomed floor at the miles of glowing rock stretching away in all directions. The complex itself had been built into the ridge of rock. Marine life—dozens of fish and exotic creatures, all glowing softly—dotted the reef. He had the feeling he was looking at something immense and powerful. "What is the Alliance doing?"

Irene stared at the bright flecks in the rock with hunger in her eyes, pressing her fingers against the glass as if she could reach through into the freezing Arctic Ocean and retrieve a shiny prize. "They're experimenting," she said. "With whatever is in the rock."

"Experimenting?" A scary thought fled across Drake's mind and took hold in his heart. "What, like, on you?"

"On a lot of us, Will." She pointed toward the surface. The Rig wasn't visible this far below, but the leviathan prison was up there somewhere. "Whatever's glowing in that rock, those crystals, they mine it and bring it into this place, then leave us in a room with a piece. Just a little bit, no more than a teaspoonful."

"Are you serious?"

"Yes. I was brought down here. They put me in a room with this fishbowl full of water and a piece of the glowing blue stuff at the bottom of the bowl, and when I touched it, the crystal sort of melted into my hand. Like it . . . dissolved into me. They kept me down here a week to see what would happen. If it would do anything."

"And that's how you were able to fix my hands?"

Irene shook her head. She casually looped a loose strand of auburn hair behind her ear. "No, not at first. From what I gather, the crystals don't work on everyone. The scientists down here observed me a week, but nothing happened. I couldn't do a thing."

"So you were sent back up?"

"Right. It wasn't until months later that I realized . . . if I concentrated . . ." She bit her lip and held up her hand. After a moment, soft blue light began to dance within her fingers, beneath the tips. She wiggled her fingers back and forth, and a trail of smoky luminescence floated through the air. "I can't always make it work, but I cut myself pretty bad a month back and . . . well, the light healed me—within seconds."

"Christ," Drake cursed. He flexed his own hands. "Are you radioactive?"

Irene smiled softly. "I don't think so."

Drake's mind raced with the implications of what Irene was telling him. He felt almost sick to his stomach with nerves. The Alliance—Warden Storm and his staff—were experimenting on inmates, on teenagers. And doing what?

Giving them abnormal abilities.

The thought was so absurd that Drake snorted laughter, but the evidence was right here in front of him. Still . . .

"Is this a joke?"

"Is the dried blood on your hands a joke?"

Drake had to concede the point. "So one small piece, about six months ago, and now you're a magician?" He shook his head. "Do you know if it'll last? Will it just . . . go away, do you think?"

"That one small piece was half a year ago, and I've only been getting better at healing in the last month or so. Getting stronger at it," she said proudly.

"Can you do anything else? Or just the healing?"

Irene frowned and grabbed Drake's hand, waving it in front of his face. "Just the healing?"

"Okay, sorry. But why didn't you say anything to anyone after you were back on the Rig? Like Dr. Lambros?"

She said that she wasn't allowed to see Dr. Lambros.

"What if it's hurting you?"

"What if I did say something and they shoved me back down here in a cage? Oh yes, there are cages down here. I'm not certain what for, but I can make a good guess."

"Do you think they're all in on it? Storm, the guards . . . They can't all be, can they?"

"Can't they? I saw Brand down here, that woman with all the muscles—"

"Stein."

"—and Hall, as well as Dr. Elias from the infirmary."

Drake knew he had uncovered something he wasn't supposed to know. Not by a long shot. The Alliance wouldn't just transfer him to another prison for knowing this secret. Would they kill for it?

"Still . . ." he said. "They gave you superpowers! This blue stuff could be doing anything to you. You have to tell someone!"

"They don't know it worked, do they?" Irene shrugged. "And anyway, the warden said that if I kept quiet, the Alliance would take two years off my sentence—which means I'll be out in eighteen months."

"You think they would have hurt you if you didn't keep your mouth shut?"

Irene nodded and exhaled. "Come on, let's keep moving. I want to find more of this stuff."

Drake stood and followed her as they crept back out into the corridor and this time took the branch forking away to the right, deeper into the complex. There were no more windows this way, just cool white plaster and high ceilings dotted with hanging lights. Trolleys and canisters of what looked like oxygen lined the walls. Crates of unmarked material were stacked two meters high next to empty crates stamped with the silver crown of Alliance Systems.

"Why do you want to find more of it?" he asked as they moved ahead with care.

"One piece gave me the power to heal," Irene said. "What would another do? Or another? I want to find out."

"You're mad," he said. "No, you're bonkers. You don't know what the hell this stuff is doing to you."

"Honestly, I've never felt better. It's exhilarating." Irene rubbed her hands together. "Aren't you even a little curious, Will? It could work on you. I know your story, you know. Escaped from half of the Alliance's juvy prisons. What if it can do more than just healing? It could help you get off the Rig."

Superpowers. He shook his head to clear those thoughts away. "I don't need some glowing hocus-pocus to get me off the Rig. I'll manage that on my own."

Drake and Irene followed the corridor down and around. At one point, a set of metal stairs led up to an overhead walkway, and they took this path. The walkway extended up and over the walls of the corridor, and as Drake and Irene tiptoed quietly across it, keeping their heads down and crouching behind the paneled railing, they heard voices ahead, echoing up distinctly.

"Is that . . . " Drake asked.

Moving with extreme caution, they took a left and emerged above a wide-open space packed with laboratory equipment, pressure pipes, scientific apparatus, and dozens of tanks containing large quantities of the glowing blue rock. Drake took all of that in quickly, before his gaze was drawn to the gathering of people below.

They had caught up to the group from the freight elevator.

Drake saw Warden Storm, Dr. Elias, Brand, and a group of ten or so men and women dressed in fine business suits. At the head of that group, wearing tinted sunglasses, his silver hair slicked back, was Lucien Whitmore—the president and CEO of Alliance Systems.

"Mr. Whitmore, ladies and gentlemen, welcome to my lab," Dr. Elias announced, his voice echoing across the vast ceiling to where Drake and Irene hid on the walkway. "Here is where your generous donations have been spent, here is where the forefront of chemical and biological science has been implemented to harness and adapt the power in the glowing mineral you saw on your way down." Elias spread his arms and gestured to the laboratory at large. "My friends, here is where we better humanity forever."

14

CRYSTAL-X

What Drake saw next changed his entire outlook on the world.

"As most of you are aware, but for the benefit of those only just brought into our select loop"—Dr. Elias smiled at Whitmore's entourage—"the Alliance has been operating this facility for just over eighteen months. We mine the glowing rock, which I'll hereafter refer to as Crystal-X, and experiment on it in a vast array of ways down here, in the privacy afforded us below the Rig."

"Do you know of anywhere else this mineral, the Crystal-X, can be found?" a tall, attractive woman asked. She stared into one of the tanks, fascinated. "Or is this location naturally unique?"

"Our leading theory is that the mineral itself is actually not natural, madam," Elias said. "We think this entire facility has been built on a gigantic meteorite. Yes, that was my reaction, too. We're standing on a massive chunk of space rock that collided with Earth some millions of years ago. And . . ."—he cleared his throat—"and it's been growing ever since."

Most of the crowd was stunned into silence, as were Drake and Irene. Drake thought, Does he mean . . .

"My technicians have been working around the clock to prepare for your arrival," Elias continued. A group of six men and women, wearing white lab coats, stood in a line behind the doctor. "This, ladies and gentlemen, is what you've traveled so far to see."

Elias flicked a switch on his workbench, and four glass display monitors hanging from the ceiling flickered to life.

The displays played footage of a dozen different tests on a dozen different subjects. Drake didn't recognize most of the boys he saw in the clips—and none of the girls—but they were dressed as he was in the Rig's green jumpsuits. One or two seemed familiar, but he was more focused on what the people in the videos were actually doing.

One girl held out her palm and created a sphere of rippling energy, like a tennis ball of lightning. She tossed it at the wall and burned a hole through the metal. Another boy lifted a massive crate over his head with one hand and smirked at the camera.

Dr. Elias provided commentary. "That weighed three metric tons."

A boy who could be no older than sixteen sat with his legs crossed. Not overly impressive by itself, but he did it two meters off the floor. He was levitating.

Irene's eyes gleamed in the half-light. She looked at Drake and grinned, as if to say *See? I told you so.*

Dr. Elias paused the footage and addressed his audience. "As you can see, the results have varied. Most subjects show zero affinity for Crystal-X. Some develop a minor talent that requires a constant source of the mineral to maintain." Elias shook his head. "We classify those as unworkable."

"Thank you, Nathan," Warden Storm said, glancing sideways at Lucien Whitmore and his entourage. "However, I think Mr. Whitmore would like to hear more about our successes."

Elias nodded. "A small percentage of the subjects tested —currently fifteen percent, although that figure could be skewed by the small sample size available, as we have to be rather selective—absorb Crystal-X and develop immediate and, often, amazing abilities. Abilities that not only last well beyond the initial dose but increase in strength and durability over time, without requiring additional Crystal-X."

Whitmore looked pleased. "How powerful are these successful subjects?"

"I've one boy who can harness the energy in his body to create physical objects out of what I've dubbed 'hard-light.' Another who can fire bolts of neon-blue energy through concrete and steel and has a minor, unconfirmed telekinetic ability. One of the girls managed to successfully guess what randomly generated picture a computer console would show three hundred times in a row. Unfortunately, she hasn't been able to repeat the feat, but we're working on it."

"She could see the future?" Whitmore asked.

Dr. Elias shrugged. "Perhaps. A split second ahead, at least."

"Remarkable," said a portly man to Whitmore's left. He was bouncing back and forth on his heels.

"The boy capable of manipulating light has so far shown the most promise. He's absorbed a not insignificant amount of Crystal-X without . . . notable detriment to his health." Elias rubbed his hands together. "In a month, he'll be eighteen, and I think a more than eager recruit into your program, Mr. Whitmore."

Drake frowned. Program?

Warden Storm smiled and tucked his hands into his belt. "Yes, Grey's coming along in leaps and bounds. Bit of a temper on the boy, but that's what you want in a good soldier, eh?" He laughed.

Grey . . . Drake swallowed hard. The knife attack in the exercise area suddenly made a whole lot more sense. Grey had created the knife out of nothing. He was a damn wizard. Drake didn't know what was worse—that Grey could conjure weapons or that the Alliance considered this a success.

Storm clapped Elias on the shoulder, clearly enjoying his opportunity to show off. "There are also weapons applications to the mineral, aren't there, Doc."

"Oh yes. If you'll allow me to demonstrate." Elias stepped over to a workbench that held a thin cylindrical glass tube about half a meter tall. "There is only a small amount of the mineral preserved inside this canister, suspended in the center here by these clasps. As you can see, the glass is sealed and full of seawater. There is good reason for this. Exposed to the air, Crystal-X becomes highly flammable and violently explosive. Please watch."

Elias picked up the tube and carried it across to the far side of the laboratory. Along the wall was a pit about two meters wide and two deep. What looked like an industrial exhaust port to Drake was built into the roof over the pit. Dr. Elias flicked a few switches on the wall, and the port began sucking in air. He then climbed down into the pit, using a ladder fixed to the wall, and emerged a moment later without the canister.

"The canister is draining now. It's designed to take a few minutes. You'll see why." Whitmore and his entourage had moved in close to the pit. Elias chuckled. "I'd advise you all to step back at least six meters."

A minute later, a great torrent of white-hot flame erupted from the pit. A wave of heat and energy knocked everyone in the lab back and rattled loose tools sitting on crates, the display monitors, and the paneled railing Drake and Irene crouched behind. Even at their distance, up and above the lab, Drake could feel the heat as if he were sitting around a bonfire.

The port above the pit sucked up the flame and kept it from spreading. Storm was laughing at the dumbfounded expression on half the faces in the room. Drake watched Whitmore, whose eyes were still hidden behind his dark glasses. The man had not even twitched.

Over the roar of the flame, Whitmore asked, "How long will it burn for?"

Elias held up four fingers.

"Four minutes?"

"No, sir." Elias smiled grimly. "Days. Four days."

A team of technicians moved in. They wore black full-body protective gear and large helmets connected via a pipe to a tank on their backs. Reflective visors obscured their faces. Each technician carried a wide silver hose strapped to a canister on a trolley behind him. They approached the roaring flame, and gouts of white steam burst from the hoses.

"Liquid nitrogen," Irene whispered. "Has to be."

"It'll take them about half an hour to douse it," Elias said. "Shall we continue to discuss the human applications?"

"How much of the mineral will be shipped this week?" Whitmore asked.

"Four crates," Brand said promptly. "About three hundred and fifty kilos. We've stepped up mining, as you requested, Mr. Whitmore. Next shipment should be in the region of six to seven hundred kilograms. Third drill comes online in two days, which should double our daily hauls."

Whitmore nodded and said nothing.

"Let's show 'em the bees, Doc," Storm said, almost bouncing on the spot. "You'll like this, Mr. Whitmore. Perhaps you'd also like to see the sharks, if you have time? No? The bees then, Doc!"

Elias straightened his coat and nodded. "Please follow me."

Casting nervous glances at each other, Drake and Irene waited a minute before moving after the group. Irene held a finger to her lips, offered Drake a weak smile, and shrugged as she moved along the walkway. They followed the group below, aware that a heavy footfall could give them away, as Elias led Whitmore's entourage through a door to the next room—another laboratory, this one filled with steel cages, glass tanks, and workbenches scattered with paperwork and tablet computers. Elias stepped behind one of these benches, and the others gathered in front.

Drake and Irene watched from above, still partially hidden by the walkway but feeling all too exposed. If Elias had reason to look up, they'd be seen.

"Here we have a glass container fitted to a crushing press.

174

As you can see, ladies and gentlemen, a small colony of bees inhabits this tank." Elias flicked a switch on the side of the tank, and a thick metal plate began to move across it. "Watch what happens."

The press slowly narrowed the space the bees had to buzz around in. Enclosed within the glass tank, the tiny insects were about to be crushed. Only . . . no. It wasn't very clear to Drake, but a few bees were now buzzing around the other side of the tank. The press kept moving, and bees kept appearing behind it, as if . . .

"Good God." One of the entourage, a tall, handsome man with sandy-blond hair, gasped. "They're flying through the solid metal!"

"Phasing through it, actually," Dr. Elias said. "We exposed these bees one at a time to a droplet spray containing six parts Crystal-X to four parts water. Of two thousand bees, three-tenths died, the rest survived. These twelve are the last test subjects. They all developed the same ability to phase through solid metal." Elias laughed. "First few nights, we'd come back an hour later and they'd be gone. Poof! Just vanished. It took us a few days to realize what was happening."

"They can't phase through the glass?" Lucien Whitmore asked.

"No, sir. For some reason, no. Metal, surely. Plastic and concrete, definitely. Glass, well, is as solid to them as to you or me."

"We've been finding dead bees all over the Rig for weeks." Storm laughed. "Mad scientist that he is, Doc here created an army of teleporting bees."

"Phasing bees," Elias corrected. "They phase."

175

"Is there anything else you'd like to show me?" Whitmore said. From his tone, Drake thought that the man had given Elias and Storm all the time he was willing to give, and his question was a conclusion to the tour.

"Actually, sir, there is one final thing, concerning side effects of human application," said the doctor.

"Now, Nathan," the warden began, "that's grist for another day's mill. Mr. Whitmore's time is val—"

"It will only take a moment, and it's something I think he needs to see."

Whitmore turned and whispered in the ear of one of his associates. Then he said, "Very well, Dr. Elias. You have five minutes."

Elias nodded and stepped briskly across the second lab and back into the first. He returned a moment later and stepped over to the rear of the lab, behind the empty animal cages, and pressed a glowing green button on the back wall. A metal roller door began to ascend, revealing another, darkened room beyond.

"They're bringing him in now," Elias said, returning to the group. "We keep this area dark—he seems to prefer it that way."

"Bringing who in?" Whitmore asked.

"Ah," the warden said. "Well, sir, there are still some problems with the human application of the mineral."

An ear-piercing scream howled from beyond the roller door, followed by a cackle that sent shivers of fear running down Drake's spine. Irene gasped and covered her ears. The sound, scratching at every corner and high ceiling of the laboratory, could only be described as insane.

Three technicians wheeled in a cage made of glass and reinforced along the edges with metal bindings. Air holes were dotted along the face of the cage, which stood just over two meters tall. The occupant inside the cage was a teenage boy. He hurled himself at the walls of his small prison, clawing and screaming. Topless, he wore a pair of torn and bloody green trousers. His upper body, below a head of long brown hair, was corded with thick muscle.

"My God . . ." Irene whispered. "His eyes. Look at his eyes!"

The boy pressed his face against the wall of the cage, glaring at the men in suits and lab coats all around him. Drake stared in growing horror. The boy's eyes were red—and glowing.

"At first," Dr. Elias said, gesturing at the cage, "the subject responded well to Crystal-X. One of the best responses we've seen so far. The mineral increased his muscle mass, his strength. He became capable of lifting weights in excess of nine metric tons. Then he developed energy-manipulation abilities, followed by the phase ability you just witnessed in the bees. That's why he is confined behind reinforced glass."

"It drove him mad," Whitmore said. He stepped forward, ignoring the warnings of his colleagues, and stood in front of the cage, looking up at the boy—face to face, almost.

"Overexposure has, in three cases now, caused irreparable damage to the brain," Elias said. "This subject is the only one of the three who has survived this far, but his condition is deteriorating."

Whitmore tapped on the glass. "Why are his eyes glowing?"

"We . . . we don't know," Elias admitted.

Whitmore stood a moment longer as the boy thrashed

in his cage. After a moment, he calmed and looked down at Whitmore, his hands and nose pressed against the clear panel. They stood that way for a long moment, staring at each other.

"I've seen enough," Whitmore said, and turned back to face his entourage, the boy in the cage glaring down at the top of his head. "Continue human trials. I want the process refined and ready to administer to Crystal Force. Send me the files on this promising recruit of yours."

"Yes, sir," Warden Storm said.

Whitmore and his men swept out of the lab and back the way they had come, toward the freight elevator. Drake and Irene stayed hidden up on their walkway, almost pressed against the cool steel. The pale, terrified look on Irene's face told Drake all he needed to know about her plans to absorb more of the mineral.

"How could they?" she whispered to herself over and over again. "How could they?"

As the technicians wheeled the boy in the cage away, he fell back against the wall of his tiny prison and wept. Just before he disappeared through the roller door, his head snapped up to the walkway. Drake wasn't sure, given those haunting crimson eyes, but he thought he saw the boy stare straight at him and smile through his tears.

15

HIDEAWAY

Drake and Irene had an easier time of it getting back up to the Rig than they had getting down. The freight elevator didn't need an access card to operate from the Crystal-X facility.

They rode the car in silence, worried about guards up top, and emerged in the junkyard, their ears popping from the pressure change, quiet and solemn. They were alone.

"Well . . ." Drake said. "That was horrific."

"I still can't believe it." Irene's pale skin, dashed with freckles, looked almost porcelain in the dull light overhead.

"Let's get out of here in case anyone else wants to use the lift."

Irene nodded. "I know a place we can talk."

They used the same overflow pipe to get around the locked, rusted doors and soon found themselves out on the lower levels of the eastern platform, overlooking the dark ocean. Flashes of orange light from the beacons strung along the outer shell of the Rig lit up the shadows.

"This way," Irene said. "There's an old control room toward the north platform, I think from when this was the only platform. Took me a few nights to clear away all the debris and get in, but it's cosy and warm—and private. I don't think anyone but me has been in there in years."

Irene led Drake down a level, past the rusted doors with the shiny padlock that hid such terrible secrets, and along a walkway toward the northern platform. He was conscious of the time as he followed her, knowing it was probably close to three or four in the morning now. He'd need an hour, at least, to follow his map of arrows back through the vents to the western platform before seven, when the cells opened for the day.

"Up here," Irene said.

"Blimey, another vent," Drake muttered as Irene lifted herself up into a vent that hung low in a bracket.

"This is how I get from the northern platform to here," she said. "You used the vents too?"

"Yeah. They rely too much on the trackers," Drake said. "As far as Control's concerned, I'm asleep in my bunk and have been all night."

Irene chuckled. "Me too." She came to a stop at an intersection in the vent, and Drake almost got kicked in the face for following too closely. "Down here."

The vent spat them out in a small room, fully enclosed from the outside, the door barred, with a single porthole overlooking the dark ocean. A sprinkling of stars could be seen through the porthole. The air smelled of rust and, as always, old oil.

Irene swiped the flashlight from Drake's pocket and switched it on, lighting up the dark. Dusty desks, old metal chairs, and a bank of flat-screen monitors, unplugged and life-less, came into view.

"Welcome to my hideaway," Irene said. "I usually don't bring boys back here until the fourth or fifth date."

Drake laughed, but it sounded forced even to him. Irene was trying to reclaim some of their earlier banter, but given what they had just seen deep beneath the sea, he wasn't in much of a laughing mood.

"It doesn't feel real," Drake said. "I mean, I know we just saw it, and you healed my hands, but I still almost can't be-lieve it."

Irene nodded. "I know how you feel. It took me a few weeks to come to terms with . . . well, with this." She raised her hand and made the blue light appear beneath her fingers again, as if the alien mineral were swimming in her blood vessels.

"From what we saw, it seems like you got off easy."

"Yeah . . ."

"Can I . . . can I touch your hand?"

Irene shrugged and nodded.

Drake brushed his fingertips against her blue fingers. Trails of luminescent smoke seeped through her skin, and she felt warm. "That's so strange."

"Will Drake, have you never held a girl's hand before?"

Drake smiled. "No, not that."

"I know what you mean."

Drake let go of Irene's hand, and soon the only light came from the flashlight. They stood in silence, and Drake stared around the small room. He thought Irene had been right; this was once used to control the platform. None of the equipment looked as if it still worked. He flicked a few switches on the panels, and nothing happened.

"So, what brings you to the Rig?" Irene asked.

"You mean the world's number one holiday destination?" Drake shook his head. "The brochure promised girls in bikinis and all the seafood I could eat."

"Fine. Don't tell me." Irene crossed her arms. "But I know you're wondering the same about me."

Drake had been. Only the worst of the worst got sent to the Rig. Or, in Drake's case, if all other cages had failed. So what had the auburn-haired girl with the magic powers done to be sent here?

"I'll show you mine," Drake said with care, "if you show me yours."

Irene snorted and elbowed him in the ribs. "Perhaps when you're older." She stared at him in silence for a moment. "Can you meet me here tomorrow night?"

"I . . ." Drake nodded. "I can try."

Time was short when they parted, Irene through her vents to the northern platform, and Drake back up and out onto the eastern platform's outer rim. He returned the flashlight to the hose in Tubes and made his way back to the vents that would take him, after much crawling, to the washroom on the ninth level of the western platform.

It was still dark when he crossed the central platform, but the sky toward the east was softening when he crossed from central to western, using the vents running under the transparent connecting corridor. Drake felt as if years had passed since he'd first come this way a handful of hours ago. He was tired through to his bones, and his elbows and knees were raw and numb from all the crawling.

Even with his felt-tip arrows to guide him, Drake managed to take a wrong turn above the empty common room on the western platform, and he had to waste valuable minutes backtracking to correct his path. He could almost feel the sun rising over the horizon, the new day dawning, and the cells about to open. Finally, after a night to remember, he was back above the outlet cover he'd first unscrewed to access the warren of vents that had led him all across the Rig. Drake let his head fall into his hands and waited.

He was dozing, just on the edge of sleep, when he heard someone calling his name.

"Will?"

Drake frowned and tried to roll over and go back to sleep. His eyes snapped open a split second later.

"Will? Drake? It's me, are you there?"

"I'm here," Drake whispered. "Is it safe?"

"Be quick—everyone's waking up, buddy."

Drake slipped his fingers through the slats in the outlet cover and pushed. It came away as easily as the night before, and he wiggled out of the pipe, arms first, then head. He was halfway out, dangling from the ceiling, when he realized that he was going to have to fall.

Michael Tristan, wide-eyed and hair askew from a night's sleep, darted out of the way as Drake wriggled out of the vent and hit the rubber floor hard, laughing and groaning.

"Good morning," Tristan said.

"Is it?" Drake muttered. "You brought it, right?"

Tristan handed Drake his tracker, and he slapped it around his wrist. The time read 0706. Six minutes into the new day, and as far as Control knew, Drake was hitting the showers early.

"Also a clean jumpsuit and towel," Tristan said. "Thought you might need a shower."

Drake was covered in dust, grime, sweat, and blood. "You will not believe the night I've had."

"How far did you get?" Tristan asked as Drake stripped out of his dirty shoes and jumpsuit and headed over to the showers. "And is this blood? Are you hurt?"

*　*　*

Drake shook his head and wasted no time stepping under the freezing cold spray from the showerhead. He gasped, but it was invigorating, and it washed away the vestiges of his little nap in the vents. "Yes, that's blood. No, I'm not hurt. A little bruised and battered, but not hurt."

"What happened?"

"Not here. Back in our cell, once I've had a chance to clean up."

The water warmed up after a minute, and Drake hung his head over the drain, washing away the night's horror. He thought of Irene and wondered if she were doing the same.

His tracker attached firmly to his wrist, Drake felt almost normal again wandering down through the tiers toward 36C on the third level. He kept his head lowered, avoided the gaze of the guards, and wondered if any of the boys he walked past had superpowers.

Back in the cell, Drake leaned against the ladder and thought about going to sleep, but it was only half an hour before breakfast. He had a long day ahead of him before he could rest—the price for leading a life outside the tracker's schedule.

"So, what did you see?" Tristan asked.

"Blimey, where do I start?" Drake took a deep breath and started at the beginning.

For simplicity's sake, and because time was short, Drake left Irene and most of the crawling through the vents out of the story, but he filled Tristan in on the rest. The junkyard, the climb down the ladder, the Crystal-X facility, and the glowing underwater ridge that was actually a bloody meteorite. He told Tristan about all of it and watched his eyebrows climb up under his bangs.

"Come off it . . ." Tristan said, but his voice was low and awed.

"Warden Storm was down there, so was Brand, and get this—Lucien Whitmore and a whole bunch of Alliance people."

He told Tristan about the mineral presentation, the things he'd seen some of the inmates do on the display screens, how the Crystal-X exploded, about Alan Grey, and what the bees could do.

"Remember you noticed that, your first night in here?" Tristan said, pointing at the window. "The dead bees."

"There was also a kid down there, in a glass cage." Drake told him what Dr. Elias had said, about how the blue mineral had overwhelmed the boy's mind.

Tristan frowned. "Did you get a good look at him?"

"Good enough. Tall, muscular. He was a big guy. Brown, shaggy hair and a sharp chin. Like, his chin could've cut steel."

All the color drained from Tristan's face. "That's Carl," he said. "Holy God, I thought he'd been sent back to the mainland. That's . . . that's . . ."

Carl?

Of course. Tristan's last cellmate. "Carl . . . Anderson?"

Tristan slumped onto his bed and held his head in his hands. "Do you think . . . maybe it's not . . . was he definitely an inmate, Will?"

Drake considered and then reluctantly nodded. "He was wearing a tattered green jumpsuit. What was left of one, at any rate."

"He was kind to me," Tristan said, and smiled sadly. "You know, tough but kind. Sort of like you are, a bit. Carl watched out for me my first few months here. Made settling in less . . . awful. Not even Grey and his gang would mess with Carl." He slammed his fist into the mattress. "I knew something had happened to him. I knew it." Tristan removed his glasses and rubbed his eyelids. For once, he looked not only his age but a lot older. Seventeen going on forty.

"He's mad," Drake said. "Like, out of his mind crazy. And his eyes . . ."

Tristan put his glasses back on and met Drake's gaze. "I want to see him."

"Mate, it's pretty hard to get—"

Tristan nodded and turned back to his bed. He reached down the side of the bunk and retrieved the magnetic key that unlocked Drake's tracker. No, this key was different.

Without saying a word, Tristan ran the new key along the seam of his tracker, and the device popped open and fell away.

"We can go tonight, Will. Please."

Drake gave a heavy sigh that turned into a small chuckle. "You cheeky bugger. Tonight, then. I was going to meet Irene in her hideaway anyway—may as well risk our lives two nights running, eh?"

Tristan secured his tracker back on his wrist. "Sure. Who's Irene?"

"Magical nurse." Drake slapped his cheeks to stay awake. "Come on, breakfast time."

16

ONCE MORE INTO THE DEEP

"Do you think she'll be mad at me?" Tristan whispered as he and Drake snuck along the outer, windswept edge of the Rig's eastern platform. The air was a little warmer than the night before, and immense, roiling storm clouds spread across the sky, blocking the stars and threatening rain.

"What? Mad at you?" Drake frowned. "For what, tagging along?"

"She's not expecting me. I don't even know her."

Drake chuckled. "Tristan, you're out of bounds on a floating prison where the guards shoot first and ask questions later. Irene's just like you, only prettier."

"She can't really do magic, can she? There's no such thing. You were just pulling my leg, yeah?"

"No."

Tristan sighed. "No. I didn't think so. Imagine what would've happened if they'd caught you down there."

"That's where we're heading again tonight, with or without Irene, so you can see Anderson for yourself. You insisted, mate, and I want a proper look around myself. Back out now, if you're not up to it."

Drake stood before the access port to Irene's hideaway. Crawling through the vents from the western platform had been far easier for Tristan than it had been for Drake. He was a lot smaller and wilier. Their trackers lay tucked under their pillows back in 36C. Tomorrow morning's walk back from the washroom was going to be interesting if they bumped into anyone—such as a guard.

"No. I want to see this." Tristan clenched his fists, fighting shivers. "Seeing is believing, right?"

"With what they're doing below this place, I'm not so sure. Quickly now, one more vent to go."

Drake had retrieved the flashlight from Tubes on their trek down, and he used the narrow beam to light their way into the old control room, buried and forgotten along the northern edge of the platform. A perfect little hideaway from prying eyes.

"I think we beat her here," Drake said, shining the light up and along the control room. "We'll give her an hour and then head down with or without her."

Tristan was intrigued by the old computer monitors, and after a moment's hesitation, he started tinkering with the cables and pulling panels off the walls to get a better look at the wiring. "Wow, this place used to run on old broadband fiber cables," he said, shaking his head. "Say what you want about the Alliance, their global nano-wireless network is spectacular."

Drake settled in one of the old swivel chairs and watched Tristan work. The little fellow stripped wires, flicked switches, plugged and unplugged cables, and was so enthralled with his work that Drake promptly fell asleep sitting in his chair.

What felt like two minutes later he was jostled awake with a start and almost slipped from the chair.

"There he is," Irene Finlay said. "Another few seconds and you would've got a slap."

Drake yawned, thought about it, and yawned again. "Good evening, Irene."

"Good evening, Will. You invite this straggler along?" She gestured at Tristan, who was almost knee-deep in wiring and dust, looking rather sheepish.

"Never seen him before in my life."

"We'll have to throw him overboard, then."

"Agreed."

Tristan started to untangle himself. "You two are hilarious."

Drake stood and stretched. "Irene, this is Michael Tristan. My cellmate, who's good with magnets."

Irene helped Tristan free himself from the knots of cable wrapped around his knees. He blushed beet red when she pulled his leg up and out of the mess. Drake almost smiled.

"You got the trackers off, then?" she asked him.

Tristan nodded. "Nothing to it, really. Drake tells me you're a witch."

"Did he now?"

Tristan read the look Irene gave Drake and stammered, "Er . . . I mean, that was a joke. You see, I'd . . . I'd like to see what you can do, if that's all right."

Irene laughed. "Oh, you're harmless, aren't you? Very well. I'll show you how I got my tracker off." She rolled up the sleeve of her red jumpsuit and held up her arm.

Drake switched off the flashlight, plunging the small control room into darkness.

A moment later Irene's hand began to shine with that ethereal blue light. Bright spots, like tiny stars, danced beneath her skin, running across her palm and up to her wrist. Drake thought that Tristan would step back, afraid, but his cellmate's only reaction was a slight widening of his eyes behind his glasses.

Irene bit her tongue, frowned, and Drake and Tristan watched an amazing thing happen. Her arm . . . lengthened. Her forearm, wrist, and hand rose up into the air—although she didn't raise her elbow at all—and grew thinner. The bone, flesh, and skin lengthened and narrowed until her arm looked comically long. Or horribly disfigured. All the while, that blue light darted with frenzy beneath her skin.

"And the tracker just slips off," she said, wiggling her arm. The elongated limb shrank back to its normal size and width. "Like magic."

"That can't be good for your bones," Tristan said once he found his voice.

Irene shrugged and cracked her knuckles. "It doesn't hurt. Tickles, mostly, and I've been doing it every night for the last few months without damage—waiting for Drake to get his act together."

"Still . . ." Tristan decided to shrug as well. "I guess all bets are off with this blue stuff."

"So what are we doing tonight, boys?"

Drake uncrossed his arms and clapped Tristan on the shoulder. "What do you think? We're going back down and having a proper look around. Tristan thinks he knows that . . . that boy we saw in the cage. With the red eyes," he added, as if they'd seen more than one poor sod trapped like an animal.

"I want to go back down, too," Irene said with a firm nod. "I've been thinking about it all day, and I believe it's about time we took our leave of the Rig."

The trip back into the Crystal-X facility went far smoother than the previous night's expedition, even with Tristan tagging along. He balked a bit at crawling through the filthy pipes and almost lost his nerve climbing up the rim of the overflow pipe hanging out over the dark ocean, but he did surprisingly well climbing down the cable to the bottom of the elevator shaft.

Drake was more than a little hesitant at first, but after some encouragement from Irene he climbed down the cable again, with her clinging to his back, and all three of them stood in the dim light at the bottom of the shaft.

"What next?" Tristan asked.

"Eh . . ." Drake chuckled. "Well, damn. Last night the elevator car came down and we snuck up and in through a panel in the bottom."

"So we wait?" Irene asked. "Or can we pry the doors open?"

Drake stepped across the shaft and approached the automatic sliding doors leading into the Crystal-X facility. He pressed his hands flat against the doors and pushed. They didn't budge. "Damn. Irene, can you abracadabra them open, or something?"

"If I could, I wouldn't need you, pretty boy."

Tristan tutted and pointed up to the frame. "Give me a boost, Will. That's the release latch up there."

Drake heaved Tristan up, and he got his hands around a triangular box stuck to the doors. A few clicks later, he pushed the latch up and the doors released. A pool of eerie blue light flowed through the gap. Drake lowered Tristan and they peeked through into the facility.

"Looks like the coast is clear," Drake said. He gave the doors another push, and this time they slid open on smooth rollers. He climbed up out of the shaft and gave Irene and Tristan a hand to do the same.

"Oh . . . my God," Tristan said, gaping in wonder at the walkway leading down into the facility and the arched glass displaying the marvelous ridge of glowing blue mineral. "You weren't kidding. This is amazing."

Drake pressed the call button for the elevator, which, as he'd hoped, reset the doors with a small hiss. "Right, let's be quick then."

Drake set off at a run, Irene and Tristan keeping up in his wake. None of them could take their eyes off the ridge outside the glass that held back the entire Arctic Ocean.

"Incredible, just incredible. And what are these? Runners in the floor?" Tristan asked, his voice just above a whisper. "I guess they haul stuff up and down this way."

"Brand mentioned something about shipments to Whitmore, yeah," Drake said. "They mine the blue stuff and ship it elsewhere, probably to some Alliance warehouse or something." He paused, struck with a realization. "Onto the *Titan* . . ."

"What?" Irene asked.

"Nothing, let's move."

The Crystal-X facility was as quiet as it had been the night before. Drake and Irene led Tristan on a similar route, down through curving corridors overlooking the vast meteorite and up onto the steel walkways above the twin research laboratories. Unlike the previous night, the labs were quiet—Dr. Elias and his squad of technicians absent.

"Through that roller door over there," Drake said. "That's where they wheeled the boy in the cage."

"Do you think we can get down there without being spotted?"

"There's no one around . . ." Tristan said.

"Which I don't like," Drake said. "You'd think there'd be some guards or the lab assistants or someone. It is pretty late, I suppose. Maybe last night was just for Whitmore's visit."

No sooner had he spoken than the double doors in the first lab swung open and two technicians entered, a man and a woman, carrying sample vials of the blue mineral and chatting quietly. They placed the samples on the workbenches and began retrieving equipment from the stores.

Irene cursed. "You were saying?"

"Let's see where this walkway leads, then," Drake said. "It curves around up ahead, down to the other side of the facility, where we haven't been yet. Maybe we can get behind that door without going through the lab."

"I know there's a whole load of rooms with beds and bathrooms somewhere around here. I stayed in one for a week."

The path did lead to the rooms Irene remembered. Much like the Rig's cells far above, the rooms were small and sealed with strong automatic doors. Drake peered in through the windows and saw that some of them looked well lived in. Candy-bar wrappers, magazines, and computer tablets littered the floors.

"I think we've found where Grey and his gang come for

'advanced lessons,'" Drake said, keeping his voice a low whisper. "Do you think—"

Shadows flickered over the wall in the next room. Drake motioned for Irene and Tristan to step back to the other side of the corridor. He approached the room slowly, taking care, and glimpsed someone he hadn't seen in a few weeks.

Mohawk sat, rocking back and forth and holding his head in his hands. Drake watched him for close to thirty seconds before Mohawk stopped moving and, quick as a flash, turned around and grinned.

Drake snapped his head back, wondering if he'd been seen. Mohawk made no sound, rang no alarm. After half a minute Drake peeked back through the window and saw him rocking back and forth again.

Drake shook his head and moved on.

The corridor of rooms ended with a set of stairs leading down into a dark and somewhat dank area. Yellow pipes ran across the ceiling, covered in condensation, dripping water every few meters. The pipes disappeared around the corner, out of sight. With no better plan, Drake, Irene, and Tristan followed the pipes.

This part of the facility was poorly lit, with a single bulb stuck to the gray brick wall every five meters or so. Piled alongside the corridor were stacks of crates, empty steel cages, and all manner of tools. Drake saw a screwdriver, a proper one with a handle, and slipped it into his pocket.

The pipes led them to a room that stank of decay, and it wasn't hard to see why. Along the wall were animal cages stacked at least six meters high. Most of them were empty, but a few held the remains of what looked like cats, maybe a few rabbits, and definitely a dog.

"Oh, that's terrible," Irene whispered, covering her nose.

Banks of computer monitors lined the other wall, glowing softly in the dull light. Tristan examined them, found they needed a user name and password, and determined there was nothing he could do without his tools back in Perth.

The yellow pipes led on, deeper down the widening corridor. Apart from the drip-drip-drip of the pipes and the splash of their feet in the puddles on the concrete floor, Drake heard nothing. He couldn't shake the feeling that they were walking down the cool, dark throat of some monstrous beast.

Up ahead, someone laughed.

Drake paused, fear gripping his heart.

"Oh, you've come this far," said a voice from around the corner. A pool of light spread across the floor—a small cone of illumination against the dark. "Come a little further, would you?"

Drake didn't think they'd stumbled across a guard. He held up a finger, keeping Irene and Tristan still and quiet, and stepped around the corner.

The boy in the glass cage stood alone in a row of similar cages. At the back of the room was a set of roller doors that, Drake assumed, led back into the laboratories. They had come full circle, almost.

"I expected you sooner," the boy said. His voice was harsh and, even muffled by the glass cage, like icicles shattering against stone.

"And later. But I suppose it doesn't matter."

"Carl Anderson?" Drake asked.

"Who else?" Anderson said with a smile. His gums were split, and blood stained his teeth. "Who else is with you? I can hear two heartbeats fluttering away in the darkness there. Step up and be counted, my little friends."

Irene emerged from the shadows, her face solemn, and Tristan followed. Anderson turned his attention back to Drake. "They're gonna have trouble stopping you," he said, and the red light in his eyes seemed to bounce as he chuckled. "Oh yes, you're going to send the Alliance a message they can't ignore, William Drake."

"How do you know who I am?"

Anderson spat on the front of his cage, a globule of blood and saliva, and began to draw patterns on the glass. "How do you know who *I* am?"

"I told him, Carl," Tristan said, and stepped forward next to Drake.

"Hey, lil' Mikey Tristan," Anderson said, still running figure eights back and forth on the glass in his blood. "What you doing down here? They didn't give you the magical juice too, did they?"

"No, Carl," Tristan said softly. "I came to get you out—"

"Not the right time for that," Anderson said, and winked at Drake. "Besides, you really don't want to let me out. No, no."

Tristan's voice was a whisper. "Why?"

"Why? Oh, because I'll rip your heart out of your chest with my bare hands."

Tristan paled and took a quick step back.

Drake didn't know what was worse—the threat, which he believed Anderson more than capable of carrying out, or the hopelessly sane tone in which he delivered it.

"But thank you for the thought. I always liked you, Mike. You don't belong in a place like this." Anderson cocked his head and looked as if he were listening to something no one else could hear. "And you'll need that kindness with what's to come." His eyes flared. "And be careful with Red here, Daddy's little girl, this one." Anderson burst out laughing and slammed his forehead against the glass.

Irene gasped and turned away. Drake could see tears in her eyes as she stepped out of the cone of light above the cage.

"How much of that blue stuff did they give you?" Drake asked.

Anderson sniffed and rubbed his eyes, leaving bloody smears on his cheeks. "Too much, you know. About ten teaspoons. They gave Grey the same. He comes down here and taunts me sometimes. Not so much lately. It's getting to him, too . . . he's gonna be like me soon."

Tristan put his hand on the latch of the cage, a determined expression on his face. Anderson grinned and crossed his arms.

"Come on," Drake said. "We can't help him now."

With a sigh, Tristan let go of the lock.

"Stay safe, Mikey," Anderson said. He pressed his bloody hand against the glass and winked. "Don't let the bastards get you down! Nine-five-four, I don't wanna be here anymore!"

His laughter echoed down the corridor as they moved on, away from the cages of dead and insane things. A new set of metal stairs soon led up to the network of walkways that crisscrossed the facility. Drake and the others headed up and to the left, following the yellow pipes overhead.

"I can smell the ocean," he said after a few minutes. The

walkway led to a concrete ramp with runners built into the floor for transporting something, most likely crates of the Crystal-X. Moving silently but quickly, Drake, Irene, and Tristan ran down the ramp and into an open, brightly lit area.

The space was as large as a warehouse, and piled high with Alliance-crested crates, shipping containers, and drilling equipment. As opposed to the equipment up on the Rig, the drill bits and machinery looked shiny and new—as if they were ready to be used. Drake tried to lift the bolts on a few of the crates to have a look at what was inside, perhaps something useful, but they were locked tight. Across the warehouse was a row of three pools, and floating in each pool was a triangle-shaped vessel.

Drake headed over that way, a surge of excitement rising in his chest.

The pools were of cold, dark seawater, which meant they were deep and, given the craft floating in the water, probably led out into the ocean. The vessels were small, about the size of the old Mini Coopers—Drake had grown up wanting one of those—with tinted windshields and single seats visible amid a myriad of controls and display screens. Attached to the nose of each craft were circular drilling bits and metal claws.

"This is how they mine the rock," Tristan said.

"Do you think . . . " Drake shook his head, having visions of stealing one of these sleek, matte-black mining submarines and escaping the metal prison once and for all.

"No," said Tristan. "I don't even know how to get inside the bloody things."

"Look over there," Irene said, pointing to the left at the

far side of the warehouse. "Through that door there's another walkway. Want to keep looking?"

Drake nodded.

The narrow walkway led out of the mining warehouse and into another space, smaller this time, with large windows framing the reef of glowing meteorite. Pale blue light flooded the area, rippling across the floor in gentle waves. The walkway, suspended two meters above the floor, was built over a tank of water that descended into the rock ridge, much like the pools that held the mini-subs back in the mining warehouse.

Dark shadows swam just below the surface of that blue water, and Irene grasped Drake's arm and breathed in sharply as they passed over the tank on the walkway. Something was alive and swimming down there. "What are they?" she whispered.

A sharp gray fin, riddled with scars, pierced the surface of the water, as silent as the night, and dipped back under.

"Sharks," Tristan whispered. "That was a shark."

"Let's get off this walkway," Drake said. A set of stairs curved around and down and brought them alongside the edge of the tank. The same shadows swam along the glass, back and forth. At least two of the creatures knew they were there, and were interested.

More crates were scattered about this room, separated from the mining warehouse by the walkway and twin sets of massive roller doors. These crates weren't as secure as the ones in the previous room, and Drake began unlatching the locks and peering inside, looking for anything that might be of use. A weapon of some sort, perhaps, or a pair of angel wings and a map back to the mainland. The first box was empty.

"Have a look through those crates," Drake told Irene and Tristan, unlatching the next one. "See if there's anything that we can . . ."

His voice trailed away as he got a look at the contents of the second crate. Something, he wasn't sure what, began screaming in the back of his head. A low, desperate wail that made him shiver and want to cry all at once.

Drake did neither.

Dr. Lambros was in the second crate. Vaguely, he heard Irene gasp and Tristan stifle a small cry.

A tiny trickle of blood that ran down from her nose and over her lips had dried on her chin. Little spots had fallen onto the collar of her white blouse. If not for the blood and the color of her skin, Drake could have pretended she was sleeping.

He was looking at a corpse.

Dr. Acacia Lambros was dead. Vicious bruising covered her neck like a purple scarf.

Drake, Irene, and Tristan stood silent for a long moment, all thinking the same thing. They were looking at murder.

For the second time inside twenty-four hours, Drake's entire outlook on the world had changed. He knew the people running the Rig were mean, even cruel, but this was something else. Evil, his mind whispered, and for lack of a better word, Drake agreed. What was happening here was evil.

And had to be stopped.

Experiments on inmates. Murdering people to keep them

quiet. Did the Alliance—did Lucien Whitmore know what was happening here? Not the gritty details, not all of them, but he knows, Drake thought. Of course he does.

"I liked her." Drake took a deep breath and wished he hadn't. The smell from the crate was none too fresh. "God, how can they do this?"

Drake recalled lying in his bunk, unable to sleep and thinking about the difference between justice and vengeance. Looking at poor Dr. Lambros, her life snuffed out long before her time, he thought again on where the line was drawn. Justice . . . or vengeance?

Right then, he felt like a touch of both.

With nothing else to do, he resealed the crate and sighed. They could do nothing to help Acacia Lambros now. But one day . . . Drake swore. He would see whoever did this punished. Although he had no proof, his mind kept picturing Brand, his hands around her neck as he choked the life out of her. Had he done it down here or up in her office?

That broken picture frame from the wall behind her desk . . .

"Are you okay?" Irene asked gently.

Drake nodded. "Well, at least we know what we're up against now. Really up against. Once and for all, the kind of people we're dealing with."

"Let's go," Tristan said. "I don't want to look in the rest of these crates, and there's nothing more we can do down here."

Drake agreed. He'd been hoping for something, something to help him escape, but short of absorbing a mineral that would turn him insane or trying to pilot a submersible drilling craft, he'd come up empty.

They walked back around the tank and climbed up the stairs onto the steel walkway, feeling defeated.

"What the—" a gruff voice snapped.

Drake, Irene, and Tristan froze—like a trio of deer caught in headlights.

Standing on the walkway over the tank was a familiar face. Officer Hall, armed and in full body armor, stared at them in shock. Hall made a sound somewhere between a startled cry and a grunt of surprise and reached for his radio.

"Was it you?" Drake spat, and ran at Hall as the guard swung his rifle up to fire. "Did you kill her?"

Drake tackled Hall, and they wrestled on the walkway over the shark tank. The guard hit the railing, his rifle fell from his hands, and the momentum of Drake's tackle carried them both up and over the railing.

Trading blows, they fell into the tank, Hall gripping Drake's hair and Drake with a hand around the guard's neck. Drake struck the water and felt a thousand tiny needles pierce his lungs. He let go of Hall and gasped, shock ripping through his every nerve. The water was ice-cold.

Something large and heavy brushed past his leg.

Drake licked the salt water from his lips. Hard shots of fear slid down his throat as something else slammed into his leg. Hall was spluttering in the water away to his left, under the walkway. The guard's eyes were wide, bulging out of his head. A fin broke the surface of the tank between Drake and Hall, and the two humans, far out of their depth, locked eyes for a terrible moment.

Hall turned and swam for the tank's edge as another fin

surfaced along with about two meters of dark gray skin. A single black eye—speckled with red stars, like a lump of burning coal—stared at Drake, and a jaw of razor-sharp teeth opened wide.

He turned and swam, knowing he couldn't make the edge before—

A pair of hands seized Drake by his sodden collar. He looked up and saw Tristan dangling almost upside down, bent at the waist over the walkway's edge, with Irene clutching his legs. Together they hauled Drake up and out of the water and back under the railing just as a red-eyed shark cut through the space between him and Hall.

The guard didn't even have time to scream before he was pulled under the frothing water.

Dripping wet, shivering, and breathing hard, Drake chanced a look back over the railing and saw nothing but dark, churning water slowly turning crimson. He looked away, sick to his stomach. That could've been me . . . he thought.

"The shark got him," Tristan breathed. "Oh God, he's dead. The shark, the shark, the shark—"

Irene clapped her hand over his mouth and whispered fiercely, "Shut up! All that made a hell of a lot of noise. We have to move and get out of here. Someone will be coming."

Drake agreed, and Tristan, as pale as a ghost, could do nothing but follow. Before he left the walkway over the tank, Drake picked up Hall's fallen rifle and slung the weapon's strap over his shoulder. He didn't know much about using the damn thing, but he thought point and shoot would work just fine if they encountered anyone else.

Is it loaded with knockout darts or actual bullets? he wondered.

For a second, he didn't care. The monsters down here were not the sharks or the boy locked away in a cage. No, the monsters down here had killed Dr. Lambros, had driven the animals and Carl Anderson insane. How many other bodies had they disposed of, deep below the ocean, never to be seen again?

But he did care, really. Drake knew he was not a killer. If he'd had the chance, he would've tried to pull Hall from the shark tank.

"I think we've seen enough tonight," Irene said. "We should try to get back up to the Rig."

"They're going to notice he's missing," Drake said, speaking almost to himself as they ran past crates, along walkways, heading down under the labs again. "Not right away, but they'll notice Hall's missing. Then what?"

He had to get off the Rig.

17

ESCAPE

Once again, Drake and Irene made it back up and out of the Crystal-X facility without being discovered. Tristan followed almost numbly in their wake, keeping his thoughts to himself. His eyes were wide and terrified as they sat in the old control room on the eastern platform, bathed in light from the flashlight.

Drake spun slowly on his swivel chair, Hall's rifle resting on his lap. He'd been fiddling with it for the last five minutes and had figured out how to eject the magazine—a clip of twelve stunning darts. *Nonlethal*, he remembered Brand saying. More's the pity.

"So what are we going to do?" Irene asked.

Drake slammed the magazine back into the rifle. He played with the safety tab on the side of the weapon and then put it down on the desk of old monitors, out of his hands, in case he accidentally shot himself or his allies.

Tristan sighed and wrapped his arms around himself. "I can't spend the next five years here, not now. I . . . I won't be able to look any of them in the eye. They'll know I know."

Drake had stripped down to his boxer shorts. His jumpsuit was still soaked through from the dip in the shark tank. He tried hard to suppress his shivering, but he was freezing. The lens of the flashlight was warm, and he kept pressing his fingers against the plastic.

"Short of swimming, I have no idea how we could escape the Rig," Irene said, casting a quick glance at Drake. "You're supposed to be good at this, Will. What have you got?"

"A canoe made of soap and shenanigans . . ." he muttered, staring into the bright light of the flashlight. He thought of Dr. Lambros alone in the dark down below, with nothing but bloodthirsty sharks for company. Someone, somewhere would be missing her . . . A husband? A child?

"Which means nothing," Tristan said, sighing into his hands. "He's got nothing, Irene."

"Well"—Irene bit her lip—"what if we could get word out about what they're doing here? We need a phone or access to a computer in the control tower or . . ." She trailed away, shaking her head.

"Who would believe it? Who would we tell? It's all Alliance-owned out there. They control the media. They control everything, even governments." Tristan laughed bitterly. "And what would we say?"

"I'm just thinking aloud here," Irene snapped. "We can't just sit—"

"Face it, Irene," Tristan replied, color rising in his cheeks. "We're stuck here, and we just better hope we can make it through the rest of our sentences without—"

"This place will get us killed!"

"Keep your voice down!"

"Don't tell me what to do, you little—"

Drake stood up and stretched his limbs, which had become stiff from the cold. Irene and Tristan turned to look at him, and he smiled sadly. "Have I ever told you," he said, "what I did to get sent to prison in the first place?"

Neither of his companions said anything. They looked at each other, shrugged, and shook their heads.

"Well, I don't like talking about it . . . bit of a long story." Drake shivered. "But, given that you're so sure the Alliance can't be beaten, Tristan, I might as well share my long story."

"Will, I—"

"Shut up and listen. I'm only going to say this once." Drake sat back down and crossed his arms over his bare chest. He could feel his heart beating, warm and true, against the cold. Taking a deep breath, he began. "You remember a few years ago, that 'miracle pill' that could practically cure most types of leukemia?"

Tristan and Irene shared another glance. The looks on their faces suggested that they were wondering if he had gone mad, and wondering what pills had to do with the price of anything.

Still, Tristan nodded and clicked his fingers. "Yeah. Something . . . Det . . . Detrol . . . "

Drake nodded. "Close, mate. Detrolazyne-V."

"What about it?" Irene asked.

"My mother is sick. Very sick." Drake shrugged, as if to say *you can't change the weather*. "About two years ago, she was dying. It's just been me and her since I was little, and there was no way we could afford that pill. You know the National Health Service in Britain collapsed eight years back, in 2018, and became privatized. I was only seven when it happened, didn't understand what that meant at the time, but I'll give you three guesses who bought it."

"Alliance Systems, of course," Tristan said, and pushed his glasses up the bridge of his nose.

"Bastards," Irene muttered.

"Right," Drake said. "Since then, health care in the UK, much like the prisons, I guess, has been a numbers game. My mum and I just didn't add up for the Alliance. She was diagnosed on the NHS, and once the Alliance took over, she couldn't get insurance—preexisting conditions aren't covered, you know. Not unless you have money, and we never did. Anyway, the doctors couldn't make her better. Just comfortable. Her sickness had advanced so far that she had maybe, at best, three months."

Irene pulled Drake's hand from his crossed arms and gave it a squeeze. "And with the medicine? The . . . Detrolazyne?" she asked.

"Years." Drake stressed the word. "In some cases, with bone-marrow transplants, even complete remission."

Tristan shared a glance with Irene. "So you stole it."

"So I stole it, yes, and burned down four Alliance warehouses getting away. Heh, my first escape. So you see, mate, the Alliance can be beat. If you're willing to take a few risks." Drake sniffed. "At least that's an easy way of looking at it. I didn't just torch a few buildings. I also put a policeman in the hospital. They caught up with me near Trafalgar Square on my way home, and I punched one of them. It sometimes only takes one punch . . . He hit his head on the curb. Lucky he didn't die. I . . . I really wish that hadn't happened."

"You were just trying to help your mum," Tristan said. "I mean, well . . ."

"How many wrongs make a right, mate?"

Irene scoffed. "The Alliance wrongs good people every day, like your mother. Or . . . or turns good people into bad people." She wasn't talking about Drake, and he knew it.

"The Alliance is scum," Drake spat, slamming his fist into his palm. "You know what I saw in that warehouse? Shelves full of Detrolazyne! Miles and miles of these little white boxes that could save my mother's life. Hell, I only needed one box."

"Is she . . . did she get better?" Irene asked.

"She was too sick to see me sentenced in London and sent to Trennimax a few weeks later. But the night I stole the drugs, she was bedridden at home, hooked up to all these medicine bags and painkillers, so I gave her the pills and moved her next door. I don't know if she even knew what was happening. Nanna Vera lived there, next door. She's not my real grandmother, but she looked after me growing up, when Mum was at work. She hid her when the police came knocking for me later that night. I went rather quietly, given the mess I'd caused."

"But your mum, Will," Tristan said. "What happened?"

Drake took a deep breath and exhaled slowly. "She got better. The pills did the trick."

"Fantastic!" Irene hugged him hard, sending them both spinning on the swivel chair.

"Yes, I bought her time." Drake gently pulled Irene's arms away and smiled sadly. "I was sentenced to two years in Trennimax. Five months into that, she sent me a letter."

Irene slumped. "Oh no . . ."

"Yeah, the cancer was back." Drake sighed. "One course, one box of the pills wasn't enough to crush it completely. She told me she had a year, maybe eighteen months, if she was lucky. That was fourteen months ago. I haven't heard from her since. If she sent me letters, I haven't been getting them."

"You think the Alliance has been destroying them?" Tristan asked.

"Maybe. Who knows for sure? No outside contact allowed on the Rig, you know that. I tried calling once while I was on the run from Cedarwood, but no one answered. Perhaps my mum died . . . but I don't think so. I think the Alliance is cruel enough to tell me if she died. And cruel enough to withhold any letters she sent me if she's still alive. I've gotta look at it that way, I guess."

Tristan nodded. "Where the Alliance is concerned, that's probably the best way to look at it."

"That's why you've been escaping," Irene said. Maybe it was just a trick of the light, but her eyes looked shiny. "You're trying to get back to London, to your mother, and what? Steal more pills?"

"Got it in one, Miss Finlay." Drake gazed through the porthole of their hideaway, out at the clear night sky and the bright stars. The storm clouds had fled, cascading now over the horizon. "And I've got four months, maybe, to do just that, or it won't matter anymore. I . . ."

Drake's voice caught, and he took a moment not to let it show. The ocean was a dark, unfathomable blanket, as much a cage as the Rig itself. How I hate it, he thought. If—no, when—he made it off this platform, he would happily never see such endless water again.

He cleared his throat and turned to face Irene and Tristan.

"I don't want my mother to die alone and afraid," he said. "The Alliance has taken a lot from me, from the whole world, but it does not get to have that!"

18

BLINK

Three days after Drake had uncovered the Rig's secrets, three days since he'd found Dr. Lambros's body and plunged into a tank of mutated sharks, he was back on the southern platform under the late-afternoon sun, dismantling the tents and tables that had served as a dining hall for Lucien Whitmore and his henchmen.

Henchmen was the right word . . . They had all expressed wonder and amazement at what the Crystal-X mineral could do deep below the ocean's surface, but Drake had not seen one of them express remorse or even a glimpse of sadness at what had become of poor Carl Anderson. Some had shown fear and, in Whitmore's case, a horrific curiosity, but none of them had cared.

Why would they? he thought. They're the Alliance. They murder and steal. In a prison full of the worst juvenile offenders in the world, not even the jailers were innocent. Drake felt cold anger and bitter frustration.

The *Titan* was back again, offloading supplies onto the Rig via the tall yellow crane on its stern. The mighty ship buzzed with activity along the deck. Dozens of men in hardhats and orange overalls were at work around the cargo hold. The hold was open, revealing the inside of the ship. Drake had a sneaking suspicion that he knew just what was being loaded onto the ship that afternoon.

"Drake, eyes on the tent!"

Tommy directed Drake and the crew as they disassembled the makeshift dining area. As the sun sank toward the west and an orange deep enough to be called red bled across a sky that was scattered with thin gray stratus clouds, they folded up the tarp of the pavilion and unscrewed the bolts in the scaffold that had held it all together.

"Good for the game this Saturday?" Mario asked as they loaded the tarp onto a small hand-operated Transpallet forklift. "We'll beat them this week, for sure."

Drake stared at Mario for a moment before he realized what the kid was talking about. His head was full of so many things that he'd forgotten about rigball. It was the fifth game of the season this Saturday, and as of last Saturday, it had become quite impossible for Tommy's team to win the league, given that they'd lost every game in the last month.

And now I know why, Drake thought. Grey's been taking the Crystal-X. His whole gang may have been in on it, which, as far as Drake could tell, meant that they may have been holding back in the rigball games. Images from the video display Dr. Elias had shown Whitmore danced through his head. Images of impossible things.

"Blimey, Mario, what makes you so damned optimistic all the time?"

Mario's smile faded. "You've had a face like a smacked arse all week, Drake. What's your problem?"

"Nothing," Drake said. Everything, he thought. "This place just gets me down sometimes, yeah."

"Well suck it up, *mi amigo*, and save it for the game on Saturday."

Drake nodded. He and Tristan hadn't ventured out through the vents these last few nights to meet with Irene. For one, after crawling back to the washroom after the shark attack adventure, Drake had been awake and on his feet for almost two straight days. He needed a good night's rest if he was going to be any use at all. For another, he didn't want to get too attached to either Tristan or Irene. When the time came to escape, he'd be going alone. As he had done since the fire at Cedarwood.

Across the platform, along a bridge the inmates never used that connected the southern platform to the eastern platform, Drake saw his suspicions about the *Titan*'s open cargo hold confirmed. Two trolleys, stacked high with the same Alliance-marked crates he'd seen down in Dr. Elias's mad scientist laboratory, were being wheeled under armed guard toward the supply crane.

Brand stood in front of the trolleys directing the movement of the electric-blue Crystal-X. The amount of mineral in the crates must have been significant because each trolley was being pushed by two masked guards. Probably just the first load of many tonight, Drake thought.

Nothing had been said of Hall's disappearance, but the guards had been on edge the last few days, more heavy-handed than usual, cracking down on even the smallest of broken rules.

As Drake lifted folding chairs off the forklift and stacked them against the wall of Processing, he watched the procession of crates move past him and the crew. The first trolley groaned under the weight, and he noticed with a start that the seal on the rear crate was broken. Drips of water seeped through the crack, pooling on the trolley and leaking over onto the platform.

"What are you lot looking at?" Brand snapped. "Get back to work!"

"Eh, Officer Brand—" Drake began, wheeling the forklift back from the storage shed. He'd seen what the mineral did when exposed to the air. If one of the crates was leaking . . . "That crate—"

"Drake, by God, boy, keep your eyes on your own damn—"

Just as the guards pushing the crates circled the Seahawk, the rear wheel on the front trolley snapped and gave way. The trolley wobbled, and the broken wheel dug into the concrete, which prevented it from going over onto its side completely. The load of crates, fastened and secured, shifted but didn't fall.

However the sporadic drips from the bottom crate became a steady trickle—and Brand noticed.

"Christ!" he roared, and turned on his heel to run. "Move away, all of you! It's going to blow!"

As the guards scattered, Drake, acting purely on instinct, turned the forklift around and dashed across the platform, running past the Seahawk and toward the broken trolley.

What are you doing? his mind screamed at him.

"Drake!" Brand growled. "You stupid son of a—"

Drake wheeled the forklift around and got one of the prongs under the broken trolley. Sweat ran down his back, and his stomach was doing somersaults. He'd seen what a small amount of the mineral, enough to fill just the head of a pin, did when exposed to the air. Given that Brand had told Whitmore that this shipment would be hundreds of kilograms of Crystal-X, Drake couldn't even imagine how large the explosion would be.

Enough to destroy the Rig, surely.

Can't outrun the blast, Brand, he thought.

At any other time, Drake would have almost welcomed the explosion. Now more than ever he hated this place and the terrible secrets rotting at its core. The prison was a festering sore, a diseased limb, and the only thing left for it was amputation. But not now—not while he and hundreds of others stood at the epicenter of what was about to be a monumental explosion.

He pumped the large handle as fast as he dared, raising the dual prongs of the forklift and the trolley into the air. The trickle of water slowed to a drip again as the trolley fell level on the forklift's prongs, but Drake was taking no chances. If the crate was leaking at all, that meant the mineral could be exposed to the air at any second.

Drake pushed the forklift as hard as he could, and the trolley began to move. His arms strained against the weight, and his shoes almost slipped along the slick concrete of the platform. He grunted from the exertion, but finally, the wheels began to turn. Once he got it moving, the forklift picked up speed, even with the heavy load.

Soon he was almost jogging, muscles screaming and teeth bared in a snarl of pure, raw effort.

As precious water continued to leak from the mineral crate, Drake pushed the forklift toward the edge of the platform, under the swinging crane from the *Titan*, and past the boxes of stores that had just been offloaded. About two meters from the precipice Drake let the forklift go and fell to his knees, gasping from the strain. The speed he'd managed to reach kept the forklift rolling right over the edge of the platform and out into the open air, plummeting toward the dark, choppy waters below.

The crates fell.

Crawling on his hands and knees, Drake pulled himself to the edge and gazed over—just as the mineral exploded. A blinding flash of light lit up the Rig as if it were midday, and a torrent of roaring flame burst up and over the edge of the southern platform. A wave of tremendous heat blew Drake back, sending him rolling across the platform like a rag doll. He struck the rear wheel of the Seahawk and came to an abrupt stop.

The fountain of bright flame receded as the crates sank, but for a brief moment it licked at the entire frame of the southern platform. Although he couldn't see it, Drake imagined an orb of almost unquenchable white-hot fire sinking below the waves, lighting up the dark depths and perhaps burning for hours.

Fire that burns underwater . . . Drake actually laughed—the first time in days. He looked himself over and patted his arms and legs, making sure he was still in one piece. His skin felt a touch burned, as if he'd been out in the sun too long, but other than that—

Brand pulled him up by his collar. The look on his face was blind fury.

"Marcus, you let him go!" A shadow fell over Drake and Brand under the blades of the Seahawk. "Why did you do that, Mr. Drake?" Warden Storm asked. He peered at Drake from under the brim of his Stetson, his expression just short of thunderous.

Drake licked his lips and swallowed. "Brand . . . Officer Brand . . . he said it was going to explode. I didn't want to explode with it, sir."

"Come with me," Storm said.

Brand grabbed him by the scruff of his collar again and dragged him through Processing, into Control, and up the stairs to the warden's office, following in the large man's wake. His tracker beeped to let him know he was out of bounds. Drake felt his eyebrows as they rose up through the tower, seeing if they were still there. He could smell burning feathers. That gout of flame had singed the hair off his arms.

"Take a seat, Mr. Drake," Storm said. "That will be all, Officer Brand."

"Sir? He—"

"Leave us, Marcus."

Brand hesitated by the door. The warden stared at him over a pair of dark spectacles for a long moment. The door clicked shut behind him.

Drake and Warden Storm had a staring contest of their own after that. Sensing a great amount of danger in that stare,

Drake tried not to fidget. He couldn't tell just how much trouble he was in. Storm's face was a mask of barely contained fury.

But fury at me? At Brand? Or because I sent his precious mineral back to the bottom of the sea?

Eventually Storm looked away and reached beneath his desk. Drake heard a door open down there and the clink of glass bottles. Storm emerged from the side of his desk and offered Drake a glistening bottle of Coca-Cola.

After four months at sea, with nothing but desalinated water and tepid apple juice, the sight of the sugary drink was, well, like water to a man dying of thirst.

"Take it."

Drake almost reached out for the soda. "No, thank you."

Storm chuckled, a sound that made Drake think of skulls rattling on the ocean floor. "Today, Mr. Drake, you have earned this treat. I doubt any of your fellow inmates, or even most of my guards, realize what you just did. You saved the Rig and the lives of everyone on-site."

Drake shrugged and, after a moment, accepted the Coke. He twisted off the cap and took a delicious sip. The fizzy bubbles rushed down his throat. First sip was always the best.

"Why did that crate explode?" he asked, feigning ignorance.

"Ah, well, it was carrying canisters of natural gas, I'm afraid." The warden sighed. "For cooking, you know."

Liar. Drake nodded along, as if that made sense, and took another sip of soda. Had this man tried to feed poor Dr. Lambros similar false tales?

"If you hadn't done what you did, we would not be having this conversation right now."

The warden turned to his computer and tapped away at the keyboard. He hummed to himself and loosened his necktie.

"I was warned about you, William," he said. "A special case. You were incarcerated in three facilities in the last eighteen months, and in each instance you managed to embarrass the Alliance. You were in Trennimax, in France. At the time the world's foremost secure juvenile facility. The Rig, as you know, holds that honor now. It took you just six weeks to escape through what was supposed to be a tunnel sealed during the Second World War. You unsealed it. One of the guards foolishly alerted you to its existence." Storm laughed. "You may already know that my staff is much less forthcoming."

Drake said nothing. He placed his half-finished bottle of soda on the edge of the warden's desk.

"Cedarwood was next, and you rigged a cart with wheels and used the train line down the mountain. Then Harronway, and no one knows how you did that. Care to share now?"

"Front door. Unlocked."

Storm sighed. "No it wasn't. But security is what it is, I guess. We can have the fanciest padlocks, the most up-to-date trackers, like the one you're wearing there. We can surround you with hundreds of miles of cold, dark ocean, but someone like you, rightly, sees all that as just tools of the system. And you don't play the system itself, William. No, no. You play its owner. You play the man."

Storm gave Drake a predatory smile, as if he were about to sink his teeth into Drake's neck.

"Every escape, every single one, has been successful for one key reason. You read people, don't you? You don't beat the locks, or the trackers, or the ocean. I imagine you've already found a way around some of my locks and maybe even my trackers, haven't you? No, don't tell me, it does not matter. Because you will never find a way through my people. Or, ultimately, through me. I know you, William Drake, I know you better than you know yourself. Would you like some advice? Do your time. Four years, seven months, and twenty-five days from now you will leave the Rig a free man, into a world vastly changed for the better by the Alliance. You will have learned a trade, a means to survive back in Britain as an honest, productive member of society. See this, my beautiful Rig, not as another prison sentence, but as an opportunity."

Drake ran a hand through his hair and frowned. He'd heard that line before, somewhere. Oh yes . . . from Dr. Lambros.

"Well, son? What have you got to say?" Storm chortled, his massive belly heaving up and down like the endless swell of the sea. "Perhaps tell me what you read on my face just now."

Drake licked his lips. "You . . . you believe that escape is impossible."

"Few things in this world are impossible, but so long as I'm captain of this ship, then yes, escape from the Rig is one of the few. Still planning on swimming back to the mainland?"

"No," Drake said, and suppressed a shudder. "I believe you about the sharks."

"Good boy. Don't waste the opportunity the Alliance has given you here."

Drake let his shoulders slump, just a little. Humble. Defeated. "Thanks for the soda."

Storm narrowed his eyes and glared at Drake, as if he were trying to read his mind. "Very well. I'll have Brand allow you the rest of the afternoon as free movement, give you a chance to rest and clean up before dinner."

Drake heard the note of dismissal in the warden's voice. He stood and turned to leave.

"Mr. Drake, thank you again for what you did today."

"You're welcome, Warden Storm," he replied without turning around. He worried that the warden would see the smile he was trying to hide.

You're welcome, you murdering bastard, Drake thought. Storm may not have done the deed himself, but he was as guilty as whoever had. As Drake left the office, he felt a shiver of honest excitement and suppressed a small chuckle. After a four-month staring contest, the Alliance had just blinked. The Rig had shown its hand and been found bluffing. *Play the man*, indeed . . .

The murky beginnings of an escape plan began to form in Drake's head.

19

CALM BEFORE THE STORM

I'll need the rifle . . . that screwdriver . . . a flashlight, most likely.

For a brief moment in Storm's office, Drake had seen all the loose threads in his mind come together in an intricate, near-perfect pattern of escape. He saw all that he had learned about the Rig over the last four months, from the *Titan* to the rotation of the guards, as a spiderweb of points that could, if he was strong and held true—if he stood against the Alliance once more—lead to freedom.

But it'll be life or death, he thought, sitting in his bunk and staring at the ceiling that night after the explosion on the southern platform and his fizzy drink in Storm's office. More than ever . . . but I'll be on my own.

Tristan snored quietly below.

As Drake played with the rough outline of the escape plan in his head, his brow settled into a frown. The more he thought about it, the more he realized that the chances of getting away unnoticed were less than zero. It was a damned near certainty.

But then the spiderweb has threads for that, too, doesn't it? Drake thought about the rifle again, about the *Titan* and her fleet of speedboats, and about Warden Storm and the Seahawk. His frown became a satisfied smile.

"Play the man," he muttered, and rolled over to sleep.

Rigball on Saturday was another crushing defeat at the hands of Grey and his gang of mineral-enhanced goons. At least Drake now knew why he couldn't knock the players down, and how they moved so fast. Working with Mario, he almost managed to score, but ended up with his nose scraped across the concrete for his trouble and Grey's gigantic knee pressed between his shoulder blades.

For a day or two after that, if he looked down, he could see a small scab on the end of his nose. It was tender to the touch.

Drake was enjoying a minor scrap of celebrity among the inmate population. Tommy and the boys had spread the story of how he had saved the Rig from a gas explosion, and even the guards seemed to give him a bit more leeway, given that he was in Warden Storm's good graces. The only guard who didn't change, of course, was Brand. If anything, Drake's quick thinking on the southern platform had soured the former Crystal Force soldier even further against him.

"That one wouldn't pee on you if you were on fire," Tristan had remarked, scooping cold green beans onto his plate in the cafeteria on Sunday at lunchtime.

"Think he'd be thankful I saved his life," Drake muttered, wishing he hadn't. He was all but certain that Marcus Brand had killed Dr. Lambros.

Knowing what he knew now, Drake committed as many hours of the day as he could to plotting his escape. It came down to two options, really. The *Titan* or the Seahawk. The ship or the chopper. He had a few rough ideas on how to make it work, but they were all risky—far riskier than any of his previous escapes. Indeed, compared with what he had in mind, his previous escapes were like finding the back door unlocked and sneaking out when no one was looking.

Drake began exploring the Rig at night, mostly on his own, but every other night Tristan and Irene, or one of the two, would tag along with him. He couldn't think of a reasonable excuse not to bring them along, and if he was being honest, he was beginning to enjoy their company.

Irene was funny and kind. More important, she had been exploring the Rig at night months before Drake had gotten his tracker off. He still didn't know why she was sentenced to the Rig, but that didn't matter as much as her knowledge of the vents and platforms. Tristan was the same kind of smart and useful. He had a keen sense of direction and could navigate the vents and the warren of pipes and tubes on the eastern platform as if he were reading from a map.

They spent a lot of time in the old control room, talking by flashlight and even playing small games. Irene swiped a pack of cards from the girls' common room and taught them how to play poker. Drake was a natural, but Tristan had a terrible poker face. He couldn't help but smile when a good hand came his way.

For the first two weeks after uncovering what lay beneath the Rig, every time they met, they spoke of escape, of course. But neither Tristan nor Irene had anything much to contribute, and Drake didn't share the rough outline of his plan with them, his glimpse of a pattern he could exploit. He didn't yet know if it was workable at all, and some of the aspects relied far too much on dumb luck falling his way.

No, when the time came, he would be escaping on his own—that much was certain—but he couldn't very well tell that to Irene or Tristan.

Still, almost against his will, he found himself looking forward to the time they spent together, particularly in the old control room hideaway, playing games and talking nonsense. He could almost pretend he wasn't in the bowels of a murderous prison built on a meteorite that, as Dr. Elias had said, was highly volatile and somewhat alive.

As March began to close in on April and Drake began to close in on five months aboard the Rig, he found himself thinking that there was only so much exploration of the platforms he and his companions could do. He knew there was no magical vent stretching back to the mainland—although, given what was under the Rig, he wouldn't be too surprised if he did find one.

He guessed that Irene and Tristan were feeling the same unvoiced frustration as they began to spend more time at night simply hanging out, broaching the topic of escape only occasionally, in the control room hideaway. Having managed to scavenge a few more flashlights and a handful of pillows, the hideaway looked a touch more homely—if you could ignore the semiautomatic rifle leaning against the far wall. Tristan had used some of his stock of credits to purchase a whole bunch of treats from the vending machines, and they were currently using M&Ms as betting chips in games of blackjack.

"Twenty-one. Blackjack!" Drake said, and collected a dozen chocolate pieces. He was the dealer, Irene and Tristan his players, and he was cleaning up.

"Well, I'm broke," Irene said glumly. "Lend me a few chips, Michael?"

Tristan shook his head. "Sorry, ma'am. I'm just not that kind."

Irene swiped a few of his M&Ms and ate them before he could protest.

"I think this game's about done anyway," Drake said. The night was still young, having barely crept past midnight. "What do you want to do now?"

The thrill of sneaking out without trackers was wearing a bit thin, Drake thought, as it became clearer that the real prison was the hundreds of miles of cold ocean trapping them on the Rig. But one night soon, I'll have my chance . . .

"Let's talk," Irene said. She folded her legs up under her and rested her hands in her lap. "We know what Drake's going to do when he gets out of here, back home in London, but what about you, Mike? Going to run all the way back to Australia?"

Tristan shrugged. "I've thought about it, but I honestly don't know. I mean, we don't really talk about it much, but we'd be living a life on the run, wouldn't we? Could we ever go home?"

Irene swatted his knee. "Oh, stop that. Let's pretend for a minute you could go anywhere, flying first class. Where would you go?"

"Nearest Burger King," Tristan said without hesitation. "Triple cheeseburger, thank you very much."

"I think I'd go with you," Irene said, and rolled her eyes.

"What's your grand plan, then?" Tristan asked her.

"Moraine Lake in Alberta. It's in Banff National Park, up in the mountains. The water is so, so blue, and surrounded by these huge trees and snowy peaks. I want to swim in that lake."

"You've been there before?" Drake asked.

Irene shook her head. "No, never. I grew up in the next province over, in British Columbia near Vancouver. But I've seen pictures." She glanced at Tristan. "We could get cheeseburgers on the way, I guess."

"It's a date," he said, then considered what he'd just said, and blushed.

Irene swatted his knee again and smiled.

"I think I'd just go back to school," Drake said, surprising even himself. "Heh, how about that? I think I'd just want to go back to a normal life, like before any of this happened."

"Boy, I can understand that," Tristan muttered. "If I ever do get home, I'd probably work outside, somewhere out in the sun, with trees, seeing as how I'm not allowed to use computers. Somewhere in the country, down south from Perth maybe, where I don't have to see, hear, or smell the ocean. Lot of vineyards down that way. I could get a job picking grapes or something."

"I always wanted to be a blackberry farmer, growing up," Drake said.

Irene snorted. "Oh bless, that's so cute. Why blackberries?"

"Why not?" Drake chuckled and shook his head. "When I was younger, before my mum got too sick to really travel, we used to go out into the country and pick blackberries. They grow wild all over the UK, you know? She'd make these fantastic pies with about a million kilos of sugar in the crust, stuffed with blackberries. And the jam, oh sweet gravy, the jam."

"That does sound nice." Tristan cleaned his glasses on his sleeve. "But you'd probably get sick of blackberries after a while."

"I'm not sure I understood what you just said."

Tristan chuckled. "So I'm working in a vineyard, Will's farming blackberries—although I'm not sure that's a thing, given that they grow everywhere—what about you, Irene? After you've swum in that lake, what then?"

Irene sighed. "Find a handsome man with a yacht and loads of cash and sail through the Mediterranean."

"Oh, sure." Tristan laughed. "That sounds great."

"What's wrong with that?" she said.

Tristan waved her protests away. "Knowing you, you'd be bored inside the first hour. Sailing on yachts and eating fancy food, that's not you, Miss Finlay."

For a moment Drake thought Irene would snap at him. Her face flickered through a range of emotions and seemed to settle on mildly confused. She stared at Tristan as if seeing him anew. The tiny smile on her face looked like a secret waiting to be shared.

The conversation drifted across midnight and into the early hours of the next day. Drake felt that the events of the last few weeks had forged a useful sort of friendship between the three of them. Oh, so you're thinking of them as friends now? he said to himself. They knew each other better in two short weeks than most people in the outside world knew each other after years. A small, nagging worry in the back of

Drake's head made him wonder what would happen to these two if—when—he escaped on his own.

"What about first kisses?" Irene asked, and giggled. "Tell me yours, Will."

"Oh, blimey. Mary. My first was Mary Mallory behind the bike shed at school," Drake said, thinking back. "We were thirteen. She was pretty." He chuckled. "I wonder if she still goes there. I've no idea what goes on at home anymore. How about you?"

"Brian Salmon," Irene said, and made little kissing sounds with her lips. "We were at Stanley Park on a school trip in downtown Vancouver. He picked me a flower."

"Did she say Salmon?" Drake asked, nudging Tristan. "She said Salmon, right?"

"Oh shut it. He was cute, and"—she almost blushed—"he could grow a mustache."

Drake laughed until his sides hurt.

"How about you, Michael?" Irene asked. "When was your first kiss?"

Tristan shrugged and looked away, embarrassed. "I've never actually . . . I was always busy at school and never, well, never really had any friends or anything."

"Really?" Irene blinked. "You're seventeen, aren't you? Well, that just won't do."

She stepped forward, grasped Tristan's head, put a hand on each cheek, and pulled him close. Irene gave Tristan his first kiss—and she made it count. She pressed her mouth against his, and Tristan gasped. His knees buckled, but he caught himself. Unsure what to do with his hands, he waved them back and forth on either side, no doubt signaling for help.

Drake burst out laughing again at the sight of him flailing.

"There now," Irene said, satisfied. She pinched his cheek and let him go.

Tristan fell back against the wall, stunned and confused. He let what had just happened sink in. Slowly but surely, a dazed, beaming smile spread across his face. "Wow," he said. "I . . . wow, Irene. Please do that again."

Irene giggled and looked between Tristan and Drake. "Boys," she said fondly, shaking her head.

Back on the western platform in his bed the next night, Tristan snoring happily below and dawn just a few short hours away, Drake thought back to that kiss with a twinge of jealousy and saw the exact moment the tiny, bespectacled boy in the bottom bunk had fallen in love with Irene Finlay.

20

FRACTURES

A few days before the first day of April, two days before the last rigball game of the season, Drake sat up in the common room flicking through the Alliance Systems newspaper, *The Crystal Globe*, thinking that Lucien Whitmore really loved the word *crystal*, when he saw the *Titan* return yet again, sailing in over the western horizon toward the Rig's southern platform.

She's coming weekly now, he thought. Hell, twice a week. A pathway on the spiderweb of escape patterns in his head lit up with cerulean-blue light. Drake followed the path, each strand a piece of the puzzle—held together only by what he thought Warden Storm would do once he set the plan in motion—and found that the light stretched all the way back to the mainland.

He gripped the paper hard enough to tear it in half. A bubble of excitement rose up from his stomach and into his throat. All that was left was to . . . try.

His excitement soured at that thought and felt a lot more

like falling into a tank of mutant sharks. Still, Drake knew his time was close at hand.

Later that night, he told Irene and Tristan that he wanted to get a better look at how they transported the crates and containers from below the eastern platform to the top of the southern platform for loading. From their hideaway they moved up through the vents, level by level, until they reached the highest point of the eastern platform.

Exposed to the night air, high above the sea, the three of them huddled together for warmth. The sky was scattered with an impossible number of stars, and the moon, heading toward full, cast a pale light on the otherwise dark ocean. Below them was the open-air bridge from the eastern to the southern platform, which Drake had never used.

Brand had brought the Crystal-X crates this way on the day that Drake had cast them back into the sea.

Concealed between vents and Tubes, Drake and his friends spoke quietly, watching the Rig in the dark. At just after midnight, about ten thousand sparks of blue light began to swim under the water between the pillars of the Rig's platforms, swaying back and forth in unison.

"I've seen that before," Drake whispered. "On my first night here. It's sea creatures, like a school of fish or something, affected by the blue mineral."

"It's beautiful," Irene said. "Like the stars have fallen into the sea." And Tristan agreed. She sighed and put one of her arms around Drake's shoulders and the other across Tristan's. "Funny what's brought us together, isn't it?"

Drake nodded slowly. "Something on your mind?"

"You both showed me yours . . ." she whispered. "Do you want to know why I'm here on the Rig?"

Tristan looked between Irene and Drake. "It doesn't matter," he said. "Irene, you don't have to—"

"I killed my father," she said.

Drake whistled low between his teeth.

"Well . . ." she whispered. "My stepfather."

Daddy's little girl, Drake recalled. That's what Anderson called her that night. He was being cruel.

"Irene, I . . ." Tristan frowned.

"He wasn't a very nice person, my stepfather," she said. Her eyes took on a shiny glaze, all the better to reflect the swirling blue light in the water below. One of the tears cut a silent track down her cheek. "He hurt me and, you know, more than hurt me. For years."

Drake felt a quiet, lethal anger stirring in his gut. Tristan's mouth was set in a fierce thin line.

"Anyway," Irene said, taking a deep breath. "One day I came home from school, and he was in the driveway working under his car. It was propped up with one of those automatic jacks, you know. My mum was there, handing him tools, and she had a shiny new black eye and a split lip and this—this miserable look on her face." Irene shook her head. "And I just snapped."

She took her arms from around Drake's and Tristan's shoulders and clapped her hands together. She looked between them both, naked fear and harsh pride warring on her face. After a long moment Drake took her arm and put it back around his shoulders. Tristan did the same.

"You know," Drake said, "the Alliance, all the police and lawyers, the judges and juries . . . They always talk about how we chose to do what we did. How we made bad choices and have to live with them." Drake shook his head. "But . . . sometimes, you know, there isn't a choice. The path doesn't lead to right or wrong. I was always going to steal that medicine for my mother. It wasn't a choice I even worried over. It was just the path I was on, because I . . . I love her."

Tristan listened to his words solemnly, and Irene pulled them both in a touch closer—sharing warmth against the cold night.

"Ah, I don't know what I'm trying to say . . ." Drake muttered. "Just, we have to live on the path that had to be taken. And that . . . that doesn't make us bad people."

For a time after that, the three of them sat in comfortable silence, watching the fallen blue stars far below darting back and forth under the surface of the ocean.

Enthralled by the light show, Drake almost missed the first shipment being transported across to the waiting crane of the *Titan*. Two small containers, about three meters high and five meters across—mini shipping containers—were being wheeled across to the southern platform.

Masked guards escorted the trolleys, pushed this time by the *Titan* crew in orange overalls and hardhats. Brand directed the movement, of course, carrying a long baton of a flashlight to guide the way. The southern platform was abuzz with activity. Drake noted that the Seahawk was missing, perhaps back on the mainland picking up more poor inmates the Alliance deemed worthy of the Rig.

For the next few hours the crew and the guards brought up

crates and containers—always two trolleys at a time—from down below the eastern platform. The *Titan*'s crane picked up the cargo, and Drake watched it disappear into the ship's hold, gears spinning in his head. *If we could get onboard, we . . .*

"We," he said aloud, surprised. When had he started thinking in terms of *we*?

"Eh?" Tristan whispered.

"Nothing, mate, nothing." His rough escape plan had a greater chance of success if he went alone. Drake knew that, he knew it, but a part of him, and not a small part, didn't like that idea anymore.

He took a deep breath and let it out slowly, releasing a warm mist into the cold night air.

The sound of whirring motors cut through the quiet. The fleet of tiny speedboats emerged from the *Titan* and began doing laps around the cargo ship. Drake shook his head, having seen enough.

It had to be at least three or four in the morning by the time the guards stopped bringing cargo up through the eastern platform. Unwilling to risk the descent to their hideaway when the platform was crawling with eyes, Drake, Irene, and Tristan had to wait them out. After a few hours, just when Drake was beginning to think they'd have to chance it if they wanted to get back to their own platforms before dawn, the *Titan*'s crane swung back over the ship and the crew reboarded. All the crates had been loaded for the night.

Just how much did they load? Drake wondered. If it was all Crystal-X—and he had no clue as to what else it could be—then the mining down below had been stepped up significantly from those first few shipments he'd seen. Tons and tons of the damn stuff . . . What did the Alliance need with so much?

Back down in the hideaway half an hour later, Tristan yawned. "Did we learn anything useful tonight?"

Drake shook his head. Irene was staring at him strangely, biting her lip. "What?" he asked her.

"I think you've got some sort of plan," she said in a sudden rush. "An escape plan, and you don't want us to know! I see how you go quiet when we talk about it, Will. Tristan thinks the same, don't you?"

Tristan opened and closed his mouth a few times like a goldfish, then settled on a nod.

"See? Tell us, Will!"

"I . . ." Drake sighed. "I don't know what you're talking about. You think I'd still be here if I had a way off?"

"That's just it," Irene said. "I don't think you would be. I think you'd leave us behind in a heartbeat if you could get away."

Drake's temper flared. "And you wouldn't?"

"I wouldn't leave my friends—"

"That's crap," Drake snapped. "Sorry, but it is. Do you think the same, then?" He turned on Tristan.

A few weeks earlier Tristan would have cowered under Drake's glare. Now he held his ground and nodded. "I think you'd feel bad about it, Will, but I do think if you had the chance . . . you'd take it without us."

Drake looked from Irene to Tristan and back again. "You two have been talking about me, then?"

"Do you have a plan?" Tristan asked.

"Just bits of one," Drake admitted. "It all depends on if I've read Storm right, and what would happen if we got caught . . ." He shook his head. "Just bits of one."

Irene shivered. "I don't know what kind of life I'll have away from the Rig, on the run from Alliance Systems, but we can't stay here, you must see that? The Rig will get us killed." She placed a gentle hand on Drake's shoulder and squeezed softly. "Please, help me escape."

Drake stared at her for a long moment, then shrugged her hand away. He thought of the fire at Cedarwood, of Aaron, who had trusted him and died for that trust. "Someone asked me to help him escape once before, about a year ago . . . And I got him killed, Irene." He stepped back with a snarl. "No! I won't. It's all just so . . . so . . . Look, we can plan, we could have the best plan in the world, but reality isn't so kind to my plans. Everything could fall apart, and you, or Tristan, could be hurt—or worse. I never want to deal with that again."

Irene sniffed. "Even if it means being alone? On the run and alone? And leaving us here?"

"You can't rely on others," Drake said bitterly. He thought of what Alliance Medicare had promised his mother, and what they had delivered. A slow death wrapped in a blaze of painkillers, when the medicine was there to treat her, sitting in large, cold warehouses. The nations of the world relied on the Alliance for so much, but the company gave so little. Look at what they were doing here! Experimenting on the inmates, forgotten kids, and changing them into something else. The ones that didn't go insane became killers to be recruited into the Alliance's own private military.

"So that's it, is it?" Irene asked, crossing her arms and scowling. "Will Drake's on his own? Just fine by himself. Tell me, how's that worked out for you so far?"

"I—"

"You're a coward." Irene thrust an indignant finger into his chest, hard enough to leave a bruise. "Do you actually enjoy acting so hard and indifferent to your friends? You're still a teenager, Will, so bloody act like one now and again!"

"Irene," Tristan said, clearing his throat. "Please . . ."

"Leave it, Tristan." Drake ran a hand through his dark hair and shoved Irene back a step, away from him. "You're not my friend. I don't need friends. I've only been meeting here because you were useful exploring this place. I don't need you anymore, Irene. You can get lost and find your own damn way off the Rig."

21

MOTHERS

Two days later, on the afternoon of the final rigball game of the season, Drake found himself still fuming from his argument with Irene. Tristan had been sulking around their cell, trying to get Drake to come out at night and apologize, but Drake was having none of it.

Perhaps we could escape together, he had found himself thinking, knee-deep in muck and grime in Tubes on Friday afternoon, the day before the game. No, we'd never get away.

"This is our game," Mario said, still sporting a black eye and split lip from the previous week's game. "You feel that, Drake? That's victory, I can taste it."

Handing out the rackets alongside the field, Tommy ruffled Mario's hair. "Nothing gets you down, does it, kid?"

"Broccoli and sprout night does," he said glumly. "But that is not tonight!"

Given the advantage Grey and the others had, Drake was sure that his own team was in for another trouncing, but it was the last chance he'd have to cause some damage. No matter what, he knew he wouldn't be there for the summer season of rigball games.

After watching the girls' matches, Drake strapped on his helmet and pads and stepped out onto the field, claiming his wing. Alan Grey stumbled onto the pitch, hulking and impressive. The helmet strapped to his head looked about two sizes too small, almost like a tiny hat sitting atop his hair. He grinned at Drake and smacked his racket against his palm.

The guard-ref blew the air horn, and the game was under way.

Since his first game, Drake had become a lot clearer on the rules of the sport and also how to play to the letter of those rules, bending them until they almost fractured. He ducked and weaved along the wing, moving in and out with Tommy and the boys, keeping the ball moving.

He took a lot of hits from Grey's team, hitting the concrete hard, but he had learned in the third game that staying down only got you trampled. He leaped to his feet as quick as he could after a hard check, racing after the ball.

The first half flew by, with Tommy's team not giving an inch—thanks in most part to Drake's fast footwork and Mario's complete aversion to self-preservation. The game was tied at nothing as they stumbled off the field for a quick break.

"Is it just me," Drake asked, "or is Grey moving a lot slower?"

Emir, surprising them all, spoke in broken English. "He slow. He no good today. This good."

"Maybe he didn't take his medicine this morning . . ." Drake muttered, thinking of when he'd last seen Grey—or rather, not seen Grey. Had he been getting the Crystal-X? Did they cut him off?

The break over, the teams switched sides, and Drake moved in close to Grey, courting a beating, to get a better look at the gargantuan boy. Grey smirked when he saw him hovering just out of reach of his racket.

"I'm coming for you," he growled, his voice deep but slow.

Drake wasn't sure, given the bright midafternoon light and the glare off the concrete, but he thought he saw twin stars of red light deep within Grey's eyes. Not as bad as Anderson . . . but getting there.

As the second and final half for the winter season began, both teams delivered crushing blows, tossing the ball not always to a racket but more at an opposing player's head. The crowd roared and cheered as the referee called foul upon foul.

With only a few minutes left to play, Grey knocked through Greg and Neil like a ball through bowling pins, sending them flying and shooting for goal.

Emir managed to catch the rigball in his racket and tossed it out to Tommy, who spun and ran for the other end of the field. Drake saw Grey take a massive leap forward and slam his racket into Tommy's leg, knocking him off his feet and hard into the concrete. A collective wince shuddered through the crowd—that had been the hardest check of the game so far.

Up close, Drake heard the bone snap. Tommy clutched at his ankle, rocking back and forth. Time-out was called as Nurse Rose and the guards saw to him. Drake and the rest of the team hung around in a loose circle, watching him writhe.

"That sounded nasty," Mario said, wiping the sweat from his brow. "There's a few minutes left. How can we win with a man down?"

"A tie's better than anything else we've had this season," Greg said.

"I want the win," Mario insisted.

"So do I, mate." Drake motioned them close. "So here's what we do . . ."

After Tommy was carted from the field, Drake's team was awarded the ball. Drake gave it to Neil from the quarter line in their half and ran up the wing. Mario was in place as well, and Greg had his part to play.

The air horn blew, and the clock continued to count down toward zero. According to the timer beneath the scoreboard, there were six minutes left of the half. This would be close . . .

Grey and his goons moved in on Drake's depleted team.

The next four minutes were a grudge match, pure and simple. Drake stayed out of most of it, keeping his wits about him, but the rest of the boys—as per the plan—took a bit of a beating. Mario was as impervious as always, but even Greg and Neil were soon sporting cuts on their cheeks, with matching black eyes. Despite the onslaught, they managed to keep the score tied at nothing.

Drake kept his eye on the clock, and as the last two minutes began to count down, he whistled loudly. His teammates acknowledged the signal and moved into position. They'd been playing defensively for most of the half, but now was the time for Drake's play.

Mario dived in and seized the rigball from under Grey's arm.

As before, Grey was too big to see him coming from behind. With three seconds to pass, Mario hurled the ball downfield, away from their goal, to Neil, who caught it and dashed across midfield, passing to Greg.

These were the three passes they needed to score.

Drake had been climbing his wing and was ready for the ball when Greg tossed it his way. He made a dash for the goal, about six meters away, and raised the racket to take a shot against the keeper as Grey and his thugs moved in to intercept.

The crowd gasped.

Drake swung—and hurled the ball to Mario across goal.

"I've got it!" Mario cried, and spun on the spot, lining up a shot.

Half of Grey's team peeled away after him, and the keeper moved out to intercept the small boy.

But Mario didn't have the ball. Drake lifted his racket onto his shoulder, the rigball still clinging to his net, and took a run at goal himself. He had never crossed the ball to Mario, keeping it firmly magnetized in his own racket. He had less than three seconds to take the shot, but that was all he needed.

Grey hadn't been fooled.

He split away from the pack chasing Mario and spun toward Drake, a snarl on his face, taking a huge stride toward him, less than two meters away.

Drake pulled his racket behind his head, took aim, and swung. As the racket fell through the air, he released the rigball into the half of the net left undefended by Grey's keeper just as the massive boy himself reacted and reached for Drake.

The force of Drake's swing kept his racket moving down, heavy and hard, and as Grey moved in close, Drake smacked the bully across the face with all the force he could muster. Drake heard something snap, saw Grey's eyes flare crimson for just a second as he spun like a top and hit the concrete hard. Blood dribbled from his mouth, and his eyes rolled up into the back of his head.

The rigball, for its part, sailed into the net with three seconds left on the clock.

Drake had scored.

Drake had won.

The crowd erupted in a wave of shocked cheers that shook the platform, echoing in the clear skies and carried away on the salty wind over the ocean even as the air horn blew and called the end of the game.

"You did it!" Tommy shouted from the sidelines, hopping up onto his good leg. "You silly bastards, you did it!"

The rest of Grey's team looked stunned by the unexpected goal and hovered around their fallen leader as Mario tackled Drake and kissed him on the forehead. "Knew you were good for something," he said, laughing.

Drake remembered thinking during his first game that rigball was not about winning, but about power and dominance. He looked over at the guard box, at the warden and his guards behind the goal, and smirked. Winning was good, but he'd been right the first time, and he'd just taken some of that power and dominance away from those men and women—and from Grey.

That was for Dr. Lambros, he thought, and felt all the old frustration and anger bubble up inside of him even as Greg and Neil slapped him on the back. No, *this* is for Dr. Lambros . . .

Drake held his racket up over his head, victorious, and acknowledged the cheering crowd. He did a slow lap of the field as Grey was carted away on a stretcher by the guards, his jaw hanging askew and bloody. Tommy and the boys cheered from the sidelines and tossed Drake the match-winning ball as he walked past. Most of the boys in the stands were on their feet and cheering as well. Taking his time, waiting for his moment, Drake strolled over and along the front of the girls' stands. He got quite a few wolf whistles and kisses blown his way.

Those made him grin. He didn't see Irene amid the sea of red jumpsuits.

As he came around to the special box filled with guards, the staff of Control, and Warden Storm, he received a polite round of applause from about half of them. Brand sat next to Storm, on his left, with Dr. Elias on his right.

Drake smiled, and Storm nodded at him. Drake pressed the trigger and reignited the current through his racket. *Whose dumb idea was it to give magnetized rackets to us lot?* Drake remembered asking Tommy that question just two short months ago.

With little preamble, Drake tossed the ball up in the air and smacked it into the guard box using every ounce of strength in his arm. The small, heavy magnetized ball hit Dr. Elias in the gut and bounced back to the nearest source—Drake's racket—where he proceeded to send it right back into the box. His aim was as good as ever, and it clipped Brand on the ear. The stands behind him, boys and girls, erupted in cheers as the guards dived for cover. Those stationed on duty around the edge of the playing field ran in, raising their rifles. Drake hurled his racket into the box, aiming for Brand again just as he was tackled by a furious-faced Stein. A hundred kilograms of angry guard slammed him into the ground, forcing the air from his lungs.

Worth it, Drake thought as the crowd erupted in renewed cheers.

He was manhandled from guard to guard and ended up being dragged down through the platform by Brand and Stein, both of them pinning his arms to his back and almost carrying him along. His tracker buzzed angrily, chiding him for being off schedule. Drake laughed.

"You won't think this is funny in a minute," Brand promised, cold fury on his face.

They dragged him back to the western platform and down the tiered cellblock to the third level and the cell he shared with Tristan. Stein threw him against the floor, and Brand stepped into the cell, cracking his knuckles.

"Don't you have work to be doing, Officer Stein?" Brand asked casually.

"You know I believe I do, Officer Brand."

She smirked at Drake and left.

"You've been pushing your luck since you got here, boy," Brand snarled, and hurled Drake up against the sink in 36C. The molded plastic dug into his back, sending pain shooting up his spine. "Get it through your head—you belong to the Alliance now, and for all that matters, I am the Alliance here."

"What happened to Dr. Lambros, Brand?" Drake asked, already knowing the awful truth. "Where did she go?" He balled his hand into a fist and delivered a powerful blow into Brand's face.

The mad guard took the punch, laughed, and spat a mouthful of blood onto the floor. "Everyone gets one free hit, boy." Brand grabbed him by the collar. "How's your mother doing?

Want to know if she's still alive? I know, Drake. Want to know how much she suffered without you?"

Brand drove his forehead into Drake's nose, and his nasal bones snapped like twigs. A torrent of blood gushed from his nostrils and sprayed in a wild arc as Drake tossed his head back with a cry and saw galaxies spinning in the cell.

"Look at me, Drake!" Brand demanded. "You. Are. Mine. No one in this world gives a damn about you, boy."

Brand punched him in the stomach—once, twice. Drake keeled over, gasping for breath. The Rig's number one guard didn't let him fall to his knees. He grabbed his shoulders and slammed his head against the steel frame of the bunk beds.

Dazed, his head spinning, Drake managed to stay on his feet. He saw two blurry versions of Brand take a step back. Speaking of mothers . . . "If I . . ." Drake frowned. Blood flowed in rivulets into his mouth from his nose. The crimson mess dribbled down his chin as he spoke. "If I wanted a kiss, Brand, I would've asked your mother."

Drake laughed, wincing through the pain. One of his ribs felt cracked. When had that happened? Brand laughed, too, and drew his ugly, black baton.

"You know, we should get you a spot in the common room on Saturday nights," Brand said, and swiped the baton across Drake's face.

Star-studded pain exploded in Drake's head. He spun and tumbled along the length of the bunk beds and saw, vaguely, one of his teeth go flying from his mouth and hit the cool floor. His cheek hit the same floor a few seconds later.

"Such a funny kid, aren't you? Should be a comedian!"

Brand kicked him—hard—in the stomach with his steel-capped boot.

Drake was laughing and crying. Vicious pain tore at him from so many places that he felt almost euphoric as his vision slipped away down a long, dark tunnel. He saw something crimson lying on the floor in front of him and tried to focus. He realized, after a moment, that it was his tooth.

"You know, Drake," Brand said, as if from a great distance. "You've been working hard lately. I reckon you should have the day off tomorrow, on me." He kneeled down on his haunches so Drake could see his face.

"You know, Brand . . ." Drake felt as if he were speaking through a mouthful of pennies. He wheezed and chuckled. "You . . . you don't deserve the . . . the bad things they say about you around here, mate."

The baton hummed as Brand pressed the red trigger, sending a cruel current coursing through the weapon. The last thing Drake felt was a jolt, and his body stiffened like a board. A string of mumbled curses exploded from his mouth, and someone turned out the lights.

22

DREAMLAND

Drifting in and out of consciousness on the floor of his cell, Drake dreamed.

He was back in Cedarwood, high up in the Alps, and the snowcapped peaks stood like silent, impassable sentinels. Towering jailers of rock and dirt, imposing and intimidating. He picked one of them up and tossed it like a skipping stone across the electric-blue waters of the Arctic Ocean. The mountain sank below the waves, burning with wicked red light the whole way down.

He was in Trennimax, and on days when the wind blew just right, he could smell lavender, carried on the air from the famed fields of Provence. None of the guards spoke much in the way of English, but that didn't matter, because he was Will Drake, blackberry farmer, and although this was his first prison, he already knew he could escape from anywhere. No place could hold him—not if he didn't want to be held. He just had to follow the web. Drake walked through the walls like a ghost and stepped . . .

. . . into the cool, clinical cells of Harronway in Ireland. This place had always felt more like a hospital than a prison. He lay on a bed of clovers, of course, and a leprechaun wearing golden glasses smiled down at him.

Drake blinked, and he wasn't in Harronway anymore. Or even on the floor of 36C. He was in Tristan's lower bunk, and Tristan himself was talking to him and dabbing his face with toilet paper that had soaked through red.

"Stay awake, Will," Tristan said. Was he crying? Yes, yes he was. "Can you hear me?"

Drake dreamed.

He was crawling through the vents of Cedarwood, something he had never done, as the temperature was often below freezing and the heating churned near boiling twenty-four hours a day. Aaron was with him. Friendly, funny Aaron. Half his face had melted away, but the accident hadn't happened yet, had it?

"The fire wasn't your fault, Will," he said, but the voice that came out of his mouth belonged to Dr. Lambros.

Another of the dead, Drake thought, unsure if he was awake or dreaming.

"Risky business, what you do," Aaron said. Flames danced within his golden hair, and his eyes were tiny bright stars of red. "Escaping. Following that web. But it is what you do. Sometimes there's only one path, so get to it, eh?"

Strange orange light played havoc with the shadows in cell 36C. Tristan sat against the wall near the sink, his head resting on his knees, fast asleep. Bloody tissue lay in spent piles all around him. Drake tried to move, but his side was on fire. Someone had filled his mouth with copper, he guessed from the taste. A dozen pennies under his tongue. He chuckled, winced, and dozed off again.

He dreamed of escape, of London, and of his mother.

"I expected you sooner," mad Carl Anderson whispered. "And later."

Drake hovered, beaten and bloody, in front of the glass cage.

"They're going to have trouble stopping you . . ."

From there, his dreams were a smooth, fizzy ride into blissful, numb oblivion.

* * *

Sunlight poured in through the large barred window when Drake opened his eyes. He groaned and blinked away tears from the harsh light. Everything still hurt, but at least he was aware of it. The memory of his nightmares still clung to the edge of his thoughts.

Tristan was there. "Will, how'd you feel?"

Drake mumbled something. His mouth felt as if it were full of cotton balls. He ran his tongue over his teeth and found a gap along the bottom row.

"Here, swallow these." Tristan handed him two white pills.

"What is it?" Drake asked, his voice cracking.

"Painkillers—Irene swiped them from the infirmary."

"How . . ." Drake shook his head. The "how" of it didn't matter. He tossed back the pills and forced them down his throat. Outside, on the open sea, he saw a massive cargo frigate sailing toward the Rig. The *Titan*, shining in the sun. "Is that thing coming or going?" he asked.

Tristan glanced out the window. "Coming, I think. Not really been paying much attention."

Drake nodded. He thought it was coming, too.

More aware of his surroundings with each passing minute, Drake looked down at himself. He was naked save for his boxer shorts. Wicked, splotchy bruising covered most of his chest and down his right side. He touched the skin there, and something twinged. A rib?

"I was out all night?"

Tristan shook his head. "Will, it's Tuesday. You've been in and out of it for a few days. Mumbling all kinds of . . . I went up through the vents on the second night, and Irene was waiting. She saw what you did at the game. The next day, she managed to pass me some pills through the barrier in the cafeteria. That was . . . that was yesterday."

"Just painkillers?"

"I think also antibiotics, but I don't know. I trusted her."

Drake noticed that a wad of toilet paper was wrapped around Tristan's index finger. "What . . ."

Tristan smiled grimly. "You bit me," he said. "Hard. I had to force the pills down your throat last night after dinner."

"They didn't let you off work to tend to me, then, eh?" Drake chuckled, and it hurt.

"God, no. Brand dragged me out of here by my hair on Sunday morning. I think . . . I think he was hoping you'd die in here."

"Wanted me to suffer a bit first."

"Yeah."

"Tristan . . . Michael, thank you. That's three times you've saved my life."

"Three? The baton — and now this? What am I missing?"

"The shark tank," Drake said. "Blimey."

Tristan shuddered. "Oh yeah, how could I forget the shark tank?"

Drake took in as deep a breath as he could. One of his ribs was definitely cracked, if not broken. He swung his legs around and sat up carefully. "Still want out of this place?"

Ready to catch him if he fell, Tristan nodded. "More than anything I've ever wanted in my life. We have to get off the Rig, Will, or we'll die here. I'm sure of it."

"Then you need to get a message to Irene at lunch or dinner today. I don't care how you do it, just get it done."

"Okay. I can do that, I think. What should I say?"

Drake stood and found that the pain in his side actually lessened a touch when he was up and moving. Maybe it was the painkillers kicking in. "Tell her tonight. We escape to-night."

23

RISKY BUSINESS

Drake spent the day in his cell, working up his strength. He was a mess of cuts and bruises, and the painkillers lasted only until lunch. Tristan had left him a stack of candy bars from the machine, which he devoured almost whole. After two days of fevered nightmares he was ravenous.

He managed to get a glimpse of his face in the reflection of the window and saw that he looked somewhat like a raccoon—two black eyes, and his tender nose, broken, had swelled to twice its normal size. He laughed at the sorry sight.

The tracker on his wrist was buzzing an angry red, informing him that he was way off schedule and had been for days. He thought of Brand and Storm, smirking at his signal on a display up in the control tower, knowing he was bloody and beaten in his cell, and watching the fines rack up. As it stood, Drake owed the Alliance nearly two and a half thousand credits for his time on the Rig.

Let's see if I can increase that debt, he thought, thinking of the night that lay ahead. There would be opportunity to cause some damage, if everything fell into place.

Drake was tempted to head out and get some dinner at half past six, but he didn't want to draw the ire of the guards any more than he already had. He knew that what he'd done at the rigball game had been careless, even stupid, and boy, had he paid for it a dozen times over, but he'd be damned if it hadn't felt good.

The high of winning the game, beating Grey, coupled with his frustration and raw, finely tuned anger at the men and women in charge of the Rig had been unleashed. If Drake was being honest, his argument with Irene may have been weighing on his mind a touch as well.

At half past seven Tristan returned to the cell and smiled when he saw Drake pacing back and forth.

"You look more like yourself," he said, and handed Drake a bread roll stuffed with the thin, poor beef the cafeteria served twice a week.

Drake seized the roll and scoffed it down in three bites. "Thanks, mate. I needed that. Did you manage to speak to Irene?"

Tristan nodded. "Enough to get her to meet us tonight in the hideaway."

"Good. That's good. We'll need to swing by there anyway. I want to pick up Hall's rifle and that screwdriver I nicked from down below."

"This is it, isn't it? We're really doing it." Tristan tried for a smile, but it fell somewhere between anxiety and fright. "I think I might be sick. Do you want to tell me the plan?"

Drake had to sit down and let the beef roll settle. He waved away Tristan's question. "Later, once we're all together. Trust me, it's a pretty awesome plan, and I'm definitely not making it up as I go along."

Just before nine that night, Drake couldn't wait any longer. Removing their trackers, he and Tristan hid them under their pillows and headed up to the ninth-floor washroom. If everything went according to plan, no one would notice them missing until they were well away from the Rig.

Follow the web . . . Drake's mind muttered at him. A shiver of nervous excitement made him chuckle.

Getting into the vents above the washroom was torture of a whole other kind for Drake. His bruised and battered ribs protested the stretch up, and Tristan had to support him from atop the sink the whole way in. Pulling Tristan up was likewise painful. Still, they got it done—and disappeared up into the network of secret, unseen passages.

Drake had to move slower than usual, so it took them close to ninety minutes to reach the hideaway. They found Irene waiting, the flashlight on, her arms crossed and her foot tapping against the floor impatiently.

"You look terrible," she said to Drake.

"You look great," he replied.

Tristan looked at them both and laughed. "Apologize, you moron."

Drake took a deep breath, which pinched at his side, and winced. "I'm sorry," he said. "I was angry and stupid the other day."

"Yes, you were. Selfish, too."

"Selfish, too."

"Cowardly selfish," she insisted. "You were a Rig pig."

Drake rolled his eyes. "Yes, cowardly selfish, and a big old idiot, and any other names you want to call me."

"You are a big old idiot," Irene said, but she smiled when she said it. "What changed your mind, then?"

"Funnily enough, it was getting my teeth knocked out by Brand." Drake grinned. "Be sure to send him a postcard from Moraine Lake once you get there."

Irene went perfectly still. "And how am I going to get there?"

Drake smiled. "Listen close, both of you."

For the next few minutes Drake outlined his escape plan, which relied heavily on the *Titan*. "We sneak into the Crystal-X facility, like we've done before, and hide inside one of those crates they load onto the *Titan*." Drake slammed his fist into his palm. "Once we're inside and aboard the ship, we can see about borrowing one of those speedboats and aiming it at a nearby continent." He squeezed Irene's shoulder. "Canada ain't that far away, yeah? We could be drinking maple syrup for lunch tomorrow."

"You mean tonight?" Irene squeaked. "We're going tonight?"

Drake touched his tender nose. "I've had enough of this place, Irene. Tonight's our best chance."

"The speedboats?" Tristan said, still processing the rough sketch of Drake's plan. "That's it? That's your great escape plan?"

"A lot better than some of my other plans, believe me. This will work." Drake tried for confidence, fell a touch short, and picked up Hall's rifle. "It's not risk-free, sure, but few things worth having are. Look, this is what I do, and I've got a pretty good record at doing it. It's like, I see this pattern in my head, and we can follow it out of here if we're brave enough. If you . . . trust me."

Irene sighed. "Oh, those are two dangerous words, Will."

"But . . . but so many things!" Tristan said. "How do you know we'll reach land? What's the range on the speedboat? Will it even be fueled?"

"All good questions," Irene said. "I'm willing to have a little faith in this plan, if it means getting off the Rig tonight. How about you?"

Tristan looked from Drake to Irene and then pulled them both into a quick hug. "I love the plan," he said.

"No you don't," Drake said.

"No, no I don't." He stared into Drake's face, grimacing at his injuries and how unrecognizable he looked. "But let's give it a shot."

24

THE GREATER GOOD

Whether it was excitement or fear, Drake felt alive as they descended the elevator shaft and entered the Crystal-X facility. He had the stolen rifle, full of stunning darts, slung over his shoulder.

He almost hadn't been able to carry Irene down the steel cable, but he found it possible after she placed her hands under his jumpsuit, on his bare chest, and he could see bright light shining through the material. The pain in his side lessened greatly as Irene gasped and fell back from the strain of using her power.

"Did that work?" she asked, her voice catching in her throat.

"A bit," Drake said. The rest of his aches and pains would just have to settle on the idea that yes, he was going to abuse them tonight and he best just go with the flow. "Was it harder this time?"

Irene shook her head, then shrugged. "No, it's just . . . Cuts and stuff are easy, but fixing things I can't see, on the inside—I'm worried I'll set your heart on fire or something."

Drake snorted. "Sweetheart, you already have."

"Shut up and carry me, Will."

The facility was abuzz with activity that night. The guards, Dr. Elias, and his lab technicians were all running back and forth through the laboratories, and Drake, Irene, and Tristan had to move slowly and carefully, clinging to the shadows. Drake kept the rifle in his hands, ready to fire at a moment's notice. He hoped it didn't come to that. Drake had never shot anyone and wasn't looking forward to discovering if he could—even if the darts *were* nonlethal.

They stuck to the network of walkways off the main floors, and they judged that it was just after midnight when they reached the stacks of crates and shipping containers in the mining warehouse. Two of the submersible craft were docked in the tunnels of water that led out into the ocean. One was missing, presumably out mining.

"This way," Drake whispered. Across the warehouse, three technicians were loading the mineral into glass tubes and tanks, making sure that none of it was exposed to the air. Stein supervised the loading, her hand on her rifle, and every few seconds she spoke into her radio.

The transmissions were too faint to hear, but Drake thought he could make out Brand's voice through the receiver. Yeah, him I'd shoot, Drake thought. A forklift was lifting heavy containers and crates onto trolleys and pushing them onto the runners built into the concrete—cargo to be loaded.

The other crates and containers were stacked in long rows and aisles across the back of the mining area. Moving with care, Drake dismissed the open and empty containers and moved toward the front rows, hoping to find one that had been filled and was ready to go.

"You check the right side," he said to Irene and Tristan. "I'll check the left of this row. We want one fully loaded, but with room to hide in."

They moved quickly, unlatching the bolts on the container doors and checking inside. Drake found the first few empty, but his fourth, stamped X-274AS, was partially filled with glowing blue mineral in seawater tanks. The next, X-776AS, was three-quarters full.

He noticed the pattern.

"These ones," Drake said, pointing down the aisle to the end of the row. "They'll be full, I'm sure of it. These are the ones going out tonight. Have to be."

Irene nodded. "Which one do we use, then?"

"Nine-five-four, I don't wanna be here anymore!" Tristan said slowly, almost reverently. "Carl . . . he said that weeks ago, remember? I've got a good feeling about this one."

Drake unbolted the latch and swung the door open on container X-954AS. Blue light from the Crystal-X, which was suspended in large square tanks secured to racks, spilled out onto the floor. My God, there must be at least five hundred kilos of the damn stuff, he thought. A narrow space ran between the racks of mineral, just wide enough to fit three stowaways.

"As good as any," Drake agreed. "Right. We can use the screwdriver to bar the door from the inside, make it look like it's latched. We're busted if someone notices it's not and locks us in."

"Do you think that'll happen?" Irene asked. Her face was a mask of worry. "What if we get stuck in here? We don't know how long it'll be before the Alliance opens this container again!"

"Worse comes to worst," Drake said, "we'll start banging on the walls and making a lot of noise. Someone will hear us."

"And send us right back to the Rig, if not worse," Tristan said.

Drake grinned. "We've got the devil's luck on our side. We have to, to have gotten this far, yeah? Point of no return—last chance to back out, my friends."

Irene smiled. "You said *friends*."

Tristan rubbed the back of his neck. "Better than staying here. Anything's better than staying here."

"Right. Then in you pop."

Irene went first, squeezing between the racks of glowing blue mineral. Tristan went next, taking up about a third of the remaining space. "Okay, I think this will work," he said.

Drake thought it was going to be a tight fit.

"Bring the forklift over this way!" a voice called from the next row of crates.

Drake's heart leaped into his throat. He closed the door to the container, sealing the latch so it didn't look out of place, and slipped around the side of the row just as heavy footsteps began to tread down the aisle toward him. He hoped Irene and Tristan had sense enough to keep quiet.

"Okay, what's going up on this run?" Officer Stein asked.

Drake heard papers being shuffled and then a familiar voice reading off crate and container numbers. "And X-stamped containers number two-four-seven, nine-five-four, and three-one-six," Marcus Brand said. "That's the last of it for tonight. Load 'em up."

Drake gripped the handle on his rifle hard enough to turn his knuckles white. They were taking the crate in which he'd just sealed Irene and Tristan. What could he do? He looked down at the rifle, shining pitch-black and ugly in his hands. No. If he shot them now, he might get the drop on them, but the crates wouldn't get moved at all. Brand and Stein would be missed before too long, and time was already short.

Trusting that his friends would keep quiet, Drake took slow, careful steps back into the dark. He was running out of time, but not out of options. So long as he remained free, there were always options. As the forklift moved in and started loading the crates and containers onto trolleys, Drake fled back into the Crystal-X facility, alone but determined.

He took the steel stairs up onto the walkway above the mining area and watched as the container concealing Irene and Tristan was loaded onto one of the trolleys, bound for the *Titan*. Brand had said this load was the last, so it would do Drake no good to hide in another container. He needed a new plan—another way to get onto the ship.

He followed the trolleys at a distance as the runners took the containers up the concrete ramp, out of the mining area, and into the network of corridors that led through the labs and, eventually, to the freight elevator.

Could he cut in front? Try to sneak in? No, he'd be seen. What then?

Drake shook his head. He had no plan for this, no fallback. If he followed the crates, maybe some option would present itself. He still had the rifle slung across his shoulder. The game wasn't over.

The trolleys were transported through the darker area of the facility, under yellow pipes overhead, and through an area Drake had never seen, having spent most of his time up on the walkways. But Brand and Stein escorted the trolleys around and back into familiar territory—the first lab Drake had seen, with the fire pit and display monitors.

The lab was empty and quiet, and Drake ducked behind the workbenches. The runners in the floor led up another ramp and around through the wall that divided this lab from the one next door. He waited for them to move on before he followed. Given the light and the walkways overhead, he was far too exposed.

Once the trolleys and the guards were out of sight, he moved out from behind the workbenches. He didn't want to take the long way up the ramp, so he decided to slip between labs using the door in the dividing wall.

Drake opened the door and ran into Dr. Elias. He bounced off the man's chest with a grunt.

Elias's eyes widened, and he made a sound of strangled surprise. Drake pointed his rifle at the doctor. "Don't you dare," he snarled. "Move back."

"What on earth are you doing down here?" Elias said as Drake forced him across the lab toward the bee cages. "This area is off-limits, you know. And you're not supposed to be out of bed after lights—"

"Save it, Doc. I know what's going on down here. What you've been doing. Sit on that chair there."

Dr. Elias raised his hands and sat. Drake scanned the lab, looking for options. He and Elias were alone, save for a few bees buzzing around in a glass cage.

"Do you know what kind of trouble you're in, son?" Elias snapped, cutting his hand down through the air. "This is a classified—"

"The kids that died?" Drake asked. "From the Crystal-X. What did you do with their bodies?"

Elias's face went still. "I'm not sure what you're talking about."

"Don't be stupid. I was here the night you showed Whitmore the footage. I was here the next night—I spoke to Carl Anderson. I know what's happening to Alan Grey."

Elias sighed and removed his glasses from his face. He rubbed his eyes. "You don't understand what we're doing down here. The advances we're making. The millions of lives we'll save harnessing the power in the mineral."

"You're killing people!"

"Nothing great can be achieved without sacrifice!" Elias shouted, and Drake's finger twitched on the rifle's trigger. "The greater good demands—"

"The greater good? There is nothing great about what you're doing, you sick bastard!"

"My wife was dying, and my research healed her! I don't expect a criminal like you to understand what it means to care for someone other than yourself, but—"

Drake slammed the butt of the rifle into Elias's face, thinking of Dr. Lambros, of Anderson, of all the others this man had ruined. Elias spun in his chair, mouth bloodied, as the roller door at the back of the lab began to open.

Three men in lab coats, technicians, walked into the lab and stopped in surprise, taking in the scene before them.

"Now, why don't you put the gun down, son," Elias said, gesturing to his staff. "There's no way out of here. We'll get the guards to take you back to your cell—"

Yeah, via the shark tank, Drake was sure, and he pulled the trigger on the rifle.

A dart shot out of the barrel and stuck Dr. Elias in the neck. He gasped, bucked in the chair, and slumped to the floor, unconscious. Drake swung the rifle over to the three technicians and opened fire. Two of the men collapsed, darts sticking from their chests. The third turned to run back through the roller doors. Drake gave chase and, given the small distance, managed to shoot him in the back. He stumbled forward onto his face.

On the other side of the roller door Drake found the control panel and lowered the door, sealing away the lab.

Now what?

The technicians and Elias would be found and the alarm raised all too soon. Drake would be trapped and hunted down, and Irene and Tristan would be stuck aboard the *Titan* without him, unable to escape the container.

Best-laid plans, Drake thought, tapping the barrel of the rifle against his palm. I need a distraction.

He was back in the part of the facility with the yellow pipes overhead, dark and dank, leaking seawater into puddles on the concrete floors. An idea occurred to him—another wonderful, terrible idea on the webbed path to escape.

He worried—a vague sort of worry—whether this idea would get him killed.

Drake ran down the corridor, following the pipes, and ran into the smell of the animal-testing room. The air stank of sweat and decay, and a cold, dark laughter rang through the room and down Drake's spine. He rounded the corner and found his terrible idea.

"You're late," Anderson said, slumped against the bottom of his cage. His speech was slurred, muddy.

"I'm here to get you out," Drake said.

"Yes, I know." Anderson stood and stretched. "Go on, then."

Drake hesitated. "What are you going to do if I open the lock?"

Anderson grinned. Since the last time Drake had seen him, most of his teeth had fallen out. They were scattered along the bottom of his cage, along with clumps of his hair. "You know what I'm going to do." His crimson eyes flared. "Now hurry up or you won't make it to the *Titan* in time."

"How do you know that?"

Anderson tapped his head. "You wouldn't believe the things I know, Drake."

Drake took a deep breath and began unlocking the cage. There were five locks—sliding bars of steel—to undo. He had to climb up on the base of the cage to get the top one. He leaped down once the bolt gave way, taking a large step back as the glass door swung open.

Anderson sniffed the air and hopped down out of his cage.

He stank of hot, burning metal. The air hummed with static as he moved, cracking his neck.

"Thank you."

"Don't mention it."

Anderson chuckled. "You've got two minutes, William Drake. Starting from one minute ago."

Drake frowned. "What?"

"Run!" Anderson snarled, and bright arcs of smoky, luminescent light burst from his palms—light as red as blood.

Drake ran.

25

SCORES SETTLED

Drake was halfway back to the freight elevator on the walkway above Elias's laboratory when the first explosion rocked the entire facility, and he stumbled and dropped his rifle.

Oh, come on, Anderson, he thought. That wasn't even half a minute . . .

The technicians and lab assistants down below, having discovered Elias and the other unconscious men, reacted with screams and cries of surprise. Drake didn't have the time or the desire to bother with them. He picked up his rifle, slung the strap over his shoulder, and kept on running. It'll be okay, he thought, and Irene and Tristan will already be up top.

Drake slid down the metal handrail on the stairs and ran up the corridor to the freight elevator. Every hurried step forced a shot of agony down his side, but time was short and getting shorter. He dashed past the large windows, paid no attention to the glowing crystal reefs and ridges, rounded the bend near the viewing platform he and Irene had hid in not too many weeks before, and burst out into the facility's entrance. Another explosion shuddered through the metal and stone, and Drake saw thin cracks spread through the plaster.

Above, walkways snapped under the strain, and a great cloud of stone and dust erupted through the high walls, raining down on Drake.

He's going to bring it down! Drake thought. It was so absurd, he almost laughed. No, he's going to drown the whole awful place. Best not be here when he does.

He entered the straight arched tunnel that led to the freight elevator, bubbled glass overhead, and saw that spiderwebs of cracks were already splintering through the glass. Drops of freezing water slipped through the cracks and splashed on his head. The tunnel moaned, and his legs almost turned to jelly. He had seconds—less than seconds. He sprinted for the freight elevator, his bruised ribs on fire, and slammed his fist into the call button.

If the elevator's up top, I'm done for.

"Drake!"

Drake glanced over his shoulder and saw Mohawk, his shaggy purple hair grown black at the roots and a snarl on his face, running down the tunnel toward him. His palms were ablaze with white light, and bright red sparks seemed to be bleeding from his eyes.

With his back against the elevator doors, Drake watched as the glass shattered and an ocean gushed into the tunnel, sweeping Mohawk away in less than a heartbeat. The elevator doors pinged open, and Drake slipped through the gap. He managed to hammer the button for the ride up as freezing water gushed through the open doors and slammed him against the back of the car.

The doors closed against the cascade, and the elevator began to rise, dragging a sodden and shivering Drake with it toward the surface. The car rose quickly, the water draining through the holes in the steel floor, but he could hear it churning up through the shaft, chasing him up to the Rig.

Drake stood as the elevator slowed and the doors slid open above the surface in the junkyard at the bottom of the eastern platform.

Alan Grey stood waiting for the elevator, not two meters from Drake. They stared at each other in dumb surprise for a moment, the Arctic Ocean bubbling up just underfoot; then Grey's eyes flashed red, and Drake brought his rifle swinging up.

He shot Grey once in the chest, and the large bully went down with a grunt as water began to pool in the car and spill out into the junkyard. Close one.

Grey sat up, and Drake screamed. He shot him again, but the massive boy ripped the dart from his neck and struggled to stand. He fell back, splashing about in the cold water.

The Crystal-X was keeping him awake . . .

Drake left Grey to it—he needed to reach the *Titan*, find Irene and Tristan, and get the hell away from this place once and for all.

At this point, after all the days in Tubes and all the nights crawling through vents, Drake knew the eastern platform like the back of his hand. He felt the floor shaking, violent vibrations shuddering through the metal walkways, and knew that Anderson was still busy downstairs. Could he bring down the whole platform? Drake raced up toward the roof and the guards' bridge to the southern platform.

Every step was agony, pulling at his side, but there was no time to stop. He flew upstairs, leaped over pipes and through mazes of machinery, relying on his memory in the poor light. It was still dark, stars sparkled indifferently overhead, but dawn wasn't far away. If he wasn't gone by then, he wouldn't be going. It was as simple as that.

Drake had to pause and catch his breath when he reached the bridged walkway to the southern platform, rifle at the ready. There were no guards on this side, no one had been sent to investigate the disturbance below—it had only been a few minutes—but that was all about to change.

He had a good view of the southern platform. The Seahawk was on the helipad, and the floodlights from Control high above cast plenty of light on the work crew loading crates near the platform's edge. The *Titan*'s crane was swinging over from the massive ship.

Standing on the bridge, Drake scanned the platform. It looked as if Irene and Tristan's container had already been loaded into the hold of the ship. In a roundabout way, they were exactly where Drake had hoped he'd be by now—although not locked inside with no chance of escape.

That was no good at all.

A tremendous shock rattled the eastern platform, and Drake was knocked off his feet. Vicious vibrations tore through the steel and pipes beneath him. He gripped the railing as the sound of screeching metal sent his world spinning.

A burst of foamy seawater exploded like a giant geyser from below, enveloping the entire eastern platform. Drake's eyes bulged as the swash hurled past him, up into the sky, and then began to fall. A deluge of cold water rained down on the platform, and to his mounting horror, the entire mass of steel, pipes, and machinery began to tilt toward the water.

The eastern platform was falling into the sea.

Someone up in the control tower must have noticed, as a piercing emergency siren began to wail across the Rig—the call to evacuate. Red warning lights flared to life along the outside of the tower, signaling distress.

Anderson, what did you do? Drake struggled to stand, clinging to his rifle and the railing. The walkway to the southern platform was still there, but buckling under the strain of the entire eastern section of the Rig, trying to tear itself free. *He did exactly what you wanted him to do . . .* Drake thought.

"Drake!" Emerging from the innards of the failing platform, Alan Grey glared at him, soaking wet. The twin darts Drake had pumped into him were gone, and the red light shining from his eyes was near blinding.

"Hello, Alan."

Drake shot him again—in the leg this time. Grey fell to one knee, howling. Drake took to his heels and dashed out onto the buckling, screaming walkway to the southern platform. He ran as fast as he could, keeping to the center of the twisting bridge. If the eastern platform moved another few centimeters one good jerk would fling him into the sea. He chanced a look over his shoulder and saw that the eastern half of the bridge had broken away from the platform.

The bolts and rigging holding the walkway to the structure weren't enough to keep it alive. Drake jumped the last two meters, landing just on the edge of the southern platform as the bridge fell away, clattering down toward the sea.

Drake looked back, breathing hard, at Grey, who was clinging to the handrail as the bridge itself struck the churning water far below. They were separated by about thirty meters of open air. Smiling, Drake offered him a quick one-fingered salute.

Grey took a large step back and ran toward the edge of the platform.

He can't be seri—

Drake watched, not quite willing to believe what he was seeing, as Grey leaped off the edge of the eastern platform, arms outstretched, and hurled himself through the air toward Drake and the southern platform. Nothing but red madness shone in his eyes. Powerful madness.

Grey's leap was impossible, but he was doing it nonetheless. He flew six meters up into the air and was almost halfway across the gap between platforms before Drake came to a swift and terrible realization.

Blimey, he's going to make it!

Taking two large steps back, Drake swung his rifle up once again, took careful aim, and fired—which is to say, he sprayed the air in the general direction of Grey and prayed to whatever gods were listening that something struck the magical psychopath.

The eastern platform sank farther toward the sea behind Grey as he flew across the gap, screaming and wailing and gnashing his teeth. His hands opened and closed out in front of him, as if he already had them wrapped around Drake's throat.

Drake kept falling back toward the Seahawk, and he turned to run as Grey struck the platform. Grey took two massive lunges forward; then his eyes rolled into the back of his head and he tumbled to the ground. Three darts stuck out of his chest, and he went down for the count a second time, groaning and foaming at the mouth. *He won't be down for long . . .* Drake thought.

Still, he breathed a sigh of relief. He'd bought himself more time, at least five seconds, and there was a lot you could do in five seconds. He looked beyond the Seahawk and saw crew from the *Titan* lashing netting around the crates to be loaded onto the ship. The crane's hook swung in the wind, over the platform, ready for the cargo.

"Drake? What the hell do you think you're doing?"

Drake snapped his head to the right, toward Processing. Marcus Brand stood across the platform, a dumbfounded expression on his face. Drake recovered quickly and reached for his rifle. The tiny dart flew swift and true, striking Brand in the chest. The impact knocked the guard back a step, but that was all it did. The dart bounced off his chest, having failed to pierce his armor.

Brand grinned. "Nice shot."

Drake fired again and was rewarded with an empty click. The clip of darts had finally run dry.

He turned and fled, disappearing behind the bulk of the Seahawk as a spray of darts erupted from Brand's rifle. Drake heard them zipping past his head and pinging off the chopper. He kept the chopper between himself and Brand as sirens wailed and more of the eastern platform fell into the sea. It was on its last legs now—literally—leaning at an angle that would soon send it crashing over.

Drake was out of ideas and ammo. He shivered in the cool night air, his jumpsuit soaked through and clinging to his skin like a suit of ice. Through the open hold in the chopper he glimpsed Brand reloading, a grim smile on his face.

Still enjoying his job . . . Drake thought. "Hey, Brand, can I ask you a question?"

Brand laughed. "Shoot. No, wait, I'll shoot."

High-pressure darts bounced off the floor of the Seahawk's hold, flicking over Drake's head. He laughed himself.

"Screw you, then!" Drake shouted. "I'm checking out of this hotel, mate. The bed was lumpy and the staff incompetent. Not once did I find a mint on my pillow!"

"I'll have a word with housekeeping," Brand snarled, and stepped into the hold of the Seahawk.

Drake rolled away and gained his feet. He had only seconds before Brand made it across the hold and leveled his rifle against his back. At a dead sprint, straining against the burning pain in his side, which forced tears from his eyes, Drake dashed across the helipad—straight toward the crates just being lifted from the platform by the *Titan*'s crane.

More darts whizzed past his head, striking two of the crew who had attached the load to the crane. They slumped, unconscious before they hit the concrete.

The crane swung the crates out over the edge of the platform, and Drake knew this was it—his last chance. Do or die, he thought.

You can't fly out of here, you know, Dr. Lambros whispered.

Actually, Drake thought he could.

He put on a final burst of speed and leaped off the edge of the platform, arms outstretched, reaching for the netting securing the crates to the crane's hook. For a split second he was tethered to nothing but open air. Dark, unforgiving ocean churned dozens of meters below. Sure death if he missed . . .

The moment he leaped was the exact moment the final pillars and supports of the eastern platform collapsed and the massive structure plunged into the sea. The platform fell screaming, and a thunderous spray of water was sent shooting into the sky, accompanied by a tremendous and hellish boom. Massive waves rippled out from the impact, rocking the *Titan* where it floated and sending the crane swaying.

With a triumphant cry, Drake snatched the webbing surrounding the crates and dangled back and forth, his arms burning, a good sixty meters above the water as the crane swung around over the *Titan*. The burst of air and water from the eastern platform's ultimate collapse rattled the teeth in his head, but he held on grimly. A wave at least five meters high rocked the southern platform as the evacuation sirens wailed. Brand was thrown from his feet, much to Drake's satisfaction.

Once the crates were over the ship, the crane operator lowered the load, and two meters above the deck, Drake waved to a very surprised crew as he disappeared into the cargo hold.

26

TITAN'S FALL

Drake descended into the cargo hold of the *Titan* and leaped off the crates onto the first walkway he saw. A group of crewmen down below were pointing and shouting at him, and he didn't want to get swarmed and held down until Brand or any other guards caught up with him.

He hit the walkway hard. Shocking all of his injuries into protest, but with no time to waste, Drake stumbled to his feet and took off at a quick jog, the best he could manage, through the ship.

The walkway led to a steel door, an exit out of the hold, and into a narrow dull-green corridor. He grabbed a fire extinguisher from the wall as he ran, looking for a way down and around. Panting hard, he slipped down the handrail on a set of stairs, slamming into a surprised crew member at the bottom and knocking the hardhat from the poor chap's head.

Drake managed to stay on his feet, and he took the next staircase down and swung left, back toward the cargo hold. Three crewmen raced toward him down the same hallway.

"There he is!" one of them barked. "Grab him!"

Drake didn't slow down. He pulled the pin from the extinguisher, pointed the nozzle at the men, and squeezed the handle.

A cloud of thick white smothering material burst from the extinguisher and hung in the air. The crew spluttered into the cloud as Drake ran past, holding his breath. He emerged on the other side covered in white powder, but still free, and tossed the extinguisher aside. The hallway led him exactly where he wanted to go — the ground floor of the cargo hold.

The stars were visible overhead, through the open hatch doors of the hold, as Drake disappeared into a maze of shipping containers and small crates, all stamped with the silver Alliance Systems crown.

Which one was it? For a moment, Drake's mind froze. The number of Irene and Tristan's container wouldn't come to him. He rolled his tongue around his mouth and cursed. "I don't wanna be here anymore . . . you little rhyming idiot . . . nine-five-four!"

That was it.

Now where is it?

The hold was at least thirty meters across, dimly lit. Wails from the Rig's evacuation sirens emanated from above, adding a sense of urgency to the chase. Drake knew that time was running out.

Panting from the exertion and the pain in his side, he ran in a pattern up and down the long aisles of the containers and crates, looking for the right one. He dismissed most of them straightaway, as they were regular-size shipping containers, far too long.

Toward the center of the cargo hold, he began to find what

he was looking for—the smaller crates and containers, wet from the sea air and fresh off the Rig.

"Nine-five-four . . . nine-five-four . . ." He ran past it twice before he saw the faded black numbers on the side. "Blimey, blind as a bat . . ."

With a grunt, he lifted and unlatched the bolt on container X-954AS and swung the door open. A pool of soft, ethereal light from the mineral spilled out onto the floor. From between the rows of glowing tanks, Irene and Tristan poked their heads up, blinking against the brighter light from outside the container.

"Will?" Tristan whispered. "Will!"

They darted out from around the mineral tanks. Irene threw her arms around Drake, smiling. "Where are we?"

"We're on the *Titan*," Drake said. "They loaded you into the cargo hold. We're right where we need to be."

"How'd you get off the Rig?"

Drake gave Irene a shaky smile. "They're a bit distracted on the Rig at the moment. Come on. We're going this way."

"I thought the plan was to hide in a container until we were away from this place and then swipe a speedboat." Tristan said.

"That was a good plan, yeah, but they know I'm here now. So hurry up, before we're—"

Something bit Drake in his left shoulder, and he stumbled back a step, a tiny frown creasing his brow. Whatever bit him burrowed deep, exploded out of the nook just over his heart, and kept flying, smacking into the glowing tank of mineral in the container. He looked down and saw a crimson stain spreading through the green cloth of his jumpsuit.

Irene screamed.

Drake fell forward into the Crystal-X container just as Grey emerged from the shadows and closed his colossal arms around Irene and Tristan. They struggled, but were no match for Grey's mineral-enhanced strength. There was no color left in his eyes save that cruel, insane red.

Marcus Brand stepped out behind Grey, a smoking pistol in his hand, and looked down at Drake on the floor of the container.

I've been shot . . . some vague and distant part of Drake's mind realized.

"Take those two up top and cuff 'em to the deck," Brand said, and handed Grey a pair of steel handcuffs. "Storm will need someone to blame for what happened down below the eastern platform. I think these two will do just nicely."

Grey pulled Drake's allies away. Irene clawed and bit at him, but he squeezed her until she stopped.

"Can I ask you a question, Drake?" Brand said, and kneeled down, passing his pistol from hand to hand.

Drake licked his lips. "Shoot . . ."

"Can you name one person who's going to miss you?"

Drops of water splashed against Drake's forehead. He kept his gaze locked on Brand, but out of the corner of his eye he saw a web of cracks spreading through the mineral tank. *Follow the web . . .* The bullet that had passed clean through him, spraying his blood across the container, had slammed into the reinforced tank—and weakened the glass.

"My friends would," Drake said, and found that he believed it.

Brand placed the barrel of his pistol between Drake's eyes,

as he had done in the exercise area a few months ago. "I mean someone who won't be as dead as you in five minutes."

Drake did the only thing that made sense. He curled his hand into a fist and punched the splintered glass of the mineral tank just behind his head. The tank shattered, and Brand leaped back with a curse as a torrent of seawater and glowing blue mineral washed over Drake, covering him in a deluge of electric-blue light.

A harsh, startled breath was all he managed before the water hit him. Jolts of pure power made him arch his back as the glowing blue rock claimed him. Wherever the mineral touched bare skin, it clung and was absorbed into his flesh. Drake bathed in the Crystal-X, and a rush of incredible energy surged through his body as he absorbed more and more of the light.

And still the mineral flowed, as if he were a sponge mopping up a spill. Hundreds of kilograms of it fell out of the tank and into the nearest source of life—William Drake.

Light.

Everything else faded away—the pain from his injuries, the fear for Irene and Tristan, and the hate for Brand, Alan Grey, and the immense, merciless Rig itself. In its place Drake felt an absurd calm, a solemn peace at the heart of the storm. He felt light, as energy from an impossible source soared through his veins and gave him strength.

Strength unbound.

He found himself on his feet, though he didn't remember standing, and tiny sparks of blue lightning danced across his skin, playing in the blood trickling down his arm from the gunshot wound. Arcs of power struck the walls of the container, scorching them black. Water about a quarter meter deep flowed past his ankles toward Brand, who turned on his heels and fled after taking one look at Drake's face.

Not so fast, Drake thought, extending his arm. The same words burst from his throat, bellowing through the cargo hold and rattling the entire ship.

A lash of pure energy whipped from his palm and wrapped itself around Brand's neck. The guard was jerked back off his feet, and he hit the floor. Drake stepped out of the container, realized with some surprise that he was actually floating a few centimeters off the ground, and hovered over Brand.

Brand's gun arm came up, and he fired three times—blam, blam, blam—point-blank into Drake's chest.

"No . . ."

The bullets struck his chest and . . . phased straight through him, as if he weren't there—nothing but a ghost. The shots pinged off the containers behind him, ricocheting away through the hold.

Brand's eyes widened. "Christ, boy, what are you?"

Drake considered, then shook his head. "Did you kill Dr. Lambros?" he asked quietly. Power thrummed in every syllable, shaking the crates all around him.

"I . . ." Brand snarled. "Storm ordered it. The bitch was asking too many questions—ah!"

Drake clenched his fist, and the noose of energy around Brand's neck tightened, cutting him off with a strangled choke. "You deserve to die."

Brand struggled against the bond of light and then slumped. "Are you . . ." he croaked. "Are you going to kill me, Drake?"

As if from across an impossible distance of time and space,

a tiny voice whispered in the back of Drake's mind. No . . . "I honestly don't know," he said.

A flash of blinding light erupted from the mineral container. Drake hadn't managed to absorb it all, and what was left in the bottom of the shattered tank had finally mixed with the open air. A wave of tremendous heat and power slammed into the two of them with all the fury of a tsunami. The explosion sent both Drake and Brand flying across the cargo hold. Drake slammed into containers, tore through them like tissue paper, and left dents in the ones he merely glanced. Blue light swam across his body, absorbing the impacts, protecting him. He was so full of energy he began to scream.

A white ball of burning fire consumed the cargo hold and began to grow as Drake came to a ragged stop against the same crate he'd used to flee the Rig not twenty minutes ago. His leg was caught in the netting, and he discovered that there were limits to his newfound power. A sharp pain tore up through his ankle. Something snapped. Drake felt it go, but the pain was a distant thing, much like that in his shoulder.

The light flowing through his arms, his entire body, began to fade away. Unsure just how he'd grasped the power in the first place, only that he'd wanted to hurt Brand, he now felt as if he'd been washed in with the tide and the tide had receded—leaving him drying under a harsh, painful sun. He came crashing back down to earth, the Crystal-X dropping him as quickly as it had energized him. Staggering pain washed over him. He had been thrown clear of the blast range from the container, but that sphere of fire in the heart of the hold was growing.

And there's another tank in there . . . he thought, not to mention the other containers.

Fear rushed through him as he realized the implications of what was happening. The *Titan* was going to explode—and soon.

Drake clung to the netting and crawled to his feet. His ankle stung when he put weight on it, but he could hobble. Pulsating heat, like the edge of a bonfire, chased him as he turned and fled toward the doorway, out of the hold, and into the corridors that would take him upstairs.

I won't make it, he thought as drops of molten metal began to rain down all around him. The hold was as bright as midday from the ball of fire. I need the power again . . .

Drake gritted his teeth and kept limping. Come on! A burst of blue light pulsed through his forearm, igniting the web of veins. He felt as if he'd crawled back into the shallows of the impossible ocean of light his body had absorbed. The pain in his ankle lessened, and he managed a slow jog, ducking for cover through the door out of the hold just as another, fatal explosion rocked the *Titan*.

To Drake, it sounded like the end of the world.

There was a mighty all-consuming roar as the remaining Crystal-X mineral, locked away in containers Drake hadn't absorbed, exploded in a geyser of white-hot superheated flame. The entire hull of the *Titan* expanded instantly. The pressure of the detonated mineral forced the seams within the ship and along the hull to burst.

Drake was thrown from his feet again and into the wall of the corridor. Rivets from the hold behind him popped out like bullets, shooting every which way. He held his hands over his head and curled up, praying that none of the deadly projectiles would strike him. He got lucky, and as the fire began to truly rage in the hold behind him, he heard a terrible scream.

He looked back.

Standing in the doorway, wreathed in smoke and flame, was Brand, on fire and screaming. All the hair had burned from his head and his armor was fused to his flesh. He fell to his knees as a wave of dark, foaming water burst through the hold—the explosions had finally ruptured the *Titan*'s hull—and swept him away.

Drake turned and fled through the nearest door, heading away from the cargo hold as fast as his injured ankle could carry him.

27

COLLISION

His ankle was broken, Drake was sure of it, but he could feel the raw power of the glowing mineral surging down through his body, into his leg, to his foot, and knitting the bone back together. Terrified at what was happening to him, he understood that he had no real control over the Crystal-X. It was in him, using him—washing him in and out on that unfathomably powerful tide. Unfortunately, it didn't seem to be doing much for the hole torn through his shoulder, but that was a dull pain. He was running on supercharged batteries now, pumped into overdrive and overtime.

Am I dying? Drake wondered. He'd absorbed more of the Crystal-X than any of Dr. Elias's other subjects. Irene had been given a teaspoon's worth, and she could heal fatal wounds. Even Grey and Anderson had received mild doses compared with what Drake had soaked up. A trickle compared with Niagara Falls. Am I dying? I've never felt more alive.

He laughed and clapped his hands together. Crackles of electric-blue lightning exploded between his fingers and left wicked, red-hot scorch marks on the walls of the corridor—a corridor that was now half a meter under rising water. Heading back the way he had come, Drake limped up a set of stairs, gripping the handrail.

He made it to the top and turned down the next corridor. Alan Grey tackled him with a snarl, and they toppled back down the stairs, wrestling and clawing at each other. The flood at the bottom broke their fall but quickly swept them down the corridor, away from the hold and deeper into the bowels of the doomed ship.

Drake spun in the surge of freezing water, his head ducking under the surface and back up as Grey struggled to pull him down. The flood spat them out on a walkway over an open space, which was fast filling with seawater. The deluge from the hold burst like a waterfall over the edge, raining down upon a sleek, idling speedboat moored in its bay. The hatch doors built into the hull were flung open.

Drake's eyes bulged—the flood had deposited him right where he'd wanted to be all along.

Grey was on his feet, and he kicked Drake in the stomach. Another explosion tore through the *Titan*, and the two boys were thrown against the railing of the walkway. The ship made a screeching sound and began to tilt, sending the open hatch doors below the surface of the water. The speedboat dock began to flood from two sources.

Drake used the railing to climb to his feet. Grey tackled him again, but he was ready for it this time, and he slammed his fist into the side of Grey's head. Blue light flared in a cone around his hand, and the punch knocked Grey back a staggering step.

"I'm going to kill you!" the bully roared.

Grey was nearly twice his size in muscle mass alone, but Drake wasn't so underpowered himself anymore. Grey slammed his fists into the sides of Drake's head and squeezed. Drake grabbed his forearms and squeezed back. A burst of blue energy rippled down his arms, and Grey let go, howling, as Drake forced him to his knees, crushing his huge arms in an unbreakable viselike grip.

"Where did you put them?" Drake shouted as the ship began to tilt toward its bow. He stumbled back a few steps as Grey squirmed in his grasp. "Where are they?"

A horrendous sound of screeching metal and tearing steel echoed through the *Titan*.

The metal support beams overhead gave way under the pressure and buckled. A ton of steel slammed into the walkway and broke it in half. Grey and Drake dived aside at the last second and rolled across the floor. Drake managed to grab the handrail—Grey did not.

The ocean churning below had buried the dock, and only about three meters of the hatch doors were still above water. Enough room to maneuver the speedboat, which had risen with the flood, if Drake had time. Grey tried to pull himself back over the railing. He was hanging only a meter above the violent current of water. The light in his eyes was dull, insane. He couldn't lift himself back up.

And Drake couldn't watch him die.

"Give me your hand!" Another explosion rocked the ship, and Drake was flung into the handrail above Grey.

"Damn it, Grey, your hand!"

Grey reached his hand up and shot a beam of pure energy at Drake, what Dr. Elias had called hard-light. Drake reared back, away from the crimson light. White spots flared in front of his eyes and cleared just in time to see Grey's grip slip on the edge of the walkway. Alan Grey fell, snarling and screaming, into the surging flood of seawater. He disappeared below the roiling waters and didn't come back up.

Damn it, Drake thought, stunned. Damn it . . .

The tilt of the ship had forced the idling speedboat against the walkway, just two meters from where Drake clung to the railing. He took a step toward the boat, then another. It would be simple to climb over the rail and onto the nose of the craft.

You could take the boat, his mind whispered. There's a GPS . . . You could make it back to the mainland.

Drake stood looking at the speedboat, at freedom, for about the same amount of time it took his heart to beat twice. Then he turned, pressed a hand against his shoulder, and limped deeper into the screaming ship, toward the stern. It was impossible to reach the stairs back down the corridor toward the cargo hold. The current was still flowing fast, the water now up to his waist, so Drake leaped over the gap in the walkway and followed it aft, hoping to find a way up to the deck.

He thought about how far he'd come in the last six months. How much he'd changed from the quiet, distrustful boy who had first landed on the Rig's helipad at twilight. Irene and Tristan had been the cause of that change, no doubt about it. Drake didn't believe there was a lot he could do to make up for Aaron's death in Cedarwood during that flawed escape attempt—where he'd decided that other people only slowed him down and that friends were a burden he didn't need—but this felt like a start. A step in the right direction, as Dr. Lambros would have put it, and it had taken only half a year in the world's most insane prison to show him that.

After all, Drake thought, what's freedom worth if I've no one to share it with?

He left a steady trail of blood in his wake, limping along as fast as he could, heading up toward the deck—and his friends.

The wrenching sound of the ship tearing itself apart was becoming far more adamant as he ascended. The crew had long since abandoned the innards of the *Titan*, no doubt evacuating to life rafts. A great, aching groan and a shocking, constant vibration almost knocked Drake on his side. The ship was listing to the right as it took on water from the bow. He had to stop halfway up the main galley as the pain in his ankle reached a stunning crescendo. He pulled up the cuff of his jumpsuit and saw tiny blue lights dancing beneath his skin. The sight of it made him dizzy—or was it blood loss from the gunshot—and he looked away.

A few moments later the pain abated and Drake tentatively put his full weight back on the ankle. His foot didn't even twinge. The bone had healed itself. Having no time, and perhaps feeling unwilling to contemplate just what Crystal-X was doing to his body, he continued his ascent away from escape and toward his friends. Too much exposure had driven Anderson mad . . . And he'd been fed only a teaspoon of the stuff compared with the ocean Drake had absorbed.

Stop thinking about that! You're still you—you're still sane.

He gritted his teeth and steeled his resolve.

Even if it was the last thing he did in his short life, he would not let Tristan and Irene die alone.

As Drake emerged on deck into a sky blurring from true

night toward dawn, the *Titan* groaned through to its very core, and the bow end began to sink fast. "Irene! Tristan!"

If they were shackled to the front of the ship, they were dead—drowned already. So Drake did all he could do and turned the other way, up toward the stern, which now almost brushed up against the southern platform of the Rig.

He saw dozens of lifeboats in the water, streaming away from the sinking ship, and winches lowering even more from the platforms of the Rig. All the inmates had been evacuated as well, it seemed.

"Irene!" he shouted against the noise of the *Titan*'s hull tearing at the seams. "Tristan!"

Blue light had pooled in the hole in his shoulder now, sealing the wound, fusing the flesh back together. A minute later, as sheer relief flooded through Drake faster than the Arctic Ocean through the ship, he found his friends handcuffed to the base of the crane.

"Howdy," he said.

Even as the stern of the *Titan* began to rise up out of the ocean, Irene and Tristan stared at him as if they were seeing a ghost. The ship was heading toward vertical as the bow took on more than it could hold and began to disappear below the water. Casting a quick look at himself, Drake had to admit he was in a bit of a state. His jumpsuit was dark green, soaked with blood and water. Tiny cuts on his arms were healing right before his eyes.

"You're alive!" Irene said.

Without thinking, Drake grabbed the chain of the handcuffs tying them to the base of the crane and melted the links. Irene and Tristan separated, wearing a cuff apiece.

"What's happening?" Tristan reached for Drake's hand, holding on to Irene with his other hand as she stumbled back against the crane.

"I kind of blew up the ship."

"You . . . you blew up the ship?"

"And a bit of the Rig earlier, but you missed that."

"Why would you do that?" Irene asked. She looked at Drake warily. "Your eyes are glowing, by the way."

Drake swallowed hard. "Red?"

"Blue. Bright, sapphire blue."

Drake didn't have the time or the desire to think too much on that. The stern of the ship was clear of the water now and still climbing. Soon the *Titan* would be vertical, bobbing in the water like a cork. But it wouldn't stay afloat for long.

"Time to go, yes?" Drake hadn't the first clue how they were going to escape this one.

"Quick, we'll jump into the water—"

"And get pulled under when the ship goes down!"

Drake looked around for anything—a lifeboat, a pair of water wings. Nothing. He clung to the crane's base with Irene and Tristan and noted with a distracted amusement that they were high up above the southern platform of the Rig, just about ten meters away. If the ship fell against the platform . . .

"I . . . I'm sorry," Drake said, and cupped Irene's cheek with his free hand. "There's nothing I can do."

"It was worth a shot," Tristan said. Through all the chaos, he'd managed to keep his glasses on. Drops of seawater dripped down the lenses.

"More than worth it," Irene said. "I—"

Drake gasped. "Follow me! For your lives, follow me!"

The boom of the crane was swinging back and forth through the air, and Drake began to climb toward it, pulling himself on his knees up and around to the ladder that led to the crane's operator box. He crawled along the crane's ladder, which was now almost horizontal above the water, as the ship bobbed, on the precipice of sinking forever.

Drake looked back. Soaked and terrified, Irene and Tristan followed in his wake.

This is going to be close . . .

The *Titan* hung vertically in the ocean, the water having finally burst through enough of its levels to drag the ship under. Clinging to the top of the crane, Drake and his friends climbed out onto the loose, swaying boom just as it swung over the edge of the Rig's southern platform.

As the ship sank, the crane swung back, but not quickly enough to avoid striking the roof of the platform with an earth-shattering bang.

Drake, Irene, and Tristan were thrown forward by the impact. The crane struck the Rig, and the tiny figures clinging to it rolled with the collision and hit the helipad hard, just missing the blades of the Seahawk.

Dazed by the crash, Drake struggled to move—his leg was caught and bleeding in the twisted steel of the ruined crane.

As the cargo ship began its final descent, the crane groaned and began to shift, dragging back across the edge of the platform.

Drake was pulled clear of the wreckage by Irene and Tristan before he could be dragged with it. They linked their hands under his arms and pulled him away. The crane dug a deep furrow in the helipad, tossing up concrete and tearing through the platform as the *Titan* drowned. Tens of thousands of gallons of foamy seawater were burned to steam by the Crystal-X still aflame in the *Titan*'s heart, wreathing the great ship in a cloud of haze as the stern sank into the cold, dark waters of the Arctic Ocean, like the eastern platform before it.

Breathing hard, having narrowly escaped death more times than he could count in the last ten minutes, Drake looked up at his friends, who were standing above him under a sky of burnt orange dawn, and burst out laughing. "Okay, whose idea was the cargo ship?"

28

AFTERMATH

"Will, oh dear, your poor leg . . ."

Irene had a nasty cut across her forehead and Tristan's glasses had snapped in the fall, but they both seemed relatively unharmed by the narrow escape from the *Titan*. Drake glanced down at his leg and almost passed out.

A sharp splint of white bone had broken through his shin, and strips of skin hung torn and bloody around the wound. His leg had been snapped in half. Blood gushed down his leg and soaked through his sock, pooling in his shoe and seeping onto the helipad.

He felt a numb sort of pain, like a dull ache. "Well, that's a mess."

Drake concentrated on the break, focusing the energy he could feel coursing through his veins. The blue magic was harder to grab this time, but it was there, waiting. He sensed a dam of energy just out of his grasp. But he had overdone it—too much too soon in the last half-hour—and all he could do was wade in the shallows of his newfound power.

Still, he concentrated, and luminescent smoke pooled around the broken bone, bright light pulsing through his leg just under the skin. The strain was almost too much, and Drake faltered. The light dulled; the bone was still broken.

Irene, her hands aglow, placed them just above and below the break. A surge of fresh energy shuddered through Drake, and he and his friends watched, amazed, as the bone disappeared back into his leg and the skin knitted itself together.

Tristan offered Drake his hand and pulled him to his feet.

"Are my eyes still glowing?" Drake asked his cellmate.

"A little bit . . ."

Irene gasped. "Where's the eastern platform?"

"Anderson decided he didn't want it there anymore." Drake stared at the broken pillars and twisted lower levels of steel and pipes, some of them aflame. The rest of the platform would have settled far below, amid the glowing rock of the Crystal-X meteorite.

"Did he now?" Tristan peered over the edge, into the depths that had claimed the *Titan*, and out to sea at the dozens of lifeboats bobbing together, thick with inmates, guards, technicians, and the *Titan*'s crew. Hundreds of people stared back at him. He waved. A few waved back. "Good work, Carl . . ."

"Well, there goes our best chance of escape," Irene said. "We're back on the Rig."

With Irene's help, Drake took a few steps. His leg still twinged when he put weight on it. "Oh, ye of little faith," he said. "That boat was never the escape plan."

"No? Then what?"

Drake stood under his own steam and closed his eyes. He

rubbed his eyelids, and when he opened them, the ethereal sapphire-blue light was gone. "Follow me along the web," he said grimly.

Drake strolled with purpose into Processing and through the corridors that led up to the control tower. The evacuation siren had stopped, but the red emergency lights were still aglow and spinning, coloring the walls with bloodlike splashes. All the doors of the Rig had released, all access was in effect. He climbed the stairs up through Control and ran into no resistance.

At the top of the tower, Drake found empty workstations and the Rig's abandoned monitoring systems flashing red. Chairs had been toppled in the mad rush to evacuate, the floor scattered with paper and spilled mugs of early-morning coffee.

"What are you looking for, Will?" Irene asked, right behind him.

"Not what—who." Drake stepped across the tower and knocked twice, sharply, on the frosted glass of Warden Storm's office door.

"Come on in, Mr. Drake," the man called.

Irene and Tristan gasped.

"He's still here!" Tristan grabbed Drake's arm. "You can't—"

"Of course he's still here." Drake could only muster a wintry smile as he opened the door. He was so tired, but there were only a few more strands on the web to follow. "This is his precious rig, as you told me yourself. Didn't you, Warden?"

"Defiant to the last, hmm?" Storm said, seated behind his large, opulent desk with his arms crossed. "Take a seat, Mr. Drake."

"Will . . ." Irene began.

"Watch the door for me, will you?" Drake said. "While I arrange our passage back to St. John's. Maple syrup for lunch, just trust me." He took a seat in front of the warden's desk with a weary sigh. "Good morning, Storm."

"This was you, wasn't it?" Storm snarled, and slammed his hand against the desk, sending a stack of paperwork to the floor. "All of this—the loss of the eastern platform, the *Titan*—was your doing."

"I played a part, yeah, but honestly, I think the Alliance had this coming."

The warden leaned back in his chair. His suit jacket fell open, and Drake saw that the man had a long, silver-barreled revolver holstered at his waist. "The Alliance is sending rescue ships from the mainland as we speak."

"Everyone's being evacuated, I take it?"

"The Rig is no longer stable. She will not be housing any criminals for the foreseeable future." The warden sniffed. "But I doubt the Alliance will give up this venture so easily."

"You mean because of the Crystal-X?"

Storm gasped. "How could you possibly . . . No—you know what, son, it doesn't surprise me that you know." His hand edged a touch closer to the gun at his waist. "Doesn't surprise me one bit."

"How could you do what you do here?" Drake asked. "Experimenting on the inmates, turning them into . . . driving them insane. If anyone deserves to be locked up, it's you."

"Ha! You've no idea what we're doing here, Drake, what advances the Alliance is making. The applications in medical science alone—"

"Dr. Elias gave me the same speech down in the Crystal-X facility only a few short hours ago. I didn't buy it then, I won't buy it now. So don't give me that 'greater good' crap, because it's not worth it—not what I saw, and not ever!" Drake found that he was almost shouting. "You should have left the mineral at the bottom of the sea, because it's not worth it if one person has to die."

"You—"

"But more than one person has died, and not just tonight—haven't they?"

Drake held up his left hand and concentrated. He wasn't sure the light would come—already his power felt like a dream, something impossible, but the energy was still there. Electric-blue fire erupted from his palm and enveloped his hand.

Storm wheeled back in his chair with a cry of surprise, striking the cabinet behind him, and reached for the gun on his hip.

"Don't you dare," Drake whispered. "Take it out slowly and slide it across the desk."

The warden scowled and made no move for his gun.

"Listen carefully, Storm. Because I'm done playing with you—play the man, remember? I absorbed enough Crystal-X on that cargo ship to send your precious Rig burning into the ocean. I could snap your neck as easily as snapping my fingers." He paused and bared his teeth. "Or as easily as you and Brand snapped the neck of poor Dr. Lambros. Oh yes, I know about that."

Drake fired a bolt of electric-blue energy, a cord of hardlight, over the warden's head. The bolt smashed through his medals and Air Force commendations and left a hole in the wall the size of a football. A cool, salty morning breeze blew in through the warden's new window.

Storm did as he was told and handed over the gun. He kept his face carefully composed. "What do you want, Drake?"

A slow smile spread across Drake's face as he slipped the revolver into his pocket. "Two things. One, you're going to help me and my friends escape this godforsaken prison. You're going to fly us out of here." He nodded to the flaming wall and the framed picture of Storm piloting choppers in Afghanistan, which was hanging askew and burning.

The warden clenched his fists. "And your other demand?"

"Give me all the soda you've got in that fridge."

29

STORM FRONT

Only an hour later, as dawn took a proper hold on the morning, Officer Stein—the last guard alive who had known about Crystal-X—escorted Drake, Irene, and Tristan to the helipad on the southern platform.

Stein led the way, with Drake behind her. He held the warden's revolver in his left hand, partially raised, and his right shone with ethereal light, energy ready to be summoned with a single thought. The revolver felt more reassuring—Drake wasn't sure just how much longer he could hold on to the power.

Warden Storm was waiting for them, already in the chopper and starting up the engines. He gave a curt nod and threw his thumb over his shoulder, gesturing for them to board.

"I'll be seeing you people again," Stein spat. Her hand twitched toward the baton at her waist.

Tristan and Irene laughed. Drake gave her a long, hard stare and was last to step up into the passenger hold of the Seahawk. The blades started spinning, the wind forcing Stein back off the helipad.

As Storm took off and headed out over the open water, Drake stood in the hold, one hand holding the rail above his head, with Tristan and Irene at either side, and watched the Rig fade over the horizon. The tiny people on the collection of lifeboats watched the helicopter depart. Drake recalled his first glimpse of the Rig from the hold of this chopper six months earlier, and he remembered thinking that the interconnected diamond-shaped platforms had resembled a giant, dilapidated demon of smoke and steel.

He had found demons here, that much was certain, and nightmares enough to last a lifetime. Murder, treachery, and greed. As if his friends had heard his thoughts, Irene slipped her arms around his chest in a gentle embrace and Tristan clapped him on the shoulder. The Rig, a living monstrosity, had not been able to crush all the good from the world.

Demons, most definitely, but also angels.

"Good riddance," Drake said, and turned away from the blinking lights. He handed the revolver to Irene. "Hold this for me, would you?"

Irene seemed surprised by the weight of the thing and quickly handed it to Tristan. The small, scrawny boy—one of Drake's only two friends in the world—held the gun at arm's length and pointed it at the floor, swallowing hard.

Drake sighed. He had been awake for more than twenty-four hours—beaten, broken, shot, and burned—and there were miles to go before he could sleep. He retrieved the warden's last bottle of soda from his pocket, twisted the cap off, and sat down to enjoy a well-earned rest.

Two hours later they flew into a storm, heading toward the west and away from the daylight in the east, outpacing the dawn. He looked out to sea, at the course ahead. Vast, mighty storm clouds obscured the sky, and not five minutes later freezing rain, thunder, and lightning threw the chopper around. Warden Storm, flying true to his name, persevered.

There was no turning back.

Half an hour later, Drake spotted the curve of the coastline and smiled at the sight of it. Tristan cheered, and Irene burst into tears.

Storm landed on a helipad at the harbor's edge in St. John's. Drake, Irene, and Tristan jumped out of the hold as soon as they were down. Sparing the warden not another minute of their time—he, and the people he worked for, had stolen months and years from them already—Tristan and Irene took off into the dark morning, toward a strip of beach that curved around the city.

Drake had just crossed the edge of the helipad when he heard his name.

"Hold it a minute, Mr. Drake," Warden Storm said. He'd unbuckled himself from the pilot's seat and stepped out into the cold morning.

Irene and Tristan looked back. "Keep going," Drake said. "Head along the beach there. I'll catch up." And he turned back to face the warden of the Rig one last time.

Storm stood at the edge of the light reflected by the floodlights above the helipad. His face was grim, almost corpselike against the wind and the rain pelting the sleeping city of St. John's. He took a few steps closer to Drake, until they were standing face to face. "You've got five minutes, and then I'm reporting the escape. There'll be an investigation by the Alliance. I know enough to keep myself safe and in control of the Rig, but I won't hesitate to tell them what you and your friends know, as well. Do you understand me?"

Drake nodded. Lightning tore through the sky directly over their heads, charging the air with static and fresh ozone.

Storm spat on the tarmac and leaned in close. His breath was hot and furious against Drake's face. "A word of advice, Mr. Drake—run. Run as hard and as fast as you can, because the full might of the Alliance is going to come crashing down on your head like the fist of the Almighty Himself."

"You won't get away with what you did on the Rig," Drake said. He held up his hand. Soft, evanescent light pooled in his palm, so bright that the warden had to look away. "I'll see to that."

"Killing me won't stop what's coming for you. You and your friends will never be heard from again!"

"I'm not going to kill you," Drake said. "I'm better than you."

Drake took three long steps back before he turned and ran, disappearing into the early-morning darkness with the warden's final threat ringing in his ears . . . Never be heard from again. The waves of the ocean on his left crashed against the shore, fighting the storm along the pebbly beach. He caught up with Irene and Tristan after half a minute.

Alone, but free, the three friends stood on the beach, the elements beating down upon them. They stared at one another in a small circle. Tristan slipped his hand into Irene's, and Drake took their free hands in his own. An invisible cord of anxiety, and of exhilaration, shivered through them all.

"We did it," Drake said. "Together, we did it."

"Look at those trees," Tristan said as lightning lit up the beach. "I'd almost forgotten how green trees are."

Irene grinned. "What do we do now?"

Drake took a long, deep breath and thought of his mother. He hadn't seen her in the best part of two years. He didn't even know if she was alive. London was an ocean away—another continent—and the Alliance controlled everything between here and there. A network of incomprehensible power and cruelty.

But then Will Drake did not consider himself so powerless either—never had.

"Run," he said. "We run."

"Okay." Tristan pushed his glasses, held together only by hope and tape, up the bridge of his nose. "But first place we see, we're stopping for cheeseburgers and milk shakes."

Irene smiled. "It's a date."

"If you two are going to start kissing again," Drake said, "I'm going back to the Rig."